D0262468

NT

Please return/renew this item
by the last date shown.
Books may also be renewed by
phone and Internet
Telford and Wrekin Libraries

BERTIE'S
❀ Gift ❀

Hannah Coates has always loved dogs — she grew up surrounded by pooches, and now has two of her own. She loves all dogs, but beagles remain her favourite.

Hannah Coates

BERTIE'S
❋ Gift ❋

HODDER &
STOUGHTON

First published in Great Britain in 2016 by
Hodder & Stoughton
An Hachette UK company

1

A CIP catalogue record for this title is available from the British Library

ISBN 978 1 473 64333 8

Typeset in Cochin by Hewer Text UK Ltd, Edinburgh
Printed and bound by Clays Ltd, St Ives plc

Hodder & Stoughton policy is to use papers that are natural, renewable
and recyclable products and made from wood grown in sustainable
forests. The logging and manufacturing processes are expected to
conform to the environmental regulations of the country of origin.

Hodder & Stoughton Ltd
Carmelite House
50 Victoria Embankment
London EC4Y 0DZ

www.hodder.co.uk

For my daughter Indigo, who adores all furry creatures

❧ ONE ❧

'Never despair — even when it's slop for dinner.'

'Wheeee!' I launch myself across the wet kitchen lino on my rump for the seventh time. The world spins brilliantly with my body, and my ears begin to lift. 'Look at me, Molly, I'm skating.'

My sister shakes her head, but she's grinning, her pink tongue hanging out. She's been enjoying the show from a safe vantage point under the kitchen table, where Mr Minton is less likely to walk past and tread on her paw or tail by accident. He's old, so it only hurts when he's wearing his heavy boots instead of his deliciously smelly slippers. But she knows I don't like her to risk it. Not with her bad leg.

Molly's bad leg is my fault. That's how I see it, at any rate.

Back when we were puppies together, skidding back and forth across another kitchen floor with our siblings, someone brought a delivery to the front door, and Mum's owner left the front door open while she carried the box through to the kitchen.

Now, Mum knew we were all brainless fur balls at that age. So she had warned us very specifically *never* to leave

1

the house, however green and tempting the front lawn seemed.

'It's not safe outside the house,' Mum told us all repeatedly, licking behind our ears as she did every morning and every evening. 'There's a busy road out there. Full of cars.'

'What are cars?' I asked excitedly.

'Big machines that go really fast and can hurt you. So don't ever go outside without a human. Do you hear me?'

Big machines that go really fast.

To me, they sounded amazing. Far too amazing to be avoided, however many times she repeated her warning while cleaning my fur.

So, of course, you already know what happened.

The moment the front door was left open, I saw my chance. I nudged Molly – the two of us never left each other's sides, even then – and whispered, 'Come on, the front door's open. Let's go and see what the lawn's like.'

'But Mum said— '

'Never mind what Mum said. She already knows what's outside, she goes out on the lawn every day, so of course she's not curious. But that's not very fair on us, is it?' I dragged her along by the ear, and she did not protest after that, but came willingly. Because Molly and I could never bear to be apart, not even for a few minutes. But she was smaller than me, the runt of the litter, and not as fast-moving. 'Oh come on, Sis, if we don't hurry, someone will shut the door again. Don't you want to see what's outside?'

What was outside was a large delivery van, reversing down our drive.

Suddenly we were outside.

Free.

Unaccompanied for the first time in our young lives.

Oblivious to the danger, I bounded across an expanse of sweet green lawn so wide and long, it seemed like a field to me at the age of three months. Grass, glorious grass! My tender paws revelled in the feel of its velvety dampness, and my nose quivered at the gorgeous fresh smell of every green springing blade it encountered. Up above our heads was the sky, the highest ceiling I had ever seen, and it seemed to stretch for ever, blue and soaring and ever so slightly terrifying.

In my heart, I had known that 'outside' would be like this. The world beyond the dreary confines of our house was phenomenal, it was like nothing I had ever known before, and all I could think was, 'What else is there? What more can I see and smell and touch?'

The lawn came to an end, but I did not stop there.

Oh no, for imbued with an adventurer's spirit, I kept running and running, with little Molly close behind me. Together, we stampeded through the soft soil of a flower bed and careered across the hard black Tarmac of the drive, barking wildly at the bombardment of smells and sights all around us.

Still reversing, the van's rear wheels missed me by a few inches.

Molly was not so lucky.

The first I knew that something had gone badly wrong was a dull thud behind me, and the squeal of the van's brakes.

Then a high-pitched yelp from Molly.

It was the kind of yelp that stays with you for ever. Sometimes I still hear it in my dreams and wake from sleep, trembling with guilt over what I did to my sister that day.

When Molly came back from the vet's surgery after the accident, one of her hind legs was tightly bandaged. She had to sleep on the sofa for days, only lifted off for food and to do her business on newspaper. Hanging my head in shame, I lay beneath the sofa all day, just to be near my sister, and cowered in abject fear every time anyone so much as opened the front door.

I thought of the outside world as a terrible, dangerous place after that, and vowed never to go outside again.

My resolve lasted all of three weeks.

You would think I should have learned my lesson after such an appalling accident. But of course, as soon as we puppies started to be allowed outside for walks and play time, I forgot my timidity and bounded about the lawn with the others as though it had never happened.

I never forgot my part in causing Molly's accident, though.

Maybe I would have forgotten in time. Except that the injury she suffered under the van's wheel that day has never entirely healed. Even now poor Molly still limps badly, and often asks me to lick her leg over the site of the old wound while she rests, as she finds that eases her pain for a few hours.

So the prospect of Mr Minton treading on her leg is a very real and frightening threat. For both of us.

Personally, I always scarper when I see old Minton

coming. His eyesight is fading, and since we're beagles and a little vertically challenged, he doesn't always spot us underfoot. Not like the bigger dogs, Jethro, Biscuit and sweet-natured Tina. But Molly is slower, not just on account of being smaller, but because of her bad leg too.

By contrast, I could never be accused of being slow.

'Bertie, careful now.' Her tone sharpens now as I skid wildly across the kitchen floor. Her eyes widen in horror. 'Too fast, Bertie. Too fast. You'll hurt yourself if you don't watch out for the —'

Too late.

Unlike the other times I've done this, I miss the softer landing of the messy pile of unwashed clothes and collide with the metal base of the cooker instead.

With a yelp, I am thrown sideways by the impact, all the breath knocked out of me. I lie there for a few seconds, staring up at the ceiling from an odd angle. It feels like my brain has turned to jelly.

'Ouch.' I get up gingerly, checking myself for broken bones. Nothing seems to be seriously damaged, but I am unsteady on my paws. I stagger away, then give myself a little shake, hoping to settle my brains back into place. 'Hmm, that wasn't supposed to happen.'

'Are you okay?'

'Think some of my brains fell out of my ear.' I shake my head again. The buzzing starts to subside. 'That wasn't such a great idea. I need all the brains I can get.'

Molly limps over to investigate. Her nose nuzzles at my face, then she gives my ear a quick lick to be sure. 'Bertie, you've got to be more careful,' she scolds me, concern in her lovely dark eyes. 'What would I do without you?'

'Oh, you'll never get rid of me,' I say cheerily. 'Even when you're old and can hardly walk, I'll be there, Sis, causing trouble for you as always.'

Molly sits back and stares at me, wagging her tail. 'I can hardly walk now,' she reminds me drily, but it's clear I've amused her.

Jethro shambles through the partly open kitchen door. A large yellow Labrador, his belly distended from too many dog treats while Mrs Minton was still alive, he gazes at us both in mild annoyance. 'What's all the noise about? You're going to wake Minton with that ruckus. And why is the floor wet?' He sniffs speculatively. 'Not wee. Did you knock over the water bowl again?'

'Welcome to my skating rink,' I say, drawing myself up magnificently.

'Your . . . *what?*'

Biscuit, an even larger yellow Labrador, pushes past Jethro, his own nose twitching with culinary excitement. 'What's up? Has Minton been cooking liver again? Damn, that smells good, smells good, smells . . .' We wait, watching him blink through other possible adjectives, but Biscuit has not been blessed with an over-large vocabulary. 'Good,' he concludes, and scratches an itchy ear, apparently satisfied with his word choice.

'Not liver,' Jethro growls. It's obvious he's bored and looking for a fight. 'Bertie's been skating again.'

'Oh no, no, no, no, no.' Biscuit keeps scratching, his paw slightly hysterical now, like it's got stuck in a loop and can't stop. 'Not the wet floor again. Minton hates the wet floor. Half rations coming.'

We fall silent at a familiar and disconcerting sound from above. It's the heavy creak of Mr Minton coming down the stairs in his boots. Probably to discover what the noise is about.

I nudge Molly. 'Boots, not slippers. Quick, back under the table,' I whisper, and she nods, hurriedly returning to her hiding place, head down, tail between her legs.

Biscuit turns too quickly and bangs straight into the door frame. 'Ow,' he mutters, looking dazed, then stumbles back into the living room.

Jethro has already vanished. He may not be the most intelligent animal in the world, but he has good preservation skills.

There is no sign of Tina, I realise. Though she probably hasn't even stirred yet today. A long-legged greyhound, Tina prefers to sleep most of the morning away in her comfortable padded basket whenever possible, aware that a walk is unlikely to be forthcoming until late afternoon. Always assuming that Mr Minton actually remembers to take us out, that is.

Not that Tina ever deigns to speak to me and Molly if she can avoid it.

'*Beagles*,' she exclaimed on the day we first arrived at 167 Park View Drive – two fluffy, brown and white puppies yapping and wriggling about in a carry-case – her thin snout quivering in outrage before she turned her back on us and curled up in her basket. 'How unspeakably common.'

A tall, elegant lady, Tina considers herself a cut above the rest of us. And she probably is, I often think. Tina would never lower herself to skid across a wet kitchen floor for fun, that's for sure.

I dart under the table, squatting rump to nervous rump with Molly, and watch as Mr Minton stomps into the kitchen.

Mr Minton.

What can I say that would endear another human to him? Not much, frankly.

Our owner is stooped and crabby, and always in a bad mood these days. Though, to be fair, that's hardly surprising. It's only three months since his wife died. I'm sure I would be in a foul mood for the rest of my life if Molly died, and she's my sister, not my life mate. And I can see his point of view when he complains about the state of the place, and how much work he has to do now she's gone. For it was old Mrs Minton who brought us here, and cared for all us dogs, and who always dropped food scraps from the meal table for us (assuming Biscuit and Jethro didn't muscle us out of the way before we could snatch it up) when her husband wasn't looking.

Then one morning she did not come downstairs like usual. And Mr Minton sat up there on his own for hours, sobbing and banging on the floor, before men finally arrived and carried her body out of the house.

'Oh no,' Biscuit had said gloomily, watching all this with only the vaguest wag of his tail. 'Oh no. Maybe she's just sleepy. I'm often sleepy like that. Maybe she'll come back soon. Tomorrow. Or . . . tomorrow.'

But none of us were so stupid we could not grasp what her abrupt departure meant. It was the end of everything we had known. The end of our comfortable life.

And the start of Mr Minton's reign of terror.

Initially, it was only our food that was affected by this change in leadership. Plastic-wrapped dog food rolls were Minton's first startling innovation. We still get them for dinner most days. Cylinders of brown pap that come oozing out of multi-coloured wrappers and land in the bowls with a horrible slopping sound. I am far too polite to suggest what it looked like. But it was not a popular decision.

'Eat it, you ungrateful mutts,' he told us, whenever he remembered to feed us that first week. 'Don't look at me like that. It's cheap. Eat me out of house and home if I let you, wouldn't you?'

Always a picky eater, Tina turned up her nose and suggested that it was actually dog meat we were eating.

As in, *other dogs*.

Molly refused to eat for three whole days after she heard that. Biscuit thought the brown pap tasted okay though, and ate her ration alongside his own and most of Tina's.

'Not bad, not bad,' he managed to say between gulps.

I was not keen either. But I was hungry. And starvation can make even cardboard seem tasty, as Molly quickly discovered, and eventually I persuaded her to eat the brown pap. 'Honestly, like Biscuit says, it's not that bad once you're used to it,' I told her, licking at her bad leg when it ached in the long, cold evenings. 'Come on, Sis, you need to keep your strength up for our walks.'

'What walks?' she asked blankly.

'I'm sure he'll take us out in a day or two,' I said, and after a minute of gloom she agreed, rubbing her nose against mine for comfort.

We both like to hope for the best. It seems the only way to deal with life's trials. Things always look brighter when you've got a smile on your face and all four paws in motion. Like trouble can never catch up with you that way.

But it turned out that Mr Minton is not a very keen dog-walker either.

That first month, we all looked up hopefully whenever Mr Minton came trudging in from his weekly shop, and our tummies rumbled with expectation. But the heavy tins with their gravy-rich contents or satisfying chunks of jelly never returned. All we had left from that time were memories of tasty scraps and meaty treats and bowl-licking goodness at meal times. It was clear early on that, however much we whined and turned our noses up at the new squishy cylinders, the delicious tins would never return. For the good old days had passed away irrevocably with Mrs Minton.

Now even Tina partakes of half a bowlful of the grim slop. So she doesn't get any thinner, I suppose, and slip down a grating while we're out on a walk.

'Better than eating poo,' Jethro often says cheerlessly, and tucks in alongside Biscuit at chow-time, neither of them being fussy eaters.

Sometimes, while waiting for the unappetizing brown slop to land in my bowl, I'm not entirely sure he's right. But I'm determined not to give in to despair.

Beside me under the table, Molly shivers as Mr Minton swears loudly over the wet floor, and stamps away in his heavy boots to fetch the mop.

'Bloody water everywhere,' he shouts, rummaging in the cupboard under the stairs. Bucket and mop and broom clatter together noisily as he slams about. 'Bloody mangy mutts. You'll be the death of me one day, just like you were the death of my poor wife.'

I feel my sister tremble and nudge her shoulder reassuringly. 'He doesn't mean it.'

'Doesn't he?'

'Life will get better,' I tell her in a whisper. 'You'll see.'

'Of course it will,' she agrees at once.

She's right. We're both right.

Things have been bad since the old lady died. Really bad. But life has to return to normal soon. When Mr Minton finally remembers to take us to the park, I think optimistically, we will see all the other dogs out with their kindly owners, and dream of a future off the lead like theirs, with pats and tasty treats and endless running after slobbery tennis balls.

One day that future will be ours, mine and Molly's. Until then, we just have to keep our paws firmly crossed.

It's a lovely dream. A tail-wagging, eyelid-fluttering dream.

But we all have to wake up sometime.

❖ TWO ❖

After the unfortunate skating incident, the sky clouds over and it rains for three days straight. Rain that runs down the windows, drips incessantly off the porch and collects in big, splashy puddles in the back yard. The kind of super-wet rain that soaks through fur in an instant, and can only be removed by a brisk, all-over shake.

For some reason, Mr Minton is not keen on brisk, all-over shakes, so he never takes us out for walks when it's raining. Instead, we get five minutes morning and evening instead, out in the back yard, with him standing in the door-way, irritably urging us again and again to 'do your business'. As if being nagged has ever helped me concentrate, especially when I'm trying to whip up enthusiasm in some soggy corner of the yard, rain trickling under my collar, my paws cold and wet. But he must enjoy saying it, otherwise he would hardly keep repeating the phrase in exactly the same tone of voice every time.

The fourth day dawns dry though, with a hint of sunshine behind the rapidly moving clouds. We all look up hopefully as Mr Minton looks out of the kitchen window after his breakfast fry-up. Will it be a walk day?

Jethro farts with expectation.

Luckily old Minton is partially deaf these days, so does not seem to hear him. Though what has occurred may soon become apparent to everyone.

Side-effects of the slop, I think delicately.

After a moment's study of the skies, Mr Minton nods and says, 'Park today, I think.'

He has learned not to say 'walk', as it sets Biscuit off.

Unfortunately, Jethro's tail begins to thump heavily against the kitchen lino at the word 'park', in anticipation of that happy event.

Biscuit stares at the Labrador's yellow tail for a moment with his head nodding in time to the thumps. His mouth opens, a little drool beginning to gather there, and he pants thoughtfully.

Suddenly a look of inspiration comes over Biscuit. His eyelids twitch and he lumbers up off his heavy hindquarters, turns round three times in quick succession, then begins to thump his own tail. Disjointedly, out of time with Jethro's, which makes me and Molly wince. He has never shared our sense of musical appreciation. On the whole, Labradors are not a hugely artistic lot.

'Park?' Biscuit repeats excitedly. 'Park? Park?'

'Park,' Jethro agrees.

Biscuit's grin widens. More drool appears at the corner of his mouth, and a long string of gloop descends slowly to the lino. 'Park,' he moans in apparent ecstasy.

Jethro turns round twice more. 'Park, park.'

Tina appears in the kitchen doorway. Stretching out her front legs, the greyhound gives a yawn of exquisite boredom. 'What on earth is going on here? With all the noise you're making, I expected to find Minton doling out the flea and tick treatment, at the very least.'

'Park,' Jethro informs her.

'Oh, is that all?'

'Park, park, park, park, park!'

In a state of near hysteria, Biscuit directs a series of high-pitched barks at Mr Minton, who is looking at him in disgust now. He bumps into Jethro, who tumbles backwards into the metal water bowl and knocks it over again.

Cold water streams across the lino like a tiny river, and we all scrabble out of its reach.

Mr Minton says a word that used to make Mrs Minton shriek with outrage. Now he can say it with impunity, I suppose. Loudly and frequently, too.

He lunges for Jethro's collar.

The rest of us escape his wrath by cramming ourselves under the small kitchen table, though there really isn't room for everyone. In the confusion, Tina treads on Molly's bad leg, and my sister yelps. I growl at the offending greyhound – I'm normally very polite, but I can't always help myself where family is concerned – and she nips my rump, which I consider to be a disproportionate response.

In the ensuing chaos, Biscuit turns to me enthusiastically, his tongue lolling out. 'What does "park" mean again?'

It takes nearly another two hours for Mr Minton's temper to soften towards us. As usual after such incidents, we hold a council of war in the kitchen, then send Tina into the living room to see if she can put him in a better mood.

It works, of course. Exactly as expected.

'Tina never fails,' I say to Molly, and she nods her agreement.

'Uncanny.'

'Indeed.' I bend round to lick my hindquarters, which are still stinging from Tina's sharp teeth. 'I can't imagine what they see in her.'

A fine actress, that's what they see.

Tina has a trick of shuffling up to any human in a chair, then laying her head in their lap and gazing up at them soulfully. Not only is she the right height for that approach – as a beagle, I have about as much chance of reaching Minton's lap from a standing position as Biscuit has of winning a dog intelligence test – but she has the perfect face for it. Big round eyes, a soft tapering muzzle and an inherently tragic expression. Like nothing could ever make her happy again. Except possibly some leftover sausage roll.

Twenty minutes later, we are in the park.

It's not much of a park, basically a small leafy square with a fenced-off playground at its heart. But it has some marvellous trails between the ranked trees, redolent of squirrel and dotted with exciting offerings from other dogs that their generous owners have not removed. Mr Minton does not always bother to collect our leavings either, though that may be because his memory is a bit shaky these days.

I often see him pat down his pockets for a doggy-poop bag, his brows furrowed in confusion, and fail to produce one.

Not his fault, of course. Old dogs get forgetful too.

But it might make our lives better if he could remember to smile more often.

And occasionally buy dog treats.

As soon as we enter the small park, Mr Minton lets us off our tangled leashes and watches helplessly as we bound away in all directions.

'Stupid old Minty,' Tina laughs, glancing back without the slightest hint of regret, then spots a large man in a suit eating a sandwich on a nearby bench, and ten seconds later is sitting beside him, head on one side, at her most appealing.

We all have our favourite parts of the park. Jethro and Biscuit love the raised flower beds around the edges – strictly off limits to dogs, and therefore irresistible to those two. Tina prefers the company of humans to her fellow canines, especially when they have food, so she enjoys peering through the railings at the kids in the playground. No doubt she hopes her thin, shivering frame and mournful eyes will attract attention sooner or later. And we all know that attention for Tina means treats: here, sticky handfuls of sweets fed through the railings by toddlers, pungent-smelling crisps from the older kids, and the occasional sandwich crust from a watchful parent.

As for me, I like to chase around between the trees, faster and faster, head down, nose to the ground, following some intriguing scent. And Molly – well, my faithful sister tends to go wherever I go. Only rather slower.

Today I run around in a circle for several minutes, wagging my tail violently, surrounded by so many stenches, smells and aromas that I'm actually dazed and can't make up my mind which to investigate first.

'Fascinating!' I exclaim, nostrils flaring as I snuffle round and round on the damp turf. 'What is that smell? And that smell? And *that* smell?'

Molly sits down in the centre of my dizzying circle and pants gently while she waits for me to make up my mind. The expression on her pert brown-and-white patched face is non-judgemental, and maybe even a touch indulgent.

She's used to me dithering, in other words.

Though strictly speaking, this is not dithering. This is me *deciding*. Which is a much more complicated and scientific process than dithering, since it involves eliminating some smells as less interesting than others so that I can selectively home in on the most alluring and provocative smells in the park.

Meanwhile, our housemates are involved in problematic decisions of their own. Walks are always chaotic, often resulting in crossed leashes and noisy altercations, but today is even less orderly than usual, probably because we have been locked up in the house for the past few days, waiting for that damn rain to stop. So within moments of being let off the leash, we are all doing something we probably shouldn't, in wildly disparate areas of the park, while Minty stands and shouts at first one, then another of us, to abso-lutely no effect.

Jethro likes to think of himself as the leader, with Biscuit as his second-in-command. So those two work together as they converge on an unsuspecting toddler with an ice cream, tails thumping greedily. His mother shrieks and tries to bat the two dogs away with her handbag. Biscuit looks startled and apologetic at the same time, which involves raising the tips of his floppy yellow ears in a surprised manner while abasing himself as though all this has been a terrible misunderstanding. Meanwhile Jethro, never very fond of abasing himself, goes to the opposite extreme and barks gamely at the toddler, who not surprisingly drops his ice cream and begins to wail.

Time for Mr Minton to intervene.

'You naughty dogs!' he shouts, and grabs Jethro's collar before he can escape. 'Come away from that ice cream.'

Jethro's eyes bulge as he is dragged unwillingly from the fallen ice cream.

'No,' he moans, and tries to slow his forced removal by lowering his capacious rear end to the ground and sinking all his claws in the mud so that, as he is dragged away, he leaves behind a Labrador-shaped trail.

'Nobody want this ice cream, then?' Biscuit asks quickly. He does not wait for an answer, of course, but plunges his nose straight into the abandoned white mess. 'Tasty but cold, cold, cold. Teeth hurt.' Then he finds the cone and crunches ruminatively. 'Oh, this is better. Like a hat.'

Molly looks at him, then at me, her head to one side. 'A hat?'

'He means, *not* cold.'

I consider going to investigate the final traces of ice cream myself. I can smell it from here, and it's certainly good. But Biscuit might not take very kindly to my interference and, besides, Mr Minton has got Jethro back on his leash and is not looking very happy. He's doing that thing with his hair again. And he doesn't have much more hair to lose.

'Do you think ... Should we go back?' Molly asks tentatively, also watching old Mr Minton struggling with a recalcitrant Jethro.

'Probably.'

But I do not move yet. It's entertainment, isn't it?

Mr Minton makes a grab for Biscuit's collar and turns to apologise profusely to the young woman with the toddler, who is now angrily wrestling her child into a buggy and promising all kinds of terrible vengeance for his ill-behaved dogs. I catch the word, 'Police,' and see Mr Minton's face change.

'I'm really very sorry,' he says, almost desperately. 'It won't happen again.'

But the woman has gone.

'Wait, one more lick, one more . . .' Biscuit too is dragged away with a lugubrious expression and a white beard, for all the world like a dog in a Santa suit. He stares in vain at the patch of mushy, ice creamy grass he has been forced to leave behind for some other lucky explorer. 'Oh damn.'

His face alarmingly flushed, Minton wheezes and bends to clip the leash to his collar. 'You bad dog.'

'Where?' Biscuit extends a large pink tongue and licks speculatively round his muzzle, trying and failing to reach the last remnants of ice cream smeared beneath his chin. His face takes on a puzzled air as he senses milky treasure close at hand, yet is unable to locate its exact whereabouts. 'Where? Where?'

While all this is happening, Jethro makes a determined break for it, but only manages to get his leash thoroughly tangled up with Biscuit's. 'Let's pull,' he pants, dragging on the leash. 'Pull, pull, pull. Come on, Biscuit.'

Swearing, his face red as a tomato, Mr Minton struggles to separate them, but the two Labradors won't stand still long enough for him to succeed. Instead, the idiots try to keep walking while tangled up together, even if it has to be sideways, like a feathery blond crab.

Molly and I watch in astonishment as the two dogs suddenly break free from Minton's grasp and waddle across the grass together, leashes trailing behind them, inextricably stuck rump to rump, like two halves of a gigantic shambling monster with eight legs and two tails. Even Tina, coming to investigate this strange creature, gets knocked aside with a yelp as they amble on towards an unknown destination, with Minton limping behind them, shaking his fist uselessly in the air.

Slowly, I lower my own bottom to the grass and enjoy the show. 'Oh, now this is fun. Can we do this again tomorrow?'

To my surprise though, Molly is not amused by their antics. Instead she is standing beside me with a worried expression, her brows pleated together.

I tilt my head, gazing round at her.

'Hey, Sis, what is it?'

Molly makes a little whining noise. 'Trouble,' she says cryptically, and lifts her head to sniff the air. 'I smell it coming.'

❧ THREE ❧

The next morning, when Mr Minton is outside in the back yard, mending a fence for the fifth time because Biscuit keeps knocking it down, I hear Jethro lumbering up the stairs. I have been sleeping on the sofa while Mr Minton is not inside to turf me off, but at the sound of his claws on the uncarpeted landing, I stir, ears pricking.

Molly is still asleep beside me on the sofa, but I see Tina glance up at the ceiling too as it shakes under his weight.

She looks at me and shakes her head. 'Minton's not going to like that. Not upstairs.'

Biscuit wanders in from the kitchen on three legs, scratching as he walks, which is a peculiar skill of his. 'Up . . . up . . . upstairs?'

'Jethro,' I tell him.

'Oh, that's not good. Not good.' The scratching reaches a peak of intensity, and his whole body shakes. Then he stops abruptly. 'Not upstairs.'

'He'd better come down before Minton finds him up there,' Tina comments, then turns round neatly in her basket and settles back to sleep.

Losing interest, Biscuit wanders back into the kitchen.

I listen for another thirty seconds, then lay my chin on my paws again, close my eyes, and try to fall asleep too.

But I'm worried.

Mr Minton really does not like us dogs to venture upstairs. That's strictly human territory, and always was, even when his wife was still alive. I have only been up there a few times in my entire life, and find it a gloomy, boring place. The toilet always smells intriguing, granted. But otherwise I can't imagine why Jethro would take it upon himself to go up there. Except that he's bloody-minded and likes to make trouble, not just for himself but for each and every one of us.

Jethro is generous that way.

I decide he will not be stupid enough to loiter upstairs, so try not to worry about it. Anyway, it's a nice warm morning, and I am sleepy . . .

But ten minutes pass, and Jethro still does not come down.

Another few minutes later, I am disturbed by a sudden clatter from overhead, then a subdued growling, as though Jethro is having a game with someone up there. Or more likely with himself, since the rest of us are all downstairs.

Even Molly looks up this time, frowning at the ceiling. 'What *is* that?'

'Jethro,' I tell her. 'In Minton's bedroom.'

'Good grief. Isn't he in enough trouble after yesterday at the park?'

'Apparently not.'

She sighs, then stretches and jumps lightly down from the sofa. 'Well, we need to get him down before old Mr Minton comes back in.'

'Leave him, he'll come down on his own soon enough,' Tina says from her basket, her voice muffled by the long paw covering her face.

Molly hesitates, then trots gently into the kitchen. When she comes back, she is looking concerned. 'Minton's nearly finished that fence,' she tells me.

'So?' I ask sleepily, yawning.

'So unless we want another scene like yesterday, and probably not even slop for tea, we're going to have to get Jethro downstairs. Because Minton will be coming in again soon.'

'Why me, though? Can't Biscuit go? Or Tina?'

Tina lifts her paw, stares at me hard for a couple of seconds, then replaces it over her eyes and pretends to snore.

Molly tips her head to one side, her expression quizzical. 'Biscuit? You want to send Biscuit to get him down? Why don't you send the tea cosy up instead? It might have a better chance of success.'

'Damn,' I mutter.

I had been having such a nice dream too. Involving a squirrel.

But I jump down from the sofa, and nuzzle into Molly's shoulder to reassure her. 'No worries. If you think we need to get Jethro down, then that is what's going to happen.'

'Thanks, Bertie.'

I hesitate. 'Tina?'

'Not a chance,' comes the answer.

I look at Molly and shrug. 'You and me then, Sis.'

'Suits me.'

I bound up the stairs with Molly slowly bringing up the rear, and onto the landing. It's gloomier than I remember from last time, but the Mintons' bedroom door is slightly open, sunlight spilling out over the bare wooden boards. Mr Minton must have opened the curtains when he got up this morning, I realise, nudging the door with my head and pushing warily inside.

Jethro is in there. The wardrobe door is ajar, and he is up on his hind legs, partially inside it, rooting around with a snuffling noise.

'What on earth is he doing?' Molly asks, bemused.

Startled, Jethro whips round. Then he sees it is only us, and that Minton isn't upstairs too, and he relaxes. His tongue lolls in an annoying grin.

'Oh, it's you.'

I try to see what he's doing inside the wardrobe. 'What have you got there, Jethro?'

'None of your damn business.'

'It's my business if we'll lose our supper because of it.'

'Get lost, midgets,' he tells us casually, and adds a rude word that has Molly staring. 'Can't you see I'm busy here?'

I growl, the short hairs bristling on the back of my neck. 'Mind your language in front of my sister,' I warn him.

'Or what?'

My temper flares, and I dash forward, knocking into the large yellow Labrador with all my strength. I only come to about halfway up his leg, so not exactly a death charge. It's also rather like banging my face headfirst into a wall, and I stagger back, momentarily dazed. Still, I recover quickly. *Where there's no sense, there's no feeling*, as Mrs Minton used to say whenever I accidentally head-butted a door as a puppy.

Anyway, my onslaught serves its purpose.

Jethro tumbles backwards, and I'm able to jump into the wardrobe while he's flailing about, trying to recover his balance.

I give a short triumphant bark, but of course my victory does not last long. Our weights are not even remotely matched, so my only advantage over a bigger dog like Jethro was surprise, and that's gone now.

'You're dead meat,' Jethro tells me, growling as he advances, his pitch deep and menacing.

I am standing on one of Mrs Minton's summer dresses in the base of the wardrobe. The old dress is all creased and crumpled, probably from Jethro's rooting. And as soon as I sniff it, I know what Jethro has been doing.

It's hard not to curl my lip at him in pity and disgust. But I suppose he has his reasons. None of us have been behaving rationally since Mrs Minton passed.

'What's that?' Molly asks, running out from where she has been hiding under the bed. Her eyes widen. 'Is that . . . one of Mrs Minton's dresses?'

'Yes,' I admit.

'What's that smell?' She slips in past Jethro, bravely ignoring his growl of warning, and sniffs at the dress too. 'Eww,' she exclaims, and then looks at him sideways. 'Have you been . . . slobbering on it?'

Jethro looks at us both in turn, vaguely embarrassed. 'No,' he tells her, then hesitates and adds, 'Maybe.' Then

26

rolls his eyes. 'All right, yes. So what? A little slobber never hurts anything.'

'Gross,' she says succinctly.

'It smells good,' he says defensively.

No argument there. The dress does smell all Mrs Mintony, a warm and comforting old lady smell of talcum powder and sweat and pockets that once held meaty dog treats. The smell makes me think of table scraps and long walks by the canal and hours of tummy-tickles on the sofa, all the things we don't get any more.

But all the same. The poor woman's been dead for months. And here he is, rubbing his gluey saliva all over one of her old dresses. I doubt even she would have understood.

'Mr Minton's not going to like this,' I tell him. 'Humans are funny about clothes.'

'In what way?' he demands.

'Well, for starters, they wear them,' I point out, and he can't exactly find fault with that, so just shrugs. 'Then they don't like slobber on them.'

'She's not here. She doesn't know about the slobber.'

'But Mr Minton will know,' Molly says gently. 'And he may not be very happy about it. He throws out rubbish, doesn't he? Things he doesn't need any more. But he hasn't thrown her dresses out, even though she's gone.'

Jethro growls again. 'I'm bored of this conversation now.'

'You mean you're losing the argument,' I say.

He lunges and grabs the dress with his teeth, then begins to drag it backwards, out from under my paws, out of the wardrobe entirely.

'Hey,' I exclaim, sliding forwards with the dress.

'Mine,' he growls, still gripping the stripy material between his teeth.

'Put it back.'

'Make me.'

There's nothing for it. My weight is not enough to stop him, and indeed another one of his powerful jerks forward and I'll fall out of the wardrobe, bringing the dress with me and probably landing on top of Molly.

I back up, bottom down, growling back at him, and grab the vanishing hem of the dress with my teeth.

Jethro looks infuriated. Like he's going to bite my head off the first chance he gets.

'Mine,' he repeats, yanking on the dress.

'Not yours,' I insist, and pull in the opposite direction.

He drags harder. 'Mine.'

'Not . . . bloody . . . yours.'

'Mine, mine, mine.'

I growl and drag hard, and he growls and drags hard, and the dress stretches between us, the thin material drawn tight.

'Please be careful,' Molly moans, watching in horror.

Suddenly there's a heavy tread on the stairs, a sound we ignore in our desperate struggle for control of Mrs Minton's clothing, then Mr Minton himself is standing in the doorway. He stares at us, three dogs in his bedroom, his private space, two of us engaged in a tug-of-war with one of his dead wife's favourite dresses.

'You . . .' He struggles for breath, slamming his fist against the wall. His face is red. 'God damn you, I should have you all put down. You . . . bad . . . wicked . . .'

He staggers unevenly towards us, swearing and repeatedly thumping his fist against the wall.

'I told you he'd be upset,' I tell Jethro, with some difficulty, as the dress is still firmly clenched between my teeth.

'He's always upset,' Jethro replies, and drags back on his end, ignoring Mr Minton and determined to be the winner.

He gets his wish.

The thin summer dress, stretched beyond endurance, tears down a seam with a loud ripping noise. I fall backwards into the back of the wardrobe. Jethro tumbles against the foot of Mr Minton's wooden-framed bed, a fragment of dress still held victoriously between his teeth.

Mr Minton gives a choking sound of fury, and lunges for his collar. 'That's it, that's the last straw!' he shouts, and smacks Jethro hard on his rump. 'Drop that. Drop it! Give it to me now.'

To my amazement, Jethro continues to growl at old Mr Minton, uncowed by this attack on his rump, refusing to relinquish the torn shred of dress hanging from between his teeth.

We all stare at him, eyes wide.

He's breaking the cardinal rule: never behave aggressively towards your owner. And he doesn't even seem to care.

Molly gives a little yelp of fear. 'Run, Bertie,' she tells me, then darts awkwardly between Mr Minton's legs and heads downstairs.

I wait a few seconds, then follow her down to our usual hiding place. Tina is already there, but silently makes room for us. Like my sister, she has a sixth sense for impending trouble.

From above, we hear thumps and thuds and barks and shouting.

Molly shivers, cowering next to me under the kitchen table. I can tell from her expression that her bad leg is aching.

'This isn't good,' she whispers. 'Not good at all.'

I start to tell my sister not to worry. My default response whenever she's feeling concerned or upset. Then I stop.

Because, for once, I am not sure how to reassure her.

I saw Mr Minton's face when he walked in and found us fighting over his dead wife's dress. And it was not a very forgiving face.

In the park, Molly said she could smell trouble coming.

I think it's here.

Sure enough, fifteen minutes later, we are all back on our leashes and trotting hurriedly down the road again with Mr Minton.

It's like a repeat of our earlier outing.

Only the atmosphere is not one of excitement and barely suppressed energy this time. We are not looking forward to a mad scamper in the park or a lazy walk beside the canal. Mr Minton has his cloth cap on and is looking grim. He has a large bag with him, stuffed with all our feeding bowls and toys and even Tina's hairy old blanket.

After a long walk in a direction we have never taken before, through unfamiliar streets busy with traffic and fumes, he stops in front of a low, dreary-looking building that smells of dogs and fear. In reverse order. I can't read the sign above the door but there's a picture of a dog, and a huge paw print beside it.

I sniff, but all I can smell are car fumes.

'In here,' Mr Minton says gruffly, pulling on our leads, and we all crowd after him through the narrow doorway, uncertain and jostling each other.

The door nearly closes on Tina's tail and she yelps.

Minton does not even glance in her direction, but marches us to the counter instead. 'I've had enough of this lot,' he tells the young woman there. 'They were my wife's dogs and she's passed away now, so I want shot of them.' He shows her the bag. 'I've brought all their documents and all this other stuff. I wasn't sure what you'd need.'

She leans over and counts us. 'Five dogs?' she asks, a little incredulous, and then smiles at Tina. 'Oh, what a sweetie.'

Tina looks back at her with a shrewd expression.

'Five, yes.' Mr Minton pauses. 'Do I have to pay?'

'No, but you may not be able to change your mind once they've been processed. So are you sure about this, sir?'

'Perfectly,' he says, not even hesitant.

The woman takes the plastic bag bulging with our possessions, then our five leashes. She pushes a stack of forms across the counter, and hands him a pen. 'If you could just fill these out . . .'

She comes round and crouches beside us, beginning to check us over like a vet as though looking for signs of disease, her touch cool and professional.

She tilts up my chin and examines my eyes and teeth. Her hands smell of latex gloves and disinfectant, an unpleasant combination I remember from when Mrs Minton used to do her spring-cleaning.

I shudder but dare not pull away in case I cause trouble for Molly.

My little sister is shaking beside me, tail tucked between her legs, awaiting her turn to be examined. 'I don't like this place, Bertie,' she whispers, staring around at the intimidating white walls and frosted-glass door panels. 'It reminds me of the vet's.'

I know what she means. The place smells like death.

'I'm here with you, Molly,' I remind her, 'I won't let anything happen to you.'

But secretly I'm not feeling very confident myself.

Jethro moans and shivers, all his earlier bravado gone. 'Is this it? Is this the final visit to the vet? Are we going to be put down?'

'Put down?' Biscuit echoes beside him, his voice hollow with terror. He scrabbles backwards a few steps, all four paws exuding sweat on the dark lino floor. 'That . . . doesn't . . . sound . . .'

'I think it's a dog shelter,' Molly whispers. 'For unwanted dogs.'

Biscuit is shaking now. '*Unwanted?*'

Tina snaps at Jethro. 'This is all your fault, you oaf. Minton wasn't perfect, and the food was appalling, but at least we had a roof over our heads there. Why couldn't you leave well alone?' Then she sucks in her ribs and turns her lighthouse beam smile on the young woman. 'Hello, hello.'

There are pictures of dogs on the wall above the counter. Sad-looking dogs. Painfully thin, starved-looking dogs. Cowed dogs, looking up hopefully.

I think it's a dog shelter. For unwanted dogs.

Before we know what is happening, Mr Minton has finished filling out the forms. He takes one last look at us all, then nods with apparent satisfaction.

'Right, that's done,' he says, then says goodbye to the woman and walks out of the building without a backward glance.

The door swings shut behind him, and we are left alone in the cool, echoing corridor, staring at the space where he was.

My legs are not trembling, but they feel decidedly shaky. I realise I cannot recall a time when Molly and I did not live with the Mintons. Even the memory of our puppy days is hazy now. Mr Minton is the only owner I know. He's *our* human.

Now he's gone.

Without even a backward look too.

Unwanted.

It's only now that I understand the full implications of that word.

The young woman goes back behind the counter, shuffling about and making odd clinking noises. Getting keys? Metal tools? Instruments of torture? She is still holding our long leashes over the counter as she moves about, and we huddle together, our necks jerking at every tug.

'Wh . . . what's going to happen to us now?' Tina asks me, and for the first time she looks genuinely frightened.

She is asking me, and none of the others, because I am famous for having all the answers. For being the smartest dog in the house. For always knowing what needs to be done in a crisis.

This time, I look at her helplessly, and say nothing.

Even I have my limitations.

'We're all going to die,' Jethro moans, 'that's what's going to happen. This is it. This is the end.'

Studying our surroundings, it's hard for once not to share his gloomy outlook.

Biscuit has no doubts at all. He listens to his friend's prognosis, then whimpers in fear, half-cocking his leg against the wall of the counter. 'Oh no, it's coming out, coming out.'

We all stare at him in consternation.

The young woman comes out from behind her counter. 'Oh for God's sake,' she says, looking at the spreading puddle.

We expect shouting and grumbling, and wait apprehensively for her reaction. That's what Mr Minton would have done.

But she does not punish Biscuit for his accident. Instead she tears a few handfuls of paper from a roll fixed to the wall, pushes him roughly aside and cleans the floor.

When she straightens, she shakes her head at him in a clearly disapproving manner, then calls down the hall, 'Sharon? Can you spare five minutes?' She throws the paper into a large bin and gathers our leashes together again, studying us with a frown. 'I'm going to need a hand with this lot.'

A few minutes later we find ourselves being dragged into a long corridor with a cold concrete floor and dozens of large stacked wire cages, some empty, but most occupied by other dogs. The noise of their barking is deafening, and the smell of the place – an unpleasant mixture of urine and bleach that burns my nostrils – is overpowering.

There are dogs everywhere, smelly and excited and dejected, pressing up against the bars to stare at us, newcomers to their prison, the enclosed space thick with barks and yelps and exclamations and insults.

I am thrust into an empty cage on an upper level, the door closed and secured before I even have time to turn around and face my gaoler.

Molly is dragged away down the block by the other woman, and stares back at me in horror. 'No, no, I have to be with Bertie,' she cries.

But the humans pay no attention.

❧ FOUR ❧

My first night in the dog shelter is hellish and seems to last for ever. The big dog next to me snores for most of the night, occasionally twitching in his sleep, but he is not the problem. No, it's the sheer number of occupied cages that overwhelms my senses. There are dogs of every kind here, moaning and whimpering and barking sporadically. Not to mention the number and variety of smells . . .

I have never smelled so many different odours, some pleasant, some bewildering, some wildly unfamiliar, some downright uncomfortable. My nostrils quiver, my brain working overtime, but I am soon dizzy trying to separate and identify each one.

I give my poor nose a rest after a couple of hours and settle my head on my paws instead, listening to the echoes and cries until my ears too become exhausted and I finally doze off to sleep. Only fitfully though, waking every half an hour or so at some disturbing whisper from a nearby cage, or a sudden burst of uncontrollable barking further down the block that sets most of my neighbours off.

It's a horrible feeling, being trapped and on show at the same time. But when I take a few minutes to investigate my prison, it turns out the cage is not as restrictive as I feared.

The back wall conceals a flap that leads to a short outside run, and for a while it is soothing to stand outside and breathe cool air, and listen to nearby traffic instead of other dogs. But I soon grow lonely, and a little scared too, and shuffle back inside where at least it is dark and I can find some comfort in the company of my fellow prisoners.

Soon after dawn, electric lighting flickers on and a moment later the shelter people come back in. A man and a different woman this time, in plastic aprons and carrying buckets with an interesting smell. They are talking to each other loudly, paying little attention to us dogs, but at least they push a little food through a flap in each cage as they pass.

The man hesitates by my cage.

'This one's new.'

The woman nods. 'Came in last thing yesterday, Sharon said. Five dogs from one household.'

'Reason?'

'It was an old man. Couldn't cope any more.'

The man has a beard and a single gold earring. He studies me. 'A beagle, I like beagles.' He smiles, reaching through the bars of the cage to stroke one of my ears. I rub myself gratefully against the bars, and his smile widens. 'He's gorgeous, this one.'

'There's another beagle, down in B Block. Same litter, but a bitch.'

'Those two should find homes soon enough. People always love a beagle.'

'Bit high-spirited though, don't you think?'

'Beagles don't suit everyone, that's true. They need plenty of love and attention, you can't leave them alone all day or they can become destructive. But if they're house-trained, and as appealing as this one . . . No, I doubt we'll keep them long. Not like some of the poor creatures that come through here.'

He withdraws his hand, and they both move on, pushing a handful of dried dog food into each cage as they go, still talking.

I press up against the unyielding bars and angle my head to follow their progress, eager to see where Molly has been caged.

What did the woman say? She's in B Block.

But what does that mean?

But when the two do not pause again in front of any of the other cages, moving on through another door that clangs heavily shut behind them, I realise Molly is not even in the same corridor as me. I sniff the air hopefully as the door closes, but cannot catch even a hint of her familiar scent from the next block. There are so many other smells here. Dozens and dozens of dogs, all exuding their own special pungent odours. But I am convinced that I could pick my sister's scent out even in a crowd of a thousand dogs, my nose is so sensitive.

I can't smell her at all though.

Which means she is not anywhere nearby.

I sink down on the floor of the cage, too despondent even to eat the handful of dried dog food the humans have left behind.

'Better eat that before it goes stale,' says a huge grey and white walking carpet in the cage next to me. He is grey and shambolic, a heaving mass that has been snoring most of the night. Two piercing eyes stare out from his hairy rug-face. His voice sounds like it's coming out of a deep pit. 'There's nothing more until lunchtime, most days, and that's only if Peter's on a full day. When he goes early, sometimes we don't even get lunch.'

'Not hungry,' I reply.

He looks me up and down. 'What's hunger got to do with it? Little fella like yourself, you need all the sustenance you can get. Otherwise you could waste away. I've seen that happen to other dogs in here. It's not a pretty sight.'

He has a point.

Reluctantly, I nose at one of the tiny star-shaped biscuits, then crunch it down. Hmm, not bad. Better than Mr Minton's slop, at any rate.

I hoover up another couple of biscuits and chew on them, suddenly starving.

'Who's Peter?' I ask between mouthfuls.

'The man who spoke to you. One of the shelter staff. He's all right. Talks to us like we're humans, you know the type. Thea's OK too, she doesn't smack. But I don't like Sharon. Or that woman just now, Elaine. She runs this place like it's a prison.' He shows his teeth. They look scarily large and sharp, if a little yellow. 'Not very efficiently either, if you ask me.'

'Right, thanks,' I say, and can't help staring at his gently thumping tail. It's so thick and furry, it looks like a

39

dead squirrel attached to his butt. 'So . . . what breed are you?'

'Old English sheepdog,' he says proudly, then winks. 'Pedigree, but it doesn't make much of a difference. Third time I've been in. I never stay long, I'm always popular.' He scratches ruminatively. 'The families who pick me up seem to bring me back very quickly though.'

I nod sagely. 'Too big?'

'That, and too damn hairy. I leave bits of myself everywhere. Folk don't seem to like that.'

I grin at his self-deprecating tone. 'I reckon five of me would fit into your skin.'

'I'm not surprised, if that's how slowly you eat. I could have eaten the whole of you in the time it took for you to eat that one biscuit.'

I pause, mid-chew. 'I'm Bertie. What's your name?'

'Gandalf.'

'Strange name.'

'The humans seem to love it. They always laugh when they hear it for the first time.' He shrugs. 'No idea why.'

'Humans have a strange sense of humour.'

'You got that right.' He watches me finish the last of my biscuits. 'Good, huh?'

'Better than slop.'

He looks puzzled. 'Slop?'

'Chow we got at my old place. Brown mush from a plastic roll.'

'Bad human, huh?'

I shrug, sitting down to gaze about myself. 'Not *that* bad.

At least he fed us. Like the staff said, Minton was just too old to cope. There were five of us, after all, and some of us were not exactly . . . well-behaved.'

I explain about the others, and how we lived quite happily at the Mintons' until Mrs Minton passed away, and Gandalf listens attentively, nodding in places, looking sympathetic in others. I get the feeling he's done this plenty of times before. Eased some new occupant into his new life in the shelter by asking a few searching questions, then listening to his story. I wonder how old he is, then decide it would be rude to ask.

When I mention Molly, he interrupts with a smile. 'You mean that charming young beagle you came in with last night?'

'That's right.' I frown, biting at an itchy spot on my right shoulder. 'I wish I knew where she was right now. B Block, they said.'

'That's through there,' he tells me, jerking his head in the direction of the door at the far end of the corridor of cages.

I stare that way anxiously. 'Is there any way to . . .'

'To get out of these cages?'

I nod, glancing at him.

He laughs humourlessly, then shakes his head. 'Not a chance, I'm afraid. We're prisoners, all right. And females are kept apart from males.'

I feel bitterly disappointed, though it is only what I expected. 'Molly,' I murmur, and rest my head on my paws. 'This is all my fault. Molly warned me to be careful. But I didn't listen, of course. Instead I started that stupid row with Jethro, and ended up tearing Mrs Minton's dress . . .'

Gandalf watches me with kind eyes. 'Don't worry, little fella. You'll probably get to see her again at exercise time.'

'What's that?'

He scratches himself, thinking hard. 'Like walkies, I suppose. Only we walk round and round the yard on leads, usually in groups of five or so.'

'And you think they may walk us at the same time as Molly?'

'Dogs that come in together usually get to walk together. I think that's to avoid scraps with rival dogs. There's no fighting allowed, by the way. Anyone caught fighting gets put back in the cages on exercise restriction.' Gandalf smiles at me wryly. 'Best to avoid getting into any other disagreements, in other words.'

To my surprise, Gandalf is right. Roughly mid-morning, the woman called Thea comes to release me from the cage, clips a leash to my collar, then walks me down to an exercise yard.

I scan every cage in passing, just in case I see Molly.

Dogs bark abuse and greetings along the way, some aggressive, others eager to say hello. I try hard not to get distracted by the strange sights and smells, I am so keen not to miss my sister if I see her.

Thea stops at one of the cages near the end of the corridor, and to my surprise I recognise Biscuit, cowering in the corner of a lower-level cage. She opens the cage and tries to coax him out, but of course he refuses to budge.

'Stranger, stranger,' he repeats, not looking at us.

Maybe Gandalf is right about us all being exercised together, I think. Which means I may be reunited with Molly in a few minutes.

Assuming Biscuit can be persuaded to leave his cage.

'Hurry up,' I tell him urgently, eager not to lose any time with Molly. 'I think it's walkies. You like walkies, Biscuit.'

Biscuit gazes at me, amazed and a little puzzled, as though he has already forgotten who I am. Then he edges towards the cage door, still staring. 'Oh, it's you . . .' His brows jerk together. 'Bertie.'

'That's right. It's Bertie. Now come on.' I try to inject some enthusiasm into my voice. 'Walkies!'

'Walkies,' he repeats, a little unsure, but allows the woman to grab him by the collar. He ducks his head as the lead is attached, then follows us down the corridor without any more argument. He seems relieved the decision has been taken out of his paws. 'Jethro go walkies too, you think?'

'Maybe.'

Thea turns a large key in a side door ahead, then pushes out into cold sunshine. There's a sharp breeze blowing, and I can smell traffic fumes, and that warm autumnal odour that bleeds from trees as they start to lose their leaves. The sky is a pale blue-white that reminds me we are heading into colder weather now, and there will be no more warm days to look forward to. It's hard to imagine what life will be like without Mr Minton. Hard and frightening too, if I am honest. But I have to focus on what's next, not what lies in the past. What else can I do?

Biscuit moans with a sudden wild excitement and thumps his tail violently from side to side. For a moment I think he must have seen food. But I have misjudged the faithful Labrador.

'Jethro,' he chokes, pulling on the lead until it nearly strangles him. 'Jethro, Tina, Molly . . . Jethro, Tina, Molly,'

I have been staring around at the outside of the shelter, studying the doors and windows, the potential escape routes. But at the sound of my sister's name I turn and leap forward, dragging on my lead with as much enthusiasm as Biscuit himself.

Molly!

My sister is on a lead too, along with our old housemates Jethro and Tina, all three of them tied up to a metal ring attached to the wall.

She jumps up at my approach, grinning broadly. 'Bertie!'

'Hey there, Sis!'

Tina looks at me disdainfully over Molly's head, then turns and continues licking her rump. 'Morning, Bertie,' she remarks. 'You know, when Minton brought us here last night, I thought it would be the start of a new life for me. A brand-new social circle. I was so excited . . . But it seems they like to keep dogs from one household together here, at least until they get rehoused. So here we all are again.' Her voice drips contempt. 'What a treat.'

Ignoring her, I nuzzle into Molly's warm shoulder, and smell her fear and nervousness at once. Right there and then, I decide not to let her see how worried I am, in case it makes her feel worse.

'Rough night, Sis?'

'Not too bad.'

She sits back, her tongue lolling, trying to look casual, but I can already tell she's favouring her right leg. Which means the left one is hurting again.

'How's your cage?' I ask, forcing myself to sound cheery. 'I swear mine's almost as comfy as the Mintons' sofa . . .'

'Liar,' Molly says, but manages a shaky laugh. 'Though I wish we could be housed in the same block. It's not fair, splitting us up like this.'

'Perhaps if we show them how close we are, they'll move us back together.'

'Good idea.'

I glance round at Jethro and Biscuit, who are joyfully sniffing each other's backsides without the slightest sign of embarrassment.

'Maybe not that close though . . .'

She grins.

I run round and round my sister, barking excitedly and deliberately getting our leads tangled 'Oh, Bertie,' she exclaims, and her ear flops over one eye as she bends, trying to extricate herself. 'Now look what you've done.'

'Just trying to show the humans we belong together.'

'You're more likely to get us in trouble.'

Thea just laughs as she releases us from our tangle though, and bends to rub both our heads. She does not seem annoyed by our antics.

'Brother and sister, aren't you? And very pleased to see each other, no doubt about that.' She gathers our leads together, and draws us both along together, with Jethro, Biscuit and Tina bounding behind. 'Well, hopefully we'll find a nice family to adopt you soon enough.'

Molly looks at me excitedly. 'Did you hear that, Bertie? A nice family.'

'I heard.'

'That would be a dream come true for us.'

Normally I drag on the lead on a walk, keen to get ahead, but today I drop my pace and stay beside my sister as we are led around the yard, aware that she is limping. 'Leg still hurting, Molly?'

'I'll be fine,' she insists happily. 'Oh, I'm so glad now that Mr Minton brought us to the shelter. I can hardly wait for us to be taken home by a lovely family. I hope they'll be kind and give us proper food and comfy baskets,' she gushes, 'and lots and lots of friendly hugging and stroking.'

I smile at her, though inside I'm uneasy. 'I'm sure they will, Sis.'

❧ FIVE ❧

Three days go by like that at the shelter, with occasional group walks followed by long hours of boredom and solitude in the cages, and then something unexpected and miraculous happens.

On the morning of day four, I am led into a small square room with a tiled floor that smells of disinfectant and has a huge window high up in the wall.

'Stay,' Elaine tells me sharply, and closes the door.

I look at the door for a few seconds, bemused by this odd behaviour, then turn to investigate my new surroundings. It seems I am alone in here with only a chewy ball for company. But hey, a chewy ball is the height of luxury after the three days I've just had, so I launch myself towards it with alacrity.

I spend the next few minutes chasing the ball round and round, hiding it under my paws, chewing it violently, and rolling on my back with it tucked under my chin. That last one is a speciality of mine, developed to amuse old Mrs Minton, and was always a favourite with her visitors too.

It's not long before I realise I am being watched through the high window.

I drop the ball and stare, panting gently.

There's a woman up there, peering down her nose at me. It's a very long nose too, in a pinched face, her skin rough and a little red in places. She reminds me of a very stern woman who once scolded Mr and Mrs Minton for letting us dogs off the lead in the park, which is apparently not allowed, even though everyone does it.

The woman is unsmiling and disapproving, and I back away from the window, a little unsure now. Perhaps I ought not to have grabbed the ball. But it was right there on the tiled floor, so I just assumed it was for my entertainment. It does look a bit mushy now, with a few traces of drool.

There's something about her narrowed gaze and compressed lips that makes me think of smacks and tellings-off and being pushed outside into the cold yard after 'bad behaviour'.

Perhaps it's her ball.

I tilt my head and stare back at her, a touch defiant now.

If she didn't want me to touch her precious ball, why leave it there in the first place? I'm a dog, and balls are my thing. Worse, I'm a beagle. You can't leave a beagle alone in a room with a ball and expect him to sit there all polite and wait for permission to maul it.

I'm not a poodle, for goodness sake!

Then the door opens.

I swing round to see Molly there, and can't help but grin at her.

'Molly,' I say thankfully.

Elaine bends to unclip my sister's lead. Free at last, Molly gives herself a little shake, then limps into the room.

'Bertie!' She inhales deeply, like she's enjoying my scent, then embraces me, shoulder to shoulder. She is warm and familiar, and I feel all my worries melting away as we stand there bonding. 'No walk yesterday. I missed you so much.'

I hate being apart from Molly even for a minute, so the past few days have been a torment for me. But I don't want to add worrying about me to her already long list of concerns.

I put a brave face on it and say lightly, 'Missed you too, Sis. How's the leg?'

'Are you fussing? You know I hate it when you fuss.'

'Someone's got to look out for you.'

She makes a face. 'I can look after myself, you know. Anyway, it only aches when you're not around to lick it better.'

'Then I'd better make sure I stick around,' I say jokingly.

'What is this place?' she asks, sniffing the air. 'Ugh, disinfectant. Why have they brought us here? And where are the others?'

'No idea.'

Curious, she glances past me and sees the ball. She raises her nose in the air again, this time with a half-smile. 'Hello, that's a tasty-smelling toy. But who's been chewing it?'

She pads over to the ball and gives it a good sniff.

'That would be me,' I admit, a little sheepishly, though she must be able to smell me all over it by now, and then glance towards the window.

The woman with the long nose and pinched face is still there, one bony hand pressed against the glass, and now

Elaine, who runs the shelter, has joined her. I am not sure I'm entirely comfortable with them both staring in at us. It's unnerving.

I remember that Mrs Minton bought a bright red goldfish as a pet one year. One of her young nieces took it away with her eventually, but now I understand how that goldfish must have felt, swimming round and round its big glass bowl with all us dogs watching it, utterly mesmerised.

Molly wrinkles up her nose. 'Eww, drool.'

'Sorry, Sis. Couldn't help it. I got excited.'

Molly nudges the ball with her nose. 'Still, it looks good and chewy. Shall we have a game, then?'

She chases the ball towards the wall, and the pinched-looking woman leans forward, watching her with a suddenly arrested expression. Something about her face makes me deeply uneasy.

'Better not, Sis. Leave it.'

She stops and looks back at me, puzzled. 'Why on earth? My leg's not *that* bad, you know. I can play ball.'

'We've got an audience.'

I nod towards the two women at the high window, and Molly stares upwards too, her brown-and-white patched ears perking up, her head tilted to one side in a characteristic gesture.

'Goodness,' she says blankly. 'A visitor. Who is she?'

'Chief of the ball police, if you ask me.'

'Pardon?'

'She didn't like me playing with that ball. Started frowning at me. I thought I was going to get a smack.'

Molly frowns, and takes a few steps forwards to study her better. She lifts herself onto her hind legs and rests her front paws on the wall, staring up at the woman. 'Hmm, she does look a little severe.'

'A little?' I grin, lifting myself up the wall to stare alongside her, both of us shamelessly studying the woman who was studying us. I'm enjoying myself more now that Molly is here. She always lifts my mood. 'I'm telling you, that face could curdle milk. I've seen cheerier bulldogs.'

'Bertie!'

'OK, that was mean. To bulldogs.'

Molly shakes her head, looking almost as disapproving as the woman at the window. 'Have you thought that she could be our next owner? That she's come to look the two of us over, to decide if she wants to take us home?'

I say nothing.

'So you'd better quit cracking jokes and start looking cute,' my sister warns me. Like this.'

Molly leaps backwards, performs a neat little somersault in mid-air and lands on all four paws at once, like some kind of dog gymnast. She really ought to have been in the circus. Then she turns and runs after the ball again with gusto. 'Otherwise she might pick somebody else. Like Tina.'

'Right.' I hesitate. 'Impressive flip, by the way.'

'Here, your turn.' Molly rolls the ball in my direction, then pretends to fight me for it. I let her knock me down and then scramble over my body, careful not to do anything that might hurt her leg, then sit up afterwards and watch her chewing ecstatically on the ball. She glances across at me, her brows pleated together, and even gives a little growl as a motivator. 'Hey, liven up! They're still watching.'

'Sorry, I'm just a bit . . .' I grab the ball off her and we chase around the tiled floor after it, mock-growling and rolling about together. 'Molly, are you sure you want us to go home with someone like that? I mean, she's not very friendly-looking.'

'She's not Mr Minton, that's all that matters.'

I grab the ball away from her and chew on it, my cheek swollen with mushed-up ball like I'm eating a gerbil. 'Mth thwo.'

She stares. '*What?*'

I spit out the ball and it rolls away, covered in saliva. 'That's true.'

Suddenly the door opens again.

The pinched-looking woman comes slowly into the room, Elaine one step behind her all the way. The woman is both very thin and very tall, wearing low black heels and a knee-length skirt of some coarse brown stuff that smells funny. I try to look up at her upper half, but it gives me a crick in the neck.

The visitor is wearing perfume, I realise, my nose wrinkling at the offensive odour. *Eau de pong*, as Mrs Minton used to say disparagingly of the Avon lady on her monthly visits. Humans do seem to enjoy overly sweet smells. Personally, I prefer Elaine's body odour, which is musty and always reminds me of old Mrs Minton's armpits. I still miss cuddling against her large, squishy body in the long evenings. But this new woman is not half as comfortable-smelling or looking.

I sneeze three times in quick succession, and recoil from her too-sweet perfume and bony hands. Unnecessarily as it turns out, because the woman is not looking at me but at Molly.

She crouches down next to my sister, and reaches out tentatively, almost as though she expects Molly to take a chunk out of her hand. 'Dear little doggy,' she says in a thin, creaking voice.

She sounds like an outhouse door in the wind.

Molly sits still and does a passable impersonation of an obedient beagle, jaws slightly open, a cute twinkle in her eye, tail wagging softly.

'Aww, just look at that, so sweet,' Elaine says, her tone indulgent. She flicks back her hair and smiles down at us both in her usual restrained way. Like smiling physically hurts her. 'How can you resist that face?'

The woman murmurs, 'Hmmm,' and glances sideways at me.

I fix her with an ironical eye.

'I must admit, she is exactly what I want,' the pinched-looking woman comments, turning her attention back to my sister.

Molly's appealing expression does not falter. If anything, her tail wags slightly more fervently. 'And this, dear brother, is how we do that,' she whispers out of the corner of her mouth.

I raise my brows. 'Good grief.'

The woman straightens up, smoothing down her skirt. 'Yes, I've made up my mind. I'm going to take your advice.'

53

Elaine simpers. 'I'm so glad. You won't regret it.'

'I'm sure I won't.'

Molly looks sideways at me, and I can see that her eyes have moistened, her tail wagging more strongly now, as though she can't help her own response. 'Oh, Bertie,' she says quietly, her voice trembling, 'I can't believe it. This is it. She wants us. We're going to have a real home at last.'

She nuzzles up to me, and I pretend to be pleased for her sake. And of course I am hugely pleased to be leaving the shelter. I just wish it could have been a family with young kids and lots of energy who adopted us. This woman does not look like much fun, and from the way she crouched down so carefully to pet Molly, I'm worried she may not be much of an outdoor person. Maybe she's even less likely to walk us in the park than Mr Minton was.

But anything's better than another night in this place.

'I suppose there'll be lots of paperwork,' our new owner says, looking worried, and tucks a stray hair behind her ear.

'It's not too bad,' Elaine reassures her, and the two women shake hands, smiling above us. 'Especially since you've fostered from us once before, so we know you. And I think you'll be very happy with Molly.'

'Yes, so do I.'

Hold on, I think, and tilt my head to study their smiling faces more closely.

My stomach sinks.

No, no, no.

Even Molly's smile has faltered as she listened to that exchange. Her wagging tail slows, and then finally stops.

She turns to me, a worried little frown on her face. 'Did Elaine just say . . . Was that only my name I heard?'

You'll be very happy with Molly.

I can't seem to move my paws. My body is slowly turning to ice. No, this can't be right. This can't possibly be happening.

'I'm not sure,' I say, instinctively trying to comfort her, but we look at each other and both know I'm lying.

'But they can't separate us,' Molly insists, her voice high with anxiety. 'We're . . . we're brother and sister. We've always been together.'

'It's a mistake, that's all.'

The pinched-looking woman glances at me vaguely. 'They're both very cute. But I couldn't possibly . . . Not two dogs at once.'

'That's fine.' Elaine bends to clip Molly's lead back on, huffing and puffing because she is quite a large woman, and begins to drag her out of the room. 'Let's go and get the paperwork started, shall we?'

The pinched woman leaves first, her heels clacking on the hard tiled floor.

Elaine follows her, jerking Molly behind her on the lead. 'Come along,' she says, adding shrilly when my sister resists, 'Now behave yourself and be a good girl.'

'No, no, no,' Molly shrieks, struggling valiantly to claw her way back to me. But she's no match for human strength, and is too polite to bite. Her claws scratch uselessly over the white tiled floor. 'Please, I can't be rehoused without Bertie. He's my brother.'

I am not polite. Not when someone is trying to separate me from my beloved sister. I growl first, then begin to bark loudly and furiously.

Nobody pays the slightest attention.

The door is closing behind them.

'Bring her back,' I shout, and finally jump up at Elaine's chunky leg in desperation. Not claws and teeth but muscle, sheer weight and momentum. All the same, I know it's forbidden. Now I am as bad as Jethro, behaving aggressively towards a human.

'Bad dog!'

Angrily, Elaine kicks me away, catching me painfully in the nose. I sprawl back into the room with a high-pitched yelp, and the door clicks shut behind them.

I stagger up and stare groggily at the closed door. The truth hits me like ice-water in the face, and I let out an agonised howl of pure despair.

My sister is gone, and I'll never see her again.

❧ SIX ❧

'Cheer up, little fella,' my hairy friend Gandalf tells me several days later, trying to rouse me from the doldrums. 'At least your sister has found a good home. Take comfort in that thought.'

I don't reply.

I'm too busy watching the heavy door into the next block. B Block.

Where Molly was housed before they took her away.

Stupid to be so blindly optimistic, I suppose. But I keep hoping the pinched-looking woman will bring her back again today. Or tomorrow. Or maybe the day after. Gandalf told me that most people take dogs home for the weekend so they can be sure the dog is right for their house and family. Sometimes dogs that are rehoused at the end of the week are returned to the shelter a few days later, tail between their legs, having failed to get on with their new owner.

But it's been longer than a few days, I can feel it.

The pinched-looking woman has decided to keep Molly. It feels like a dark cloud has settled around my head, and I can't seem to shake it. Hopelessness. Though not quite. Because I'm still hoping Molly will misbehave or cry all night without me and end up being placed back in the shelter, even though she's been gone for so long.

I don't want her to be punished or feel like a failure. But then we could be together again.

It's a selfish hope, I tell myself. After all, it would mean Molly returning to this awful place. To the constant barking and the smell of despair. But at the same time, I know how much she must be missing me, out there somewhere on her own, everything unfamiliar, in a new house with a new owner. And I know how much Molly depends on me. If I'm not there, who will lick her bad leg in the evenings to stop it aching? Who will be there to keep her spirits up on a long walk when she starts to hurt?

That woman with the thin, pinched face won't know about my sister's bad leg. How could she? She'll probably drag Molly along on the lead at too fast a pace, and then curse her when she can't keep up.

She looked so stern, as well. Too stern for Molly. I can already imagine what a cold and cheerless household she must run. Clean, sterile floors and everything stinking of disinfectant. And she probably has endless strict rules about no mud in the house and no sleeping on the sofa and no barking when the doorbell goes – not to mention terrible punishments for Molly if she does something wrong.

My heart aches as I think of my beloved sister out there without me. Alone and friendless. Maybe she's being punished right now, with no one to protect her or bring her comfort.

'You're whimpering again,' Gandalf points out kindly.

'Sorry.'

Sighing, I lay my head down on my crossed paws, and try not to feel so depressed. Gandalf is right. I should be comforted by the fact that Molly has found a home. Even if I could have hoped for a kind and boisterous family to brighten her life instead of That Woman.

Perhaps I shall see Molly again in my dreams.

It hasn't happened so far, but I have dreamed once or twice of my mother. A dim and distant memory of a large, warm, shambling body and a sense of total safety. The sweet smell of milk. Then of course I have woken up to this place.

I close my eyes and sleep fitfully again, twitching at the barks and whines from other dogs on our block. The bright overhead lights are so intrusive, I cover my face with my paws and curl up, trying to burrow deep into my own chest.

I'm finally slipping into a deeper sleep when Gandalf sits up abruptly, banging his head on the top of his cage, and gives a deep, warning bark.

I keep my eyes closed.

'Bertie,' Gandalf says, and nudges the cage wall that separates us, his bulk shaking my little enclosure. 'Ahem, little fella. You've got a visitor.'

A visitor?

I open one eye, frowning, and look out from between my paws.

Two human eyes stare back at me, slightly lower than the top-level cage I'm in. Two small hands grip the cage bars either side of my head. A wedge of pale-yellow hair falls aslant the eyes, a serious expression. Thoughtful, considering.

A human child.

Probably male, though I often find it hard to tell when they're still young.

I raise my own head a little, consider him in return. He's not that young, at a second glance, but not that old either. Freckles and a pert nose, lips that curve gradually into a smile as he studies me. A friendly little face, but tinged with something . . . sadness?

My ears flop sideways, and the boy's yellow fringe follows the same line, our heads tilting in unison as we stare at each other.

'This one, Dad,' he says, but there's a question in his voice. Like, *is this one right for us?*

Or perhaps, *if I choose this one, will I be allowed to take him home?*

The boy glances over his shoulder, and I follow his gaze.

'Dad' is a tall, fair-haired man in a grey suit, with one of those restrictive-looking ties men wear round their necks sometimes, like collars.

Mr Minton used to wear a tie on Sundays or to funerals, but he never looked very comfortable in them. This man looks like he wears ties all the time, though from the frown lines on his face, I'd say he is not very comfortable in them either. So he is the type of human who worries, I guess.

Right now he is smiling at the child though. He is clearly the boy's father. The two humans look perfectly alike, except for the height difference and the absence of worry lines in the boy's face.

'You like this one?' he asks, glancing in at me with an indulgent expression.

'I'm not sure. What type of breed is he, Dad?'

The man comes closer. 'Beagle, I'd say.'

'Are beagles nice dogs?' the boy asks, a little hesitant, looking back at me. He does not try to stroke me through the bars.

I watch him curiously. So many expressions in that small face. Fear, excitement, hope, and a strange blankness when he tries not to feel any of those things. I shift to see him better and see him take a wary step backwards. I get the impression this young human in the past has come up against dogs who bark and bite.

Gandalf thumps the cage wall with his heavy tail. 'Sit up properly, fool,' he grates. 'Wag your tail. Make an effort.'

I stare at him.

Then realise what he means.

You like this one?

I turn my head, looking back at the boy and his father. This is a family looking for a shelter dog to rehouse. And the child has stopped in front of my cage.

Are beagles nice dogs?

The man is talking quietly to his son, head bent, one hand on his shoulder. The boy is already pulling a disappointed face, but he is not resisting.

He is ready to move on, to look for a different dog.

A better dog.

I catch a few words as the man gently starts to steer the child past my cage, and realise my chance of a new home is slipping away. 'They need a lot of exercise . . . pack dogs . . . a bit destructive . . .'

I jump to my feet, wagging my tail for all I'm worth. This is it, as Molly would say. This is where I do my thing.

'Hello, hello,' I say brightly, head on one side, and give a muffled bark. More of a yap, really. A kind of, *look at me* yap.

The boy stops, looking back at me.

My heart starts to race.

Right, I've got his attention again. Now what?

I can chase my tail, round and round in ever-decreasing circles, until I'm dizzy. In fact, I am rather skilled in that department.

I start to turn, making myself as small as possible in the narrow cage, and then chase my own tail with as much excitement as I can muster.

'Hey, look at that!' the child exclaims.

I keep going, round and round, faster and faster, until my head feels like it's going to explode. I stop, horribly off-balance, and stagger sideways, banging into the cage wall.

The boy laughs.

Behind him, his father frowns down at the boy's fair head. Then he raises his troubled gaze to my cage.

'You like this one?' he repeats, a note of surprise in his voice.

The boy comes back to the cage and stares in at me again. I shuffle forwards, very careful not to look threatening, and sniff at his hand on the bar.

The boy looks back at his father. 'He's so cute. May I touch him?'

The man shrugs.

Tentatively, the boy reaches in and strokes me between the ears. I keep very still and look back at him, panting softly, hoping I seem friendly and fun, the kind of dog any boy would want to take home.

I suddenly understand why Molly got so excited and choked-up at the thought that she would soon be going home with someone new. Because I'm feeling choked-up too now, though I dare not let myself hope. Not yet. After all, what if the father says no, or the boy sees another dog on the way down the block and changes his mind . . .

'This is the one I want,' the boy says, more firmly.

The man stands looking at me for another minute, then nods. 'Right, then we'll go and find someone who can tell us his name, and all about him.'

The boy grins. 'His name is on the cage. See?' He points to something I can't see on the outside of my enclosure. A board of some kind. 'He's called Bertie.'

'Bertie.' The man laughs, then shrugs. 'Odd name for a dog. If we take him home for the weekend, and then decide to keep him, you can change his name if you like.'

'No, he's definitely a Bertie.' The boy withdraws his hand and studies me again, more closely. 'Anyway, how would he know we were calling him if we use a different name? That wouldn't be very fair.'

The man says, 'Come on, let's go and find a member of staff. I think they're all out at the front desk.'

The two humans walk away, the boy glancing back at me occasionally, his face suddenly lit up.

I know how he feels.

I bark and rear up against the cage bars, watching until the two have disappeared out the door at the end of the corridor.

I can't quite believe my luck. I've got myself a family. A new home. A real, proper home. I could be sleeping somewhere new tonight, and not in a smelly old cage any more. Just like Molly.

I turn in another excited circle, unable to help myself, and grin broadly at Gandalf, then at all the other dogs in the cages around us.

'I'm getting out!'

Gandalf looks pleased, though a little sad too. 'I knew it wouldn't take long before you were rehoused. Cute little fella like you.'

I stop and look at him. 'I'm sure someone will ... I mean . . . You'll get a family one day too, I'm sure.'

'Of course I will. So don't you give me another thought.' He gives a deep bark that resonates down the full length of our block, and laughs when I chase my tail with pleasure again. 'But once you escape from this place, don't forget to keep an eye out for your dear Molly.'

Molly!

I stop chasing my tail, and swallow hard. A thought has just occurred to me, and it's not a very comfortable one.

'If that horrid woman brings Molly back before you're rehoused, Gandalf, will you tell her what happened to me? Tell her that I . . . I found a new family?'

The big old dog nods his head. 'You can rely on me, Bertie. It would be my pleasure. But maybe you'll see Molly yourself first. Out walking in one of the parks. Or maybe at the vet's.'

I sit down, staring at nothing, worried now that if I leave with that boy today, and Molly is brought back to the shelter, I may lose my chance ever to see her again.

'Hey, cheer up.' He nudges the cage. 'This is your big break. Do you know how lucky you are? You've got a lovely young family to go home with, and there's still a hope you may see your sister again one day.'

I have to agree with him. 'Yes, of course.'

'Remember, this isn't the end, my diminutive friend.' Again I catch that wistful note in his voice. 'It's only the beginning.'

He's right.

But it doesn't make me feel any better about leaving.

I sit down and look along the rows of identical cages, listen to the dogs all around us on the block, and then sniff the air for any last remaining traces of my sister's familiar scent.

Nothing.

There's nothing here to remind me of her.

All the same, I can't forget that this is the last place where Molly and I were together. To leave the dog shelter is to break the last remaining link in the chain that used to bind us, and I can't help but be sad about that.

Suddenly, I remember that faraway look in the boy's eyes as he reached through the bars to stroke my head.

He is sad too, I realise.

But what could a boy like that possibly have to be so sad about?

❧ SEVEN ❧

The boy's name is Sam, I soon discover.

Sam Green.

Elaine uses their names several times at the counter, and treats the man as someone very important, smiling constantly, which is unusual for her.

'I hope Bertie gets along well with your family, Mr Green,' she says as Sam leads me out of the front entrance on a brand-new lead that smells of gorgeous fresh leather. 'Please let us know at once if you need anything. Bertie's a very special little doggy. We've loved having him here with us.'

Huh, I think, glaring back at her. Whatever.

'Thank you, I will,' Mr Green agrees.

'Someone will call round after the weekend, if that's OK,' she says, and shakes his hand. 'To make sure he's settling in okay with you and Sam. Thank you again for your very generous donation.'

The day is dry again, but with a light breeze that makes me shiver. Autumn is well under way now, a real nip to the air, the ground chilly under my paws. In a short while we will have frosts in the mornings again, I think, and cold-edged leaves and spiders' webs in the park. I don't mind winter but I do prefer the summer, its long endless days of warmth and sunshine, when walks are plentiful and there's no shouting about muddy paws on the furniture.

The Greens have a large, shiny car outside the shelter. I am put on the back seat next to Sam, and settle at once on the very comfortable cushions. Leather again, and a bit cold and slippery under my bottom. I try hard to behave. But as soon as Sam bends to tie up his loose shoelace, I sniff around with my highly sensitive nose, unable to help my curiosity. There are all sorts of delicious and intriguing smells to process, but at least it's clear I am the first dog ever inside this car.

Am I going to be an only dog?

I've never been an only dog. It has always sounded to me like rather a lonely life.

Still, Sam seems to be a nice boy. I can imagine him wanting to run around the garden or the park with me, to throw balls and let me chase them. So maybe I will not need any other company but him. And I will always be lonely without Molly, so I might as well get used to the idea.

The thought makes me sad again, suddenly.

Then I catch a few sudden whiffs of cat as Mr Green closes the boot. I wrinkle up my nose at the pungent smell. More than one cat scent, and quite recent too.

So the Green family has cats. This is not exactly welcome news.

Still, nobody's perfect.

It's quite a long drive to their home, as I discover they don't live in the town itself but in a small village beyond the river. I suppose I expected to find a rambling townhouse like the Mintons', the only home I have known since I was a tiny puppy. Instead, the Greens live in a large, old-fashioned house with a broad driveway and ivy on the walls. Rows of plants in ornate pots line the drive and sit beneath the front windows, still tangled with the remains of summer growth.

There's no front garden, I realise. Only pot plants.

My heart sinks, though I keep wagging my tail, eager not to look ungrateful.

But when Sam opens the car door on my side and I jump down, I spot a metal side gate through which I can see a large expanse of lawn edged by trees and shrubs.

A back garden!

I bark excitedly and drag on the lead.

'Bertie, no,' Sam exclaims, pulling me back. 'This way.'

I really do mean to behave impeccably, yet somehow my excitement gets the better of me and I jerk forward, eager to explore.

Sam drops the lead. 'Dad!' he shouts, and watches help-less as I dash away across the drive to the side gate, the lead trailing after me.

Mr Green comes running after me, and picks up the lead. I can tell from his face that he is not impressed with my behaviour.

Oops.

'Now, Bertie,' he says sternly, 'that's not right. You can't just go tearing off when you feel like it.' He raises a finger, using a very deep voice. 'Sit.'

Panting, I sit down and look up at my new owner with what I hope is an apologetic expression on my face.

But damn, the back garden does look amazing. And it smells . . . Well, actually, it stinks of cats. I've never been a big fan of cats, though as long as they don't spit, I can tolerate them. But underneath the feline whiff, I can smell all manner of wild creatures, squirrels and birds and rodents and so on. Best of all though, I can smell dustbins.

I draw in a huge breath and savour the proximity of their two wheelie bins, one for household rubbish, one for garden waste, both neatly arranged in the narrow side passage between the front and back of the house. Their odour is unspeakably delicious and mysterious.

I gaze longingly through the metal gate.

Sam has followed me too, but slower, shuffling his feet. He stares down at me, a little worried. 'I'm sorry, Dad. Was that my fault?'

'No, it's fine.' His dad hands the lead back to Sam. 'But keep a tighter hold in future, OK? Bertie may be small, but he's strong and clearly determined to have his own way. So you'll need to be very strict with him. You don't want to risk him running into traffic, do you?'

'No, Dad.'

I turn my head again and stare through the bars of the gate, trying to decide which parts of the back garden I want to investigate first. The bins, of course. That's a given. But there are also some interesting trees at the far end, clustered together. Trees and woodlands are always excellent for games of hide-and-seek. Then there's a stone pond in the middle of the back garden, with what looks like a statue of a huge fish at its centre, twisting in the air. Water is pouring from the fish's mouth back into the pool below. It looks very refreshing and great fun too.

I can hardly wait to splash into that pool, then jump out again and do my lovely all-body shake. The kind that sprays everyone and everything with water.

Oh yes, this is going to be good.

'Let's take him indoors to meet Granny M,' Mr Green says. He gives his son an encouraging nod, as though the boy is not very confident. 'She said she wanted us to bring home a small dog, so she's going to love Bertie.'

Granny M?

I pull on the lead, heading straight for the front door to the large, ivy-covered house, and Sam follows, laughing again. 'Look, I think he understood what you said, Dad.' He lets me drag him forward, though I notice he is careful not to drop the lead again, keeping it wrapped twice about his wrist this time. 'He can't wait to meet Granny M, either.'

The front door opens as we approach, and a tall, grey-haired woman stands there, arms open in welcome. 'Oh, what a sweetie she is!' She wipes her hands on her apron, then claps them together in delight. 'A beagle too. I love beagles. How clever of you, Sam, to bring me such a perfect little doggy.'

She?

Bristling, I try not to be offended. The lady is clearly quite old, around Mr Minton's age, and I am used to old people getting things wrong or muddled.

Below the front step, I look up and stop dead at the sight of her vast, staring eyes. Then I realise that Granny M is wearing large-rimmed glasses, like the ones old Mrs Minton used to wear. She has a long nose and a small mouth, and wispy grey hair tied up in a bun, with a few strands hanging down loose. Oddly though, she has powdery streaks on her face, and smells of flour and sweet spices.

My tail begins to wag furiously.

I know *that* smell.

Granny M has been baking!

To my relief, Sam corrects her mistake immediately. 'It's a boy dog, Granny,' he tells her, his tone indulgent as though he is accustomed to pointing out such obvious things, 'not a girl. You don't mind, do you?'

'Oh no, I love boys.' She reaches down and ruffles his head. 'I love you, don't I? What's the doggy's name?'

'Bertie.'

'What a lovely name. He looks just like a Bertie. A little mischievous too, I'd guess.' Then she glances at Mr Green over the boy's head. 'No problems, John?'

'Sam chose the dog on his own, and sat in the back of the car with him all the way home from the shelter,' Mr Green tells her, a touch of pride behind the words. 'No nerves at all.'

'Why would I be nervous?' Sam asks at once, sounding defensive as he stares from his father to his granny. 'Oh, because of that dog bite when I was little? But I'm not scared of dogs any more. It was only a tiny nip, and that was three whole years ago. I'm ten years old now, you know.'

'All grown-up,' Granny M agrees, smiling. 'Of course you are. Silly of me to worry.' She looks down at me. 'I'm Granny Margaret, Bertie. Pleased to meet you.'

Sam tilts his head to one side, staring at her. 'Dogs can't talk, Gran.'

'Is that so?' She winks at me knowingly. 'Well, why don't you bring Bertie inside for a bowl of water and a dog treat? I've made a little bed for him near the range, with a blanket and some toys, and he can trot out into the garden anytime he wants during the day. I'll leave the back door open all today, so he knows where to go for his business.'

'Thanks, Gran.'

'You're very welcome, Sam.'

She may still be smiling, but there's a strain in her voice. Some kind of worry about the boy, as though he's delicate in some way. I pick up on it, and glance back at Mr Green, who is also frowning slightly.

Why are they so concerned about Sam? He looks robust enough to me.

But my worries about the family are soon pushed aside. Once over the threshold, my nose quivers delicately. Already I can smell something sweet and moist in the oven.

Cakes!

I knew Granny M had been baking!

My belly rumbles and I rush forward into the hallway, dragging Sam along behind as I follow the impossibly delicious scent of baking. He gurgles with laughter again, and I hear Granny M say wonderingly to Mr Green, 'Is that Sam . . . *laughing?*'

'Yes,' Mr Green replies. 'It certainly is.'

Then we are in the kitchen, and the back door is standing open, and I can see the neat lawn outside, and the pool with its big stone fish spitting water. The baking smell is gorgeous. But damn, the garden looks so inviting too.

'I think he wants to explore the garden. Can I take him off the lead?' Sam asks eagerly as his father enters the kitchen.

'Absolutely. We're home now.'

The boy fumbles to unclip my lead while I crouch low in my best big-dog impression, then spring up at his jeans, making it as much fun as possible for him to free me.

'Hold still, Bertie,' he complains, but still laughing, so I know he isn't really angry, just pretending. 'You silly dog!'

I dance about on my hind legs, a move my sister taught me that always gets humans giggling. Well, the young ones, anyway. I don't think Mr Minton thought much of it.

At last I am free.

I give a little yapping bark, not loud enough to scare the child but enough to show my appreciation, and bound away across the patio and onto the lawn. Sam follows me across the grass, laughing and shouting my name again and again, while Granny M and his father stand in the doorway to the kitchen, watching.

I suppose they are still worried I might bite.

Though there's something else worrying them too, I'm sure of it. Something that's put that permanent frown on his father's face.

Is that Sam . . . laughing?

I give a little backwards kick, out of sheer pleasure. It's fantastic to feel soft grass under my paws again, not the hard concrete of the exercise yard at the shelter. It's like I've escaped from prison. Bursting with irrepressible energy, I race to the very end of the garden and almost bump into the mossed stone wall around it.

'Here, Bertie,' Sam calls, trying and failing to whistle with his fingers.

Not wanting him to be disappointed, I dash back towards him, then weave in and out of his legs, and race back again to the trees.

I haven't finished my exercise yet.

'Hey!' the boy shouts, then laughs, shaking his head.

Ignoring him, I twist between the low, clustered apple trees, enjoying myself for the first time in ages. But I don't want to be sent back to the shelter for disobedience, so when he calls me again, I turn and bound back towards him.

Stopping in front of my young master, I sit and pant, grinning my appreciation of the garden.

'Good boy,' he exclaims, and crouches to pat my head.

Granny M is hurrying across the lawn too. She is surprisingly nimble for an old lady; nothing like Mrs Minton, for example, who could hardly move about without huffing and puffing like Jethro panting up a steep hill. 'Throw a stick for him,' she calls, and points to a fallen branch lying on the grass nearby.

Sam runs to pick it up, then hurls it with all his strength across the lawn. It lands near the side wall in a clump of bushes.

Without even waiting to be told, 'Fetch!' – a command that figures high on my list of favourite words – I dash after the stick as fast as I can. Which is pretty fast.

I hear Mr Green shout something from behind me, but pay no attention. The stick has been thrown, the challenge made. From now on, the stick is everything. I need to retrieve it, and promptly too, or I shall have failed in my essential skill as a hunter of thrown items. I know that truth as well as I know my own name.

I run across a stretch of slightly damp grass, and stop beside the wall.

No stick.

My nose quivers.

It must be behind the shrub, I decide, turning to consider its thick, shiny-leaved bulk. Behind it, or possibly inside it. It's hard to tell.

I search, but there's nothing behind it except the wall and a few fallen leaves.

Undeterred, I muscle my way into the fragrant depths of the shrub, oblivious to the scratch-and-tug of its thin, spiteful branches. Where is it? Where is the stick? It must be here. There is nowhere else it can have gone. So I rub my sensitive nose along the dirty ground, casting here and there, sniffing hard, alert to any trace of my new master, to the peculiar smell of a freshly thrown stick.

Then I shoulder my way out the other side, and come up against the rough wall. There's an unpleasant smell, and it's getting stronger, but it's not the stick so I disregard it. I can feel mossy, lichened stone in front of me. Broken edges sticking out. Still no sign of a stick. Determined not to be beaten by this obstacle, I clamber along the wall as far as possible, head and nose down, snuffling on the trail of Sam's lost stick, ignoring everything else, until I reach the end of the shrub.

Suddenly, the air is filled with a threatening hiss.

The aromatic shrub smell is forgotten as my nose is filled with an only too familiar stink instead. I stop at once, coughing and sneezing in protest at the pungent smell, and look up in horror.

Cat!

On top of the wall is a large, round-bellied tabby with malevolent eyes. Her stripes are quite distinctive, smooth and glossy, probably designed to intimidate dogs like me. Her body language is fairly intimidating too. She's watching me intently, her tail and back fur already puffed out with animosity. Her worryingly long claws are unsheathed, her body is crouched in pre-attack position, and she generally does not look too friendly. In fact, it looks like she intends sharpening those claws on my tender muzzle. Any second now.

Faced with a cat, a dog has two choices. Bark and give chase, or run away.

Buoyed up by my success at finding a new home, and then being given a mission to find a nice damp stick, I feel emboldened and am half-inclined to choose the barking and chasing option. This garden is my legitimate territory now, after all.

Then I meet the cat's eyes.

Wow.

Not. Friendly.

Warily, I lower my head (largely to protect my eyes in the event of a full-frontal attack) and start to back away. I don't want to lose face with young Sam, but equally I'm not keen to replay a violent cat encounter I had during my first year at the Mintons', an incident I can never recall without my eyes watering.

But it seems the cat on the wall has other ideas.

Not to mention an accomplice.

'Going somewhere?' a voice drawls from behind me.

I stop backing away and whip my head round, horrified. It's like having double vision.

Two tabby cats.

One tabby on the stone wall, still watching and no doubt ready to pounce on me with all the advantage of height. The other crouched among the fragrant lower branches of the adjacent shrub, motionless and on my level, but no less dangerous-looking than its counterpart above. If anything, the cat under the bush is even larger and fatter than the one on the wall.

The smell of cat is everywhere, and overpowering.

'Such a very *little* doggy.' The cat on the wall has a single black slit in each one of her large, yellow eyes, focused directly on me. 'And it's trespassing in *our* garden.'

EIGHT

Thankfully, before either of these would-be dog-killers gets the chance to gouge out my eyes, the bushes above us part and a hand reaches down to retrieve me.

'Come along, Bertie,' says Mr Green in a weary tone, dragging me out by the collar with scant regard for my dignity in front of the watchful cats. 'Better forget the stick. I think it must have flown over into next door's garden anyway, the way Sam threw it. It's long gone.'

No stick?

The cat under the shrub meets my gaze and sniggers.

I growl at the tabby, and watch in satisfaction as his fur rises along his stripy back and tail.

Score.

Mr Green scoops me up into his arms as though I weigh nothing. Which, thanks to the tasty treats old Mrs Minton used to feed me, is not entirely the case.

'Looks like you've met your new friends, Kitty and Rico,' he says. 'I hope you're all going to get on very well and not cause me any trouble.'

Trouble sounds about right. As I am carried away like a handbag, my paws sticking out in an embarrassing manner, I stare back at the two cats, wondering which one is Kitty and which Rico.

I don't have long to wait for an answer.

The tabby on the wall jumps down and weaves herself between his legs as Mr Green tries to walk back towards the house with me in his arms. 'Kitty!' he exclaims, frowning, and then gently toes her away. 'That's not very helpful. You and your brother need to be very well-behaved towards Bertie, do you understand?'

Rico comes sauntering after us, too fat to run. His eyes mock me. 'Bertie?'

'Bertie?' his sister repeats scornfully, looking up at me with huge yellow eyes. 'What kind of name is that? It sounds like a name humans would give to a cockatoo.'

'Mrs Brooks next door had a cockatoo,' Rico remarks.

'Only it didn't live very long,' Kitty says, and licks her lips in a menacing way.

My hackles are beginning to rise. I growl in response to the cats, but very quietly. I don't want Mr Green to think I am growling at *him*. That would be awful.

'Birdie,' I say fiercely. 'That's probably what you heard them saying next door. Not Bertie. What are you, a couple of idiots?'

Pacing ahead, her tail high in the air, Kitty turns and spits, 'Did you hear what that mutt just said, Rico?'

'Yeah, I did,' Rico agrees slowly, and blinks his large eyes. 'I never thought of that possibility. How fascinating.'

She hisses at her brother. 'That's not what I meant.' The fur ripples along her back. 'But maybe you really are an idiot, Rico.'

Sam comes running up to us, my new lead in his hand. 'Let me take Bertie,' he says, his eyes pleading, his face a little flushed. 'Please, Dad. I'm sorry about the stick. I didn't realise it would go so far.'

His father looks at him thoughtfully. 'Well, OK,' he says, and sets me down on my four paws again, much to my relief. 'But no more throwing things for him to fetch. Not until Bertie's had a chance to get used to our garden.'

'Yes, Dad.'

'He might have jumped over the wall, looking for the stick, and that could have landed me in serious trouble with Mr and Mrs Brooks next door. You know how furious they get about Kitty and Rico doing their business in Mr Brooks' prize vegetable beds, as if there's anything I could do to stop them.' He gives a lopsided smile. 'Seeing a dog in his garden too would probably kill Mr Brooks.'

Granny Margaret has already returned to the house, perhaps because she was getting cold outside. She is waiting for us at the kitchen door, her hands all delicious and floury. I can smell cakes now, gorgeous and fresh from the oven, and have to restrain myself from rushing inside and begging for one.

'I'm so sorry,' she tells Mr Green, remorse in her face, 'that was entirely my fault. Please don't blame Sam. It seemed like a good idea at the time, I just didn't realise what a strong arm young Sam has.'

His dad hesitates, then shrugs. 'Perhaps we should take Bertie to the park later this week. He can run freely there, and chase sticks for as far as you can throw them. That's what I used to do when I was your age, with my Yorkie Buster.' He manages a proper smile at last. 'He was a great dog.'

I'm a great dog too, I think, looking up at them all. But they ignore me. I suppose I shall have to prove my greatness first. I just don't know how to do that.

Other than by ignoring Rico, who is currently sniffing my butt.

I growl under my breath.

'Oh yes, please!' Sam is saying, his eyes shining. 'That sounds awesome.'

But his grandmother is looking worried. 'John, I'm not sure if you're allowed to take dogs off the lead at the park any more. They changed the by-laws. There's a council notice on the park gate now.'

'Oh, right.' Mr Green makes a face. 'Damn.'

Sam stares from one to the other. 'But that doesn't matter. People let their dogs off the lead at the park all the time. Harriet says she and her dog have races. And he's a Labrador, much bigger than Bertie. Honestly, no one will care.'

His father puts a hand on his shoulder. 'I know it seems harsh, Sam. But the law is the law.'

'But if other people do it . . .'

'Sam, I'm a lawyer. I can't be seen to break the law.'

'But Harriet says —'

'I know you like Harriet. But just because other people break or bend the law, and get away with it, that doesn't make it right.' He hesitates. 'Do you understand what I'm saying?'

Sam's lip trembles. 'No.'

'Look, it's the law. Nothing I can do about it. Though I don't see what the problem is. We can still take Bertie to the park. You won't be able to throw sticks or balls for him, that's all, and he'll have to stay on his lead the whole time.'

Sam's whole face crumples into tears at this gloomy picture. He dashes back inside the house, past his grandmother, past a startled-looking Kitty, leaving me behind on the patio as though he has forgotten my existence.

'I hate you,' he shouts back at his father. 'I hate you, I hate you, I hate you.'

I hear the sound of his running feet going upstairs. Then a door slams shut somewhere. Presumably his bedroom door.

Mystified, I look up at Mr Green, who is running a hand through his hair and cursing under his breath. I recognise the same words Mr Minton used whenever Biscuit peed on the carpet.

You won't be able to throw sticks or balls for him, that's all, and he'll have to stay on his lead the whole time.

Hmm, not exactly the idyllic picture I envisaged when I first heard the word, 'park'. Frankly, it's hard to disagree with Sam's disappointment. There's nothing I like better than stretching my little legs by running halfway across a park after a thrown stick or chewy ball. But maybe 'hate' is a little strong. And now Granny Margaret is looking at Mr Green in an accusing way, which makes me wonder what I'm missing.

There seems to be something else going on here – besides a row over walks in the park – that I have failed to grasp.

'Oh my,' Kitty says from a nearby patio chair, and raises a disdainful paw to her lips. 'You've only been here five minutes, Bertie, and already you're causing trouble.'

I knit my brows together, puzzling over that. Is the cat right? Was this argument, that just seemed to blow up out of nowhere, my fault?

My shoulders slump.

The thought of causing a row makes me sad and rather uncomfortable. But the more I consider it, the less credible it seems. Yes, I ran after the stick and couldn't find it. But the tension between father and son seemed to have been there before any of that happened. In fact, now I think about it, I spotted signs of unhappiness in Sam's face at the dog shelter. So this can't be entirely down to me.

I look to the humans for guidance, but there's a tense silence on the patio now. Mr Green glances at Granny M, then walks past her into the house without saying a word.

The old lady stands there a moment, staring after him, then turns back to me with a determined smile. 'Well, Bertie, what a first day in your new home!'

Indeed.

I wait patiently to see what will happen next, but all she does is gaze out across the chilly garden, her expression wistful. She plays with the long beads twisted twice about her neck, her fingers pale and wrinkly, just like old Mrs Minton's were. Yet this old lady seems much younger in spirit.

'Oh dear, oh dear. What are we going to do?'

I can't answer that question, unfortunately. But I can try to comfort her. With that in mind, I move closer and begin to wag my tail encouragingly.

Granny M looks down, hearing my tail thump against the stones of the patio. Her expression softens, and she clicks her fingers at me. 'Come on, Bertie, let me show you where you're going to sleep. And I'm sure you could do with a nice dog treat too.'

Now *that* sounds good.

'Not to worry,' she adds, as though reassuring herself rather than me. 'Ten-year-old boys can be difficult creatures at times. I expect Sam will soon come around.'

I wag my tail more cheerfully, and follow her inside.

She closes the door, leaving the two cats outside. Instantly the kitchen is darker and warmer, more cosy-feeling. The heat pouring off the range is lovely, just right for warming my damp paws. I pad eagerly towards the little bed she points out to me. It's essentially just a piece of old cardboard laid out on the floor, covered with a blanket. A thick, hairy blanket that feels soft as a cushion to the touch, and miraculously does not smell of cats. There are some toys tucked into the blanket too. A brand-new chewy ball like the ones we used to fetch in the park, and a pretend bone, nicely squishy and rubbery-smelling.

I nose the toys, give a quick nip and lick to my rump, which has been itching since I got caught up in that scratchy shrub, then turn my attention to the dog treats she has placed just beyond the blanket.

Granny M fills her kettle and puts it on the range – which is similar to the huge metal oven one of Mrs Minton's friends had – and it soon begins to make its quiet bubbling noise as it heats.

She sets out some cups and busies herself preparing some drinks and food. I turn around on my new blanket, and try to get comfortable. I guess it must be nearly time for one of their human meals, which means no games or walks until later. Humans seem to eat so many meals, I think, but accept it with resignation. They are much larger than dogs, after all. It stands to reason they would need more food. I just wish more scraps would come my way. Human meals always seem to smell so much tastier than the food they put down for us.

I brighten up quickly though. Maybe this is a good thing. Maybe in the Greens' household, scraps will come more readily than at the Mintons'.

I watch my new mistress curiously, munching on a particularly tangy treat with a strong aftertaste of liver. Granny Margaret strikes me as a very capable person, always buzzing about, doing this or that, never content just to sit and stare at the wall, which Mrs Minton did regularly. She fits this house too, which is tidy without being obsessively clean, and is crammed with pretty little ornaments and unusual objects. The kitchen smells of cats and fresh flowers and baking too, not even a hint of disinfectant.

Granny Margaret has been bending to a low cupboard, sorting through a stack of clean plates. Suddenly, she closes the cupboard with a loud snap, as if she's changed her mind.

I look round, startled.

'Damn,' she says in a thick voice.

Then she covers her face with her hands and starts to make a distressed noise. Like a cat choking on a fur ball.

I stop munching, and swallow hard.

'Jenny,' she sobs.

I wag my tail, but she does not notice this time.

'Jenny, oh my darling Jenny.' She sinks into the high-backed wooden chair at the end of the kitchen table, grey head bent, still crying. The kettle bubbles and whistles noisily behind her but she does not seem to notice it. It's as if she is talking to someone, even though the kitchen is empty except for me and her. 'I wish you were here. What on earth am I supposed to do about them?'

I hesitate, and tip my head to the side, one ear flopping down. I don't understand why my new human is making that noise. But she's clearly in distress.

Molly would know what to do, for sure. Only Molly is not here.

Thinking about my sister makes me sad too.

For a moment I contemplate joining her in a heartfelt and highly vocal expression of grief. I haven't had a good long howl in several days.

But we can't both be sad.

I trot over there and sit beside her instead. When Granny M does not look down, I give a little whine, then gingerly place one paw on her knee.

Startled, she stares at me. Then she gives a shaky laugh, and pats my paw. 'Thank you.'

She reaches into her sleeve and pulls out a hanky, then blows her nose with it. Gently, I withdraw my paw, but keep watching her. She does seem very upset. But after a short while, she hides the hanky again and forces her shoulders back.

'Yes, quite right, Bertie.' She gets up and marches to the range. There, she deals briskly with the kettle, making several steaming drinks. 'Silly to keep living in the past. What's done is done and cannot be undone, and all that.'

But her gaze keeps straying to a framed photograph on the wall opposite. It's of a woman with curly, shoulder-length hair and a huge smile, standing in the back garden next to a much younger-looking Sam. She looks like Granny Margaret might have done when she was younger. Behind her is the fish statue in the fountain, spouting water, and it looks like full summer, the branches of the trees are so thick with glossy leaves.

I guess the woman must be Sam's mother, the family resemblance is so strong.

Jenny, she called her.

I study the picture. Sam looks very happy there, standing next to his mother. Much happier than he looked today at the dog shelter, his eyes and mouth drawn down mournfully like a Pekinese's.

If that is Sam's mother, where is she now?

And will she be coming back?

I wag my tail, and follow Granny M about as she sets out spicy-smelling biscuits and a plate of freshly baked cakes, then goes to the stairs to call Mr Green and Sam down for tea. She says nothing more about the mysterious Jenny. But when Sam trails downstairs for a hot drink and slice of cake, his shoulders are slumped and he looks dejected. His father looks just as miserable when he arrives, hardly saying a word at the table and nibbling on a biscuit with as much enthusiasm as if it's made of cardboard.

I study the family as I hover, hoping for a few crumbs of cake or maybe half an unwanted biscuit.

Sam helped me by bringing me here from the shelter. So now I should help him in return. And it's obvious what he needs.

His absent mother.

I know how he feels. Molly's absence is an ache under my heart that never seems to go away, however much I focus on treats or nice smells or this new house. I shall never see her again. And there's not much use pretending I will. I'm a dog, not a human. I have little chance of getting out on my own to search for Molly, and even if I managed it, they would probably brand me a troublemaker and cart me straight back to the dog shelter as soon as I was recaptured. Which would be about five minutes after I made it over the wall.

So I can't get Molly back.

But perhaps I can find a way to solve Sam's problem.

The real issue is, I don't know if it's definitely Jenny he's missing so badly. I know almost nothing about the Green family and their history, and it's clear that even Sam's grandmother feels unable to sort out their problems. Otherwise why would she be crying in private like that? If there was a simple fix to the boy's unhappiness, she seems to me the kind of practical human who would have found it by now.

'Here, Bertie.' Granny M turns in her seat to slip me a crumbly home-made biscuit, as if she can read my thoughts, and I wolf it down eagerly. 'There's a good boy.'

I glance at the back door to the garden, which is made of glass. Outside I see two dark shapes lurking behind huge plant pots on the patio, crouched and watching me through slitty eyes. The Greens' tabby cats, Kitty and Rico. My new deadly enemies. And my position as newcomer has not been helped by the undeniable fact that I've been allowed inside, but she's closed the door against them, the loyal mouse-hunters and sofa-warmers. In fact, I can practically smell the resentment coming off them in waves, like the constant heat from Granny M's range.

Those cats are probably planning to get me alone at night, possibly when I go outside to relieve myself, and then mount some kind of violent attack. Maybe get rid of me for good. I'm no coward, but I've seen the aftermath of a cat attack and it's not pretty. Missing whiskers, bleeding ears, torn muzzle, even eye-watering damage to the lower parts . . .

Nothing is sacred.

I don't mind a light-hearted chase around the garden, and maybe some rough play. Dust and a lick. Molly and I have often rolled about together for fun like that, pretending to be puppies again. But I hate real tooth-and-claw scraps. That's not my strength. Besides which, there are two of them and only one of me. A short one, at that.

I lick tasty crumbs off my muzzle, thinking hard. Like it or not, I'm a stranger here. So if I want to reunite Sam with his mother, I'm going to need inside help.

And I'm looking at my best chance of success.

❧ NINE ❧

It turns out the cats are not terribly cooperative.

About an hour after the Greens have eaten their tea and cake, and dispersed about the house, Granny M lets me out with the old familiar command, 'Go and do your business!'

It's getting dark by then, so I take advantage of this natural cover and scuttle away behind the trees and shrubs at the far end of the garden. Quickly, since I am busting after so long indoors, I cock my leg against a convenient trunk, then perform some random but oddly satisfying scratching motions on the loose soil round about.

I guess my ablutions must have been visible from the house, because Granny M whistles from the back door as soon as I've finished.

I ignore her, and trot further into the cover of the trees.

I am waiting for company.

It's a cold autumn evening, and the air is slightly chillier than in the town centre. I've also grown accustomed to the heating in the dog shelter, which kept us unnaturally warm at night and made hairy dogs like Gandalf shed like an old rug. But I have a thick hide and am not afraid of a little cold air.

Behind me, the kitchen door creaks shut. No doubt

Granny M is trying to keep the heat in the house while she waits for me to finish.

Good. There's nothing worse than trying to make friends with the local felines while some over-protective human is hanging around, interfering and drawing all the wrong conclusions.

I drop my sensitive nose to the ground and root around in the bushes at the back of the garden, making a loud scuffling noise. Stink of cats everywhere. Unpleasant, but necessary. I back into a large shrub and rub my itchy bottom on its lowest branches. The whole shrub moves, rustling noisily.

Deliberate, of course. I want the cats to know where I am.

Sure enough, I am not alone for long.

'You again,' says a sharp voice from the darkness above me. Two yellow eyes glow, staring down from a tree branch.

Kitty.

It's dark but, thanks to my acute canine night vision, I can make out her outline. Right down to the angrily whisking tail. 'I thought we'd made our position clear earlier, mutt,' she hisses. 'You're not welcome here. You need to misbehave. Bark all night. Tear up a few cushions. Scratch all the doors. Do whatever it takes to get them to send you back to that . . . *dog shelter* you came from.'

She shudders at the words *dog shelter*, as though it sticks in her throat to mention such a lowly institution.

The other cat appears from under a bush again, but says nothing, merely stares at me. Her brother Rico, framed by fragrant leaves. He must have a thing for shrubs. Either that or he's trying to soften that infernal cat smell with a little aromatic herbiage.

It's not working.

I nod in his direction. 'Rico.' Then, more cautiously, at his sister. 'Kitty.'

I am trying to be friendly, in the hope that it will filter through to them.

Again, it's not working.

'Are you learning impaired?' Kitty demands, glaring down at me. 'Or perhaps it's arrogance. You think a couple of house cats can't run you out of here.'

'Oh, I believe you capable of anything,' I say.

'Then why are you still here, dog?'

'I prefer Bertie,' I say, introducing myself properly, and sit back with a grin, my head to one side. It's important in these situations to remain as unthreatening as possible. And a sitting beagle with a sideways grin is about as non-confrontational as it's possible to get.

'Look, I can see you've got a problem with dogs. And I'll be honest with you. I've got a problem with cats. It's the smell, mostly. But since it looks like we're stuck with each other, at least for a while, what do you say we work through our differences and try to be friends?'

'Friends?' Kitty hisses.

She leaps down from the branch and lands just in front of me, an arching spitting demon in the darkness.

It's an impressive sight. And a little frightening too.

I swallow hard.

'Yes, friends,' I repeat with what I hope sounds like total calm, and turn my head slowly toward where Rico is still crouching under his beloved shrub, never once removing my gaze from Kitty's. Those lethal claws may be sheathed at the moment, but all that could change very quickly. 'You'd like that, wouldn't you, Rico?'

There's a short silence.

Then Rico mutters, 'Erm . . . I think so, yes. Why not?'

Kitty shrieks, 'Rico!'

The male cat shuffles out from under the bush. Maybe there's something in his weird fetish, because he definitely smells less . . . *catty* than his sister. 'Hey, I don't want any trouble,' he says, avoiding his sister's glare. 'War, you know. Blood and claws. It's all too much hassle. And it's a really cold night, you know? I'd rather find somewhere warm to curl up and have a snooze.'

Kitty shakes her head in disgust.

I begin to relax. Two cats in a spitting rage is a challenging situation. One cat in a spitting rage and the other one zoning out under a fragrant shrub is a different matter altogether.

In other words, there's room for manoeuvre here.

'I don't want trouble either,' I say.

'Dogs always say that, and then they always do.' Kitty still looks like someone's taken a foot pump to her, like the one Mr Minton used for his car tyres before he gave up driving. Her eyes glow from the centre of a large fluffy cushion. 'What proof do I have that you won't chase me up the nearest tree as soon as I let my guard down?'

'None whatsoever,' I tell her cheerfully. 'But look on the bright side. It could make life exciting, never being entirely sure.'

She hisses.

Not the response I'd hoped for. But at least her fluff halo is slowly subsiding, shrinking Kitty back down to the size of an ordinary tabby.

'The reason I actually came out here, apart from the obvious,' I continue in a friendly manner, 'is that I want some information.'

Rico looks surprised. 'What sort of information?'

'Don't tell him a thing, Rico!'

I ignore Kitty and focus on her brother. As cats go, he seems fairly mellow. Maybe that's something to do with the shrub.

'About the Greens.'

Rico contemplates me for a moment, then says, 'You're very short, aren't you?'

Kitty sniggers.

He glances at his sister, then adds hurriedly, as if only just realising that his comment was not exactly polite, 'But perhaps you haven't stopped growing yet.'

'I'm a beagle,' I say. 'I'm the correct height for a beagle. This is about as high as we get.'

'Oh.'

I raise my brows.

Kitty licks a paw, then examines it carefully, as if considering unsheathing those long claws in my honour. 'He just means you're shorter than Pepper.'

I blink. 'Pepper?'

Now her brother is looking embarrassed. His large eyes half-close, staring at her, then he shifts uncomfortably. 'That's not what I meant at all.'

'I'm sorry, who is Pepper?'

Kitty smirks. 'Next door's dog.' She rolls a sinuous shoulder towards the house on the opposite side from where she and Rico pinned me down earlier. 'She's a poodle.'

Oh marvellous, a *poodle*.

Not my favourite breed. They all tend to worry too much, and those long, rangy legs make me feel a touch inferior. No wonder Rico thinks I'm short. Next to a poodle, especially if she's one of those tall, elegant varieties, I must look like some kind of scurrying rodent with odd splodges on my ears.

Pure muscle though, I tell myself. And wiry as hell. Like most beagles.

'I look forward to meeting her,' I say politely.

Again, Kitty sniggers.

Behind us in the darkness, the kitchen door creaks open and Granny M whistles a few more times, then calls, 'Bertie!' in a high-pitched voice.

She's getting impatient. And so am I.

'Look, I need to know something about the Green family,' I tell them.

Kitty's eyes narrow. 'Such as?'

'Where's Sam's mother? Is she Jenny? I overheard Granny M crying before, and she said that name. It's obvious she's left Sam and Mr Green. So I was hoping we might somehow be able to find her and bring her back, make Sam happy again.' The cats are looking at each other, their expressions inscrutable. 'What?'

Rico looks miserable, his whiskers drooping. 'She didn't leave, Bertie.'

'Where is she then?'

They do not answer. So I press them, aware of Granny Margaret's whistle and cries growing louder. I can hear her footsteps shuffling over the cold, damp grass. She must have put her outside shoes on so she can come all the way down this long garden to find me. It's such a chilly night too. I don't want to keep the old lady outside any longer than I must.

But this is important.

'What, is she sick?' I remember old Mrs Minton used to be sick quite regularly. Sometimes an ambulance would come for her, noisy and with bright flashing lights, and all us dogs would watch from under the kitchen table as she was carried out. 'Did they take her to the hospital?'

'Worse than that,' Rico tells me unhappily. 'Sam's mother is dead.'

It takes me ages to get to sleep that night, and not simply because I'm saddened by the way things have turned out with Sam's mother. It's a strange bed, a strange room, a strange house, and it's surprising how quickly I adjusted to all that noise at the dog shelter, the sighs and whimpers in the darkness, and even Gandalf wheezing next to me all night. Then there was the dull roar of traffic passing on the main road, and a train rattling by at regular intervals, like the one we could see from the back yard at the Mintons'. It was never quiet in the dog shelter, in other words.

I always fell asleep in the end though, despite the constant noise. I suppose even sensitive ears like mine can get used to any level of abuse.

Here, we are out of the town centre. There is little passing traffic. No rattling trains. I am the only dog, and the cats appear to sleep in other parts of the house, since I saw them stalk past as the lights were being put out downstairs and disappear into the shadows.

Here, I have nothing to compete with my need for sleep. Here, everything is warm and comfortable and absolutely silent.

Except for a large round clock on the kitchen wall.

TICK

TICK

TICK

TICK

TICK

I get up, turn around on my hairy blanket three times, then try to resettle in the same position. Only with a paw over my ear.

TICK

TICK

TICK

This is going to be a very long night.

I'm still mulling over the worrying problem of Sam's unhappiness, given the impossibility of fixing it by getting his mother back, when a creaking noise makes my ears perk up. Someone is coming down the stairs, I decide, my ears now so attuned to silence – and the incessant ticking of the clock – that I can easily identify the source of any sound in the quiet house.

I raise my head.

The person begins creeping across the hallway.

I tip my head to my side, listening.

A very light tread. Not Mr Green. Slippers?

No, bare feet.

Granny M does not strike me as someone who wanders her house at night in bare feet. Which only leaves one other person.

The door into the kitchen opens slowly. A narrow beam of light picks out the ceiling, the walls, then drifts across the range and down, right down to where I am lying on my blanket on the kitchen floor, momentarily blinding me.

I thump my tail on the floor.

Sam.

The torch wavers in his hand as he closes the door behind him. Then its thin light wobbles across the floor towards me.

I smell the boy before I actually see him. It's the scent of bath time, toothpaste, freshly laundered pyjamas, plus his own particular smell, the one I remember from sitting next to him in the car. Sam smell, interesting and pleasant on the nose. There's a pad-pad-pad of small bare human feet across the kitchen floor, and here he is, looking down at me in the darkness.

'Hello, Bertie,' he whispers, and drops to his knees before me. 'I wanted to . . .' The boy stops, and gulps. He's been crying, I realise. His young voice quivers. 'I can't sleep. How about you?'

I stand up, looking at him. My tail wags harder as I nuzzle into his shoulder. Sam pats my head, then embraces me clumsily, a little uncertain, like he is still not quite sure of me.

'I had a . . . a nightmare.'

I lick his face.

'I was with my mum in the hospital that last day. I kissed her goodbye, and told her I'd come back to see her the next day, but then . . . Then I never saw her again.' Sam gulps, then wipes his face with the back of his hand. 'It was horrible.'

I think of Mr Minton, howling in torment after he found the body of his wife, and how we dogs had huddled together for comfort under the kitchen table.

'It was my fault she died,' he says hoarsely, right next to my ear. 'My fault, Bertie.'

I wag my tail a little harder, to indicate that Sam must be mistaken, that this cannot be the truth.

But Sam does not seem to notice. Instead, he sniffs and wipes his wet face again. 'You see,' he gulps, 'if it wasn't for me, Mum would still be here.'

Ah, I think, this is guilt talking. His mother got sick and died, and he thinks it must be his fault. But he is only a young human. He cannot possibly have caused her death. I recall what Granny Margaret said, that ten-year-old boys can be temperamental at times. Perhaps this is simply one of those times.

I wag my tail even harder, trying to distract him.

'If I had been a good boy,' he whispers, then falls into a series of gasping sobs, clinging on to me, 'if I hadn't caused her so much trouble, then maybe . . .'

The boy stops speaking and cries loudly instead, his small frame shaking.

I want to help him.

But as I stand there, trying to comfort Sam with my warmth and undemanding silence, my sister Molly comes into my mind.

If I had behaved better, if I had not tangled with Jethro so often, if we had not fought like that over Mrs Minton's dress and ripped it in half, perhaps Mr Minton would not have lost his temper and taken us to the dog shelter that day. Then we would all still be living together at 167 Park View Drive: me, Molly, Biscuit and Tina, and even the irascible Jethro.

My wagging tail falters, and my ears droop.

I think of my darling Molly and wonder where she is now. Is she still stuck with that nasty, pinch-faced woman who looked so stern, or back in the dog shelter again, alone and in despair? I cannot bear to think of my sister as unhappy, as missing me in the same horrible way that I miss her. But that is what I have to face if I am honest with myself. She did not get adopted by a nice family like the Greens. She was taken away by someone who may have turned out to be a monster, the kind of cruel owner who uses a stick when a dog makes a mistake or withholds food as a punishment.

I shudder at the thought of what poor Molly may be going through right now. And I have no way of knowing where she is or how to rescue her.

Was it my fault we lost each other?

Suddenly I hear more footsteps on the stairs. Heavier feet, a more lurching gait. Mr Green, not the grandmother, not bothering to be quiet. There's even a hint of impatience as he crosses the hall and shoves open the kitchen door.

The bright overhead lights come on, dazzling me and illuminating Sam on his knees beside my little bed. He gives one last strangled sob against my fur, and turns his head, a look of apprehension in his eyes. Perhaps even fear.

'Dad?'

Hurriedly, he lifts his pyjama top and dries his face with it. I watch with interest. The boy does a good job. His eyes still look red-rimmed but it's not obvious he's been sobbing his heart out.

Mr Green comes over in slippers and dressing gown, and stares down at his son. His own eyes are a little red-rimmed too, his hair is standing on end as if he has been clutching it, and he does not look impressed. 'Sam,' he says curtly, 'it's two o'clock in the morning. What on earth are you doing down here?'

'I had to check on Bertie.'

'Nonsense.'

Sam struggles for words, stammering a little. 'It's not n . . . nonsense. Granny M said I should check on him. She said that Bertie might be lonely on his own. His first night in a new place.'

'I'm sure Granny M didn't mean you should check on him at this ungodly hour.'

He blinks. 'What does ungodly mean?'

'Too damn early.'

I sit and thump my tail helpfully against the floor.

Sam glances round at me, surreptitiously taking that opportunity to wipe the last trace of tears from his face. 'See? Look at Bertie's tail. That means he's pleased I came down. Harriet at school says dogs wag their tails to show they're happy. So Granny M was right. He *was* lonely.'

'Well, you've cheered him up now.' His father grabs Sam by the arm and hauls him to his feet. Not roughly, but without any sign of tenderness either. 'I'm tired, Bertie's tired, and I'm sure you must be tired too. Time to get back to bed.'

'But Bertie might need to go outside . . .'

Mr Green looks down at me sternly. 'Bertie, do you need to go outside?'

I know that tone of voice. It was one of Mr Minton's favourites whenever he was near breaking point.

Lying down on my blanket again, I look up at him mournfully.

'Excellent.' Mr Green leads Sam firmly back to bed, snapping the lights off on his way out of the kitchen. 'Goodnight, Bertie.'

'Night-night, Bertie,' Sam chants, then adds, 'Don't let the bedbugs bite.'

❖ TEN ❖

After my trial period is up, I am ecstatic when the Greens decide to keep me. Ecstatic and worried too, in case Molly has been returned to the dog shelter in my absence, and is wondering where I am.

To mark their decision to keep me, they buy a grim, new-smelling, high-sided basket. 'To keep out the draughts,' Granny M says with evident satisfaction.

The new basket is hard and cold against my back, and I can no longer see the whole room at night simply by opening one eye. Not surprisingly therefore, I prefer the old arrangement. To communicate this fact to my new owners, I keep dragging the hairy blanket out of my new basket onto the kitchen floor, and sleeping on it there instead. This infuriates Granny Margaret, who pulls me off the blanket every morning with scant regard for my comfort, and tucks it back into the basket. I wag my tail apologetically while she's doing this, as I don't like to annoy her. Then I wait until everyone's gone to bed that night and pull it out again.

It becomes a standing joke between us, a daily tussle between in and out, between the basket and the floor.

Luckily, Granny M seems amused rather than annoyed by my obsessive behaviour, and I can see it's also serving to keep her mind off the family troubles. By which I mean Sam's unhappiness. And his father's too, I suppose. Because I can see in Mr Green's face that he is unhappy as well. Not just in the downward turn of his mouth, which seems almost permanent, but a certain look in his eyes sometimes when he's alone in the kitchen or garden with me. The same faraway look that reminds me of my mood in those early days after I lost Molly.

I know only too well that there's no cure for that kind of look.

But perhaps time will make things easier for me, and for Mr Green and Sam too. Though the cats tell me it's been nearly two years since Sam's mother died. But I suppose that kind of wound takes a lot longer to heal.

After all, Molly isn't dead. And at the back of my mind is always the hope that I may see her again one day. And while it's unlikely, it's still a possibility.

What the Greens want isn't possible though. It's a dream that can never come true. And it's a regret too. Like the deep regret I feel whenever I remember the role I played in splitting up our happy household at the Mintons'. I share Sam's sense of guilt then at the way things have turned out, and find little pleasure in going out for a walk or being allowed to play upstairs in Sam's cosy bedroom. I think about Molly, and my reckless stupidity in not taking better care of her, and the whole day turns grey for me, and the autumn drizzle that runs down the kitchen window seems like a reflection of my mood inside.

It's when I think awful things like that, and hang my head in shame and unhappiness, that I have to remind myself that our household at the Mintons' was not that happy. Not really. Not after old Mrs Minton died, anyway, and the brown slop made its first appearance in our dinner bowls.

Soon after the Greens decide to keep me, I meet next door's dog, Pepper, the dreaded poodle, and learn that not all poodles are snooty know-it-alls. But she is a little wired. Not to mention weird.

'Hello,' she says the first time we meet, her on one side of the garden fence, me on the other, with a curious audience of cats, 'you must be Bertie. Rico's told me all about you. I have to be honest, I don't much like boy dogs. All that leg-cocking and butt-sniffing. It's so common, and besides that, it really gets on my nerves.'

She pauses, studying me.

Unlike the high stone wall between us and the Brooks, the fence dividing our garden from her owners' property is only a picket fence, with wide gaps between strong-smelling wooden slats, so she's able to get a good look at me.

'Look, could you possibly pretend to be a bitch like me,' she asks suddenly, 'whenever we're together? You wouldn't need to squat, or anything. Just act a bit more . . . girly.'

I stand up on my hind legs, leaning on the nearest two fence slats with my front paws, and try to look her in the eye. Which is a challenge, given our relative difference in height.

'No.'

Her funny little mouth clamps shut at that response. I get the feeling Pepper is used to having her demands met without question.

The poodle frets for a moment, turning around on the spot several times. The ground under her neat paws is all churned up in that area, which makes me think it's a manoeuvre she often performs when looking through the fence at the Greens. She looks quite outlandish, but I try not to stare on the grounds that she may jump over the fence and intimidate me with her height and her furry bobble if I annoy her. Her fur has been closely shaved except in a few choice places, with a ruff round her neck and a fat bobble on the end of her short, upright tail. The tail bobble sways dangerously as she whisks her muscular body around, then she stands still and stares at me again, her small eyes bulging.

'Very well,' she concedes, with a failed attempt to sound magnanimous. 'You won't be a girl. Even though I've asked so nicely. But I can always pretend. You won't mind if I call you Bertina, will you?' She hesitates, and there's a danger-ous flash in her eyes. 'I mean, you can't mind *that*, surely?'

'My name's Bertie,' I tell her firmly.

'Oh my goodness.' She flounces up and down on the other side of the wall. Then seems to come to an abrupt deci-sion. 'Very well. If you won't be a girl, and you won't let me call you Bertina, despite my extreme politeness in asking first, then I suppose . . . I suppose I shall simply have to call you B.'

'B?'

'You can assume it's short for Bertie, if you wish. But I shall know it's short for Bertina, and thus integrity will be maintained on both sides.'

I frown at her, my head on one side. It does not seem an unreasonable request. 'Um, OK, you can call me B if you really must.'

'Oh, I must. I really must.'

'B it is, then.'

She performs a little bob of gratitude, her tail bobble dancing. 'Thank you, B.'

'You're strange, do you know that?'

Rico, who has been listening to this exchange from a nearby tree branch, smiles with obvious satisfaction. 'Yes, she is.'

Pepper tosses her head. 'Hard words already? Well, I suppose it's only to be expected. From a beagle.'

I grin, and wag my tail in agreement. 'Pesky blighters, ain't we?'

'Huh,' is all she says. But I can see the poodle's not as bad as she likes to make out. Just a little flighty. And probably insane.

The days pass slowly as I grow used to my new home, but before I know it, the air grows cold and autumn slips inexorably into winter. My morning walks become brisker and chillier, especially on my paws. Granny M knits a woolly hat and scarf for Sam to wear to school, and he doesn't come home some evenings until it's nearly dark. I begin to wish she would knit me a vest, or some woolly boots, but instead Mr Green gets me a tight, slightly itchy coat to wear out to the park. I scratch at it furiously when he's not looking, but can't seem to dislodge the damn thing. There's a nip to the air outside, but the Greens' house remains warm and comfortable inside, the old range constantly heating the kitchen, an open fire in their large and homely lounge – something I have never seen before, and watch with fascination the first time it is kindled – and huge sofas where I am allowed to stretch out and sleep in the darkening afternoons while Sam is still at school.

We go for long walks in their local park, which is a much larger open space than the park in the town centre, and even along the canal too, which is great fun and seems to stretch on for ever. I come back muddy and exhausted, but always content, and Granny M makes a clucking noise, drags off my coat and takes a damp sponge and towel to my legs and paws. She does not complain like Mr Minton used to, or shout at me when I trot across her kitchen floor with dirty paws. But although she smiles, and even laughs when I nuzzle mischievously under her skirt while she's towel-drying me, I can see Granny M is not as happy as she would like Sam and Mr Green to think.

I look into her sad eyes, and remember the first day I arrived at their house, when she sat at the kitchen table with a bowed head, and cried, 'Jenny!'

I thought the old lady might cheer up now that she has a cuddly dog like me to care for, but it seems even my wagging tail has its limitations.

One afternoon she sits with me on the sofa, and puts on a film where I can see Sam and his dad playing football together in the back garden. But it's a much younger Sam, only a very small boy, with spindly legs and a chubby face. He is laughing and kicking the ball, and missing it sometimes, which makes his father laugh. Then the woman from the photograph on the kitchen wall, the woman she called Jenny, runs up and kicks the ball instead, and Sam giggles and runs after it with her.

The picture is a little shaky, but I can see it's Jenny. I can also see how much Sam and Mr Green have changed since this day in the back garden.

Jenny is exactly as I imagined she would be. She is wearing a summery dress and sandals. Her legs are bare and slightly tanned. She looks young and strong, bouncy fair hair that curls at the ends and falls to below her shoulders, a healthy glow about her skin, and a big grin on her face that reminds me of Sam when he's playing with me.

And Mr Green is watching the two of them run about the garden, hands sunk in his jeans pockets, smiling like I've never seen him smile before. He looks young too, and carefree, and as though his life is perfect.

In other words, totally different to the man he is today.

Then Granny M strokes my ears and murmurs, 'That's my Jenny. You see her, Bertie? That's my lovely Jenny. Gone now, bless her.'

And she cries.

She watches the film several times over, crying all the time. The cats are nowhere to be seen that day – probably playing with Pepper next door – so I cuddle against her and wag my tail, and when she strokes my ears again, I turn my head and lick the back of her hand.

'Oh, Bertie,' she says, and draws a handkerchief out of her sleeve and blows her nose noisily.

Getting the back of her hand licked by a beagle, however enthusiastically, can't be much of a comfort to a sad old lady. Yet what else can I do?

The perfect solution would be to bring Jenny back to the Green family.

But that's impossible.

Jenny is dead.

That means she's gone for ever.

But still . . .

If only there was something I could do to make them all happy again, I keep thinking, helpless in the face of their invisible, unspoken despair. And sometimes it feels as though the solution is right there, right on the tip of my tongue. But then it slips away into the demanding schedule of my new daily routines, into walkies and meal times and bath times, into trips to the vet or around the shops, into wrestling matches with Sam upstairs in his bedroom, and silly games of football with him and Mr Green in the back garden, when I naughtily hog the ball instead of bringing it back to them as I should.

Then, one day, Mr Green comes home early from work.

There's the sound of familiar car tyres crunching on the gravel drive. Then Sam glances out of his bedroom window while we're playing a tug-of-war game with his school

jumper, abruptly lets go of his end – sending me flying backwards under his bed – and gives a little squeal of
excitement.

'A Christmas tree! Dad's brought us a Christmas tree!'

Sam leaps over the army of toy soldiers scattered all over
the carpet and throws open his bedroom door.

'Come on, Bertie!'

❧ ELEVEN ❧

Sam charges out of his room and thuds down the stairs at a tremendous pace, and I follow him to the front door, barking fervently to show my solidarity. Though, to be honest, I have no idea why the thought of a Christmas tree should excite him so much.

I remember our last winter at the Mintons' with little pleasure, except for the memory of being there with Molly. Mr Minton brought down the Christmas tree from the attic and set it up in the lounge. Mrs Minton blew dust off the baubles and tinsel garlands, and draped them over its plastic branches like fake leaves and fruit, and then the tree sat there for a few weeks, while we were all warned not to go anywhere near it. (Jethro ignored this injunction, of course, and there were regular shrieks from Mrs Minton whenever he toppled it from its lightweight plastic stand.) Then one day Mr Minton took the tree down again, and boxed it up elaborately, and dragged the whole thing back up to the attic.

A strange ritual, we all thought. Especially since everyone who visited the house would clap their hands and exclaim in apparent delight at this fake tree. It clearly held some special significance for the humans.

We just had no idea what.

Granny M holds me back by my collar at the front door. 'Look at this, Bertie,' she says, a hopeful smile on her face.

I pant, watching as ordered. She seems to think this tree may help to make Sam happy again.

I have my doubts.

But once Mr Green has wrestled the tree out of his car and into the lounge, with Sam's dubious help, and cut the thick net holding it all together, I understand why she hopes this may cheer her grandson up.

For this is no fake tree with unlikely, plastic-smelling branches.

This is a real tree.

A pine tree, sturdy and freshly cut from the forest. Quite tall, too. With long, sweeping branches that unfurl and drench the air with a sweet heady fragrance. It makes me think of long walks in the woods and scurrying rabbits in the distance and soft, diggable earth, the kind that flies upwards through my back legs when I burrow into it.

After some discussion, a large pot is found and the Christmas tree is 'planted' in it like it is still growing, which it clearly is not, since its pine needles are already starting to drop. Then it is placed in front of the bookcase in the lounge, to one side of the open fire, which is crackling away with a satisfying warmth. Granny M fusses about the base of the tree for a while, then fetches down a large box of tinsel garlands and baubles like the ones Mrs Minton had, but bigger and newer, and definitely more shiny.

'Would you like to help me decorate the tree, Sam?' she asks.

'Yes, please,' he says at once, his eyes glowing. 'One year, I helped Mum do the tree.' Then his voice falters. His eyes fill with tears. There's a short silence, then he swallows and adds shakily, 'Dad helped too.'

Mr Green's eyes look teary as well, but he forces a thin smile to his lips. 'Well, this year Dad is rather too tired to do the tree, I'm afraid. It's been a really tough week at work. So I'm planning to have a drink and relax instead, while you two do the tree.' He hesitates. 'If that's all right with you, Granny M?'

'Of course,' she says, but I can hear her disapproval.

He nods and leaves the room, heading for the kitchen. I hear the clink of a glass as he makes himself a drink. It's becoming a familiar sound.

Granny M turns and busies herself in the box of ornaments for a moment, then straightens, looking rather flushed. 'Right, well, let's get started,' she says loudly. 'Sam, tinsel or baubles?'

'Tinsel, please.'

She throws him a large armful of bright, shiny garlands. 'See what you can do with them. Be as artistic as you want. Then you can try a few baubles.'

'Thanks, Gran.'

She and Sam walk about the tree, strewing it with thick, glittering tinsel strands and glassy coloured balls that catch the light as they spin.

'Have your friends at school got their trees up yet?' she asks him.

He shrugs.

'You don't know?' She hesitates, watching him. 'What about that friend of yours . . . Harriet? The pretty girl who helps her mum with the newspaper round some weekends.'

'Harriet? She's not my friend.' Suddenly flushed, Sam throws some tinsel at the tree in a haphazard fashion.

'But you like her.'

Again he shrugs. 'What difference does it make? Harriet never notices me.'

'I'm sure that's not true.'

But Sam does not answer, just continues rearranging the strands of tinsel so they stretch all the way round the tree. I watch for a while, my head on one side. Then I get bored and decide they need a helping hand.

I run about the tree, and then under the tree, and get underfoot, enjoying the general hilarity, and even allow Sam to wind a string of scratchy tinsel round my collar so that it trails after me everywhere like a shimmering lead.

'Good boy, Bertie,' Sam says, and encourages me to chase him round the tree.

'Careful,' his grandmother tells him.

He dangles tinsel in front of me, and I jump up to try to catch it. Then take a few stumbling steps towards it on my hind legs, my front paws outstretched.

'Look, he can walk on two legs!'

Granny Margaret laughs and shakes her head. 'What a clever doggy.'

'He's a clever Bertie.'

I sit and grin round at them both, panting. It's surprisingly hard work, this business of decorating the Christmas tree. Especially when games are involved.

Sam disappears round the other side of the tree, then pops his head back, teasing me. 'Here, Bertie.'

I run round but by the time I get there, he's gone again.

I bark and pant, staring round for him.

A second later, he reappears on the far side of the tree, and laughs at my confusion.

'Sam, don't get him too excited.'

'He's fine,' Sam insists.

'Perhaps you should take Bertie outside in the garden. I expect you could do with some fresh air too. You've both been cooped up indoors all day.'

Sam glares at his grandmother, aggrieved. 'But Bertie's enjoying himself. And I'm enjoying myself. It's only a game.'

Granny M hesitates, but then smiles. 'All right, just another few minutes.' She fetches more baubles from the box and begins to hang them up on the tree.

'Over here, Bertie,' Sam urges me again, and I duck under the sweet-smelling tree to get to him faster. Only the tinsel strand becomes caught on something, and I don't stop, but tug hard, then harder, eager to be free, to get to Sam before he can escape me again.

Abruptly, the tree lurches sideways towards the window. I catch a glimpse of Sam's shocked face through the fragrant branches, then I'm free.

I dash out through falling branches.

Granny Margaret shrieks, 'Bertie, watch out!' but it's too late.

The beautiful Christmas tree topples over, catching me fleetingly across the back. I yelp and dart out of the way of its cruel, heavy branches. Baubles roll away across the floor, stars shining on the carpet, and tinsel is scattered everywhere. The room smells like a forest, all sweet disturbed pine and earthiness.

Deeply shaken, I scurry out of the lounge and run upstairs with tinsel trailing after me, while Sam shouts hoarsely for me to come back.

Mr Green emerges from the kitchen, glass in hand, and demands, 'What was that crash? Sam, what on earth is going on?'

Something tells me it would not be a good idea to hang about and see Mr Green's reaction to the chaos I've just caused in the lounge.

I trot up the last few stairs, bang wildly through Sam's bedroom door, and bury myself deep among the toys under his bed.

Stupid tree.

I hear shouting from below for a while, and then Granny M's quiet tones, trying to calm the situation down. Finally there's the sound of feet coming up the stairs. Fast, angry feet, stamping hard on every stair.

Sam comes into his bedroom, breathing hard, and slams the door behind him.

He pauses. 'Bertie?'

I wag my tail apologetically to let him know I'm hiding in there, and that I'm very sorry but I'm not moving.

'Are you under my bed?' Sam drops to his hands and knees, and peers under the bed. He has to move several toy bags before he can see me, right at the back, behind an old crate of plastic bricks. His eyes meet mine. 'Sorry about . . . about the Christmas tree, Bertie. Gran says I shouldn't have tied the tinsel round your collar. That it made you . . . excitable.'

To my relief, he does not seem angry. I creep forward on my belly, which is about the only way I can move in this narrow, confined space, until I'm just past the plastic bricks, but I do not come out yet. Tinsel or no tinsel, I am still a little concerned that I may be blamed for what happened downstairs.

In fact, it was probably my fault. If I had been more patient, if I had not tugged quite so hard on the tinsel when it got caught on that tree branch . . .

'Dad's really mad at me now.' He sniffs, and rubs his face with his hand. I guess Mr Green was not very happy about the tree falling over and has made his feelings known. 'He says . . . He says he's going to send you away if I can't control you better.'

Oh, that doesn't sound good.

I crawl further forward, and he reaches in, grabs my collar, and tries hauling me out from under the bed. I resist at first, unsure if it's a good idea for me to leave my hiding place. Then I decide it's OK, that he's not going to punish me.

This is Sam, after all. He's not Mr Minton.

I have to remember that.

I scrabble out and he lets go of my collar, then hugs me. 'Are you hurt?' he asks, and feels along my back with surprisingly gentle fingers. 'Gran said the tree hit your back and I have to check . . .'

It's true, my back does ache a bit where I was caught by the heavy tree as it toppled over. But it's nothing serious, and I expect a day or two should see it right. Certainly it's not like the time Biscuit brought the bookcase down on me when I was a young dog, still a puppy really, and there was blood trickling from a gash behind my ear, so they had to take me to the vet.

Mrs Minton used to say I was never quite right in the head after that.

I wag my tail a little harder.

'I can't feel any bumps,' Sam says, relief in his voice, 'and you don't seem hurt.'

Then he puts an arm across his face and sobs.

'I'm so stupid,' he gasps, his words muffled by his arm. 'Stupid, stupid, stupid.'

I look at him in surprise.

'This is why Mum died. Because I'm so stupid. I never think . . .'

There are more footsteps on the stairs. I glance at the door, wagging my tail, and Sam gets the message. He reaches for a tissue and dries his eyes.

It's Granny Margaret. I recognise her light, slightly shuf- fling step on the landing. Then she knocks on his door.

'Sam?' She hesitates. 'Is Bertie in there with you?'

He takes a deep breath, then answers, 'Yes, Gran,' as if he has not just been crying.

'Is he hurt?'

'I don't think so.'

'May I come in?'

Sam gets up and looks down at me, his face wretched. 'Yes.'

The door opens quietly, and Granny M is there, smiling at us both. She bends to ruffle my ears when I trot forward to greet her. She smells good, as usual. Flowery and sweet. Almost edible. The double-twisted strings of beads about her throat clack together as she straightens, and her heavy skirt rustles.

'I'm so glad you're OK, Bertie,' she says, using that special soft voice that she reserves just for me. Though I sometimes think she ought to use it on Sam occasionally. He could do with knowing that she cares for him too. 'That tree caught you pretty hard. Perhaps I should take a proper look, just in case.'

Sam watches miserably as she examines my back, then makes me sit while she feels along my spine. Her fingers are very careful.

'Yes, I think he's been lucky,' she tells Sam.

'It was my fault.'

'Well, perhaps next time no tinsel for Bertie.' She winks at me. 'He's handsome enough without it, don't you think?'

The telephone rings downstairs.

She sighs, and pats Sam's head. Like she patted mine. 'That'll be for me,' she tells him. 'I'm hosting the Christmas raffle at the village hall tonight.'

'You're going out? Again?'

Her brows twitch together. 'I'm sorry, darling, but it's for a good cause.'

'It always is,' he mutters.

'It's to raise money for . . .' She hesitates, then adds, 'For charity,' and looks at him awkwardly. I get the feeling she was going to say something else. 'Anyway, I won't be out that long. I've left a cold supper for you and your dad in the fridge.'

Sam's shoulders slump.

Downstairs I hear Mr Green answer the phone in a deep, curt voice that tells me he's still annoyed about the Christmas tree incident.

'It's for you, Gran,' he shouts.

She hurries out of the room, looking guilty. 'If that's Sandra,' she calls down to him, 'tell her I'm very sorry to be late. I'm just changing, then I'll be on my way. Better tell her there was a . . . a hold-up.'

'She'll be on her way to the hall in a few minutes,' he repeats dutifully into the phone. 'Sorry about the delay. The Christmas tree fell over.' He pauses, then says impatiently, 'That's very kind of you, Sandra, but it's fine now. I've set it all up again.'

I wonder if he's picked up all those glassy baubles too. Maybe he's missed one. Easily done, after all. And it might be rather fun to find one under the coffee table tomorrow and chase it round the room.

Once Granny Margaret has gone into her own bedroom to change, Sam kicks the door shut behind her and throws himself onto his bed, face-down.

'A cold supper again,' he repeats without enthusiasm. 'Oh, goody.'

I wag my tail hopefully.

Cold supper usually means unwanted crusts, often with butter smeared across them, and the occasional hint of mayonnaise. There might even be a slice of ham going spare. Or a prawn. I have discovered that I like prawns. Especially smothered in that sweet, tangy sauce Granny M pours over them before setting the dish on the table. The Mintons never had prawns the whole time I was living with them, but they are a regular delicacy in the Green household.

Unfortunately, the cats like prawns too. Really, really like them, I've noticed. And they don't seem terribly happy when I grab the last one on offer. Apparently that's always trad-itionally been Kitty's share. *The last prawn.*

Or so Rico advised me last time it happened, and Kitty inexplicably tried to spag me in the head with her claws.

I decide I would prefer that not to happen again. So if it's prawns tonight, I'll have to make sure I'm somewhere else when the last one is held out as a scrap. Assuming I can work out in advance which one will be the last one, that is.

'It's my fault,' Sam says suddenly.

I lean back and scratch my ear, frowning with concentra-tion. I hate being itchy.

'It's always my fault,' Sam continues in a hoarse voice, possibly talking to me, possibly to himself. 'I'm such a loser. I wish I'd never been born.'

I stop scratching and gaze at him. This sounds serious. I trot to the edge of the bed and nudge his leg, just in case he's talking to me. His arm is still across his face though, so it's hard to tell.

He must feel my nudging, because he sits up and looks down at me. His eyes are wet, his face screwed up with some desperate emotion. 'Can I tell you a secret, Bertie?'

I sit and wait.

'It was that football match, you see,' he says slowly, not looking at me any more. He's turned his head and is looking at a photograph of his mum, framed and sitting on his bedside table. 'I know it was. If I hadn't made Mum come and watch me play that afternoon, she wouldn't have got sick. And if she hadn't got sick, she would never have gone into hospital.'

He pauses, then bursts out, 'That's why Dad's always so angry with me. Because it's my fault, Bertie. It's my fault she died.'

There's a soft knock at the door.

Sam sits up, staring.

He rubs his eyes, then says, 'Who is it?'

'Dad.'

'I'm busy. Reading a book.'

He grabs a book off his bedside table and opens it. I study it curiously, ears perking up. I recall that Mrs Minton was always reading books, and wonder why there is an upside-down picture on the front of this one.

'I just want a quick chat.'

'Go away.'

But Mr Green does not go away. He pushes the door open a little and peers round it at Sam on his bed. Then he glances down at me.

I wag my tail.

His eyes do not seem to see me properly. Mr Green looks back at Sam, then he too studies the book with its upside-down picture on the front.

He smiles. But it's a sad smile.

'Look, Sam,' he says, 'I'm sorry. Really sorry. I lost my temper.'

Sam does not say anything.

'What I said about the dog . . . It was wrong of me. I didn't mean it. Of course you can keep Bertie.'

He glances at me again, but that faraway look is in his eyes again. Like he's remembering, living in the past, not quite here with us. I wonder if I look like that too when I'm thinking about Molly and the carefree times we used to have together.

'But you must try not to excite him so much,' he adds.

Sam's lip is sticking out. It's quivering now, like he wants to cry. Only he does not cry. He looks down at his book instead.

'Told you, I'm reading.'

Mr Green hesitates, then nods. He glances at me again. An odd, sad look. Then he withdraws, closing the door behind himself.

❧ TWELVE ❧

I soon discover that next door's dog, Pepper, has a habit of sidling through a gap in the fencing near the end of the garden, and coming to the kitchen door in search of Rico. The over-coiffured poodle seems to have a crush on the tabby, and it's obvious from the way Rico fusses and preens himself when-ever she is around that the feeling is mutual. Personally, I can't understand the attraction – cats smell so odd, for start-ers; like old wet rugs, only less pleasant – but whatever, it's none of my business. Pepper makes it clear she is still a little suspicious of me. I am the interloper, I suppose, here to reduce her likelihood of wheedling snacks out of Granny Margaret, and also perhaps to come between her and Rico. (Not remotely likely, but I can understand her insecurity. I used to feel something similar for a lady bulldog we would see in the park, whom Jethro also liked.) But her company makes for more interesting walks in the garden. Now there is another dog to run about with me, and splash in and out of the foun-tain – which we quickly learn, on turning up at the kitchen door soaked and muddy, is absolutely forbidden.

The thing is, I suppose, I have spent my entire life with other dogs, and being the only dog in the Green household has been a strange and unsettling experience for me.

With Pepper around, even regarding me occasionally with suspicious eyes, I can pretend for an hour or two that the full burden of dogship has not descended on my narrow shoulders. Wiry and pleasingly muscular shoulders, no doubt, but undeniably narrow. And unused to any kind of responsibility.

Now I wake in the night and, instead of scratching at my fleas and rolling back to sleep in a desultory fashion, I sit up and listen hard, wondering what woke me.

I sleep like a guard dog now, in other words. Lightly, worriedly, and with one ear permanently on alert. Because I'm uneasily aware that I am the first and last obstacle if a thief or assassin comes calling. That the safety and well-being and happiness of every one of the Greens ultimately rest with me.

It's a sobering realisation.

At the Mintons', I did not need to worry about thieves and assassins. Firstly, no serious burglar would have bothered with such meagre pickings as could be found in that ramshackle household and, secondly, even a mindless thug would have to be crazy to break in somewhere with five dogs. Especially a dog like Jethro, who would have liked nothing better than to imitate a German Shepherd and take a chunk out of some fleeing evil-doer.

Five dogs!

The sheer number of us in that tiny house is staggering to me, now that I have grown used to being the lone canine in a much larger property. How did we not go completely insane? Well, maybe Biscuit did. But the rest of us managed to stay reasonably sane, somehow, and vicious rows like the infamous one I had with Jethro on our last day there were really quite unusual. When I think of it now, the way the five of us lived, shoulder to rump, often crowding together in fear under that grimy kitchen table . . . Well, it's astonishing we weren't handed over to the dog shelter a lot earlier than we were.

The morning after the Christmas tree incident, Granny M is busy on the phone to someone about her Christmas raffle for something called a 'hospice'. I try, but can't seem to get her attention even by tugging on the hem of her skirt.

'Not now, Bertie,' she says, glancing down at me with a harassed expression. 'Go and play in the garden, there's a dear.'

I hesitate, looking over my shoulder.

She's left the back door ajar, where she's been cleaning out the cold frames on the patio. So I give up trying to engage Granny M in a game, and run outside in the sharp winter sunshine instead. To my surprise, I find Pepper already in our garden, drinking from the pond. She looks up as I approach and barks for joy, almost as though she's been waiting for me.

Which is a worrying thought.

'Hey, B,' Pepper says chirpily.

B?

I am tempted to say, 'Hey, P,' in response, but decide not to.

It is almost Christmas, after all.

Rico is hanging about by the fountain too – like Pepper's shadow, only shorter and with pointier ears – and even Kitty has turned up. She is looking depressed. That is, she's not smirking at me as she normally does, but is regarding one of her own paws in a disgusted manner.

I glance at the tabby, surprised. 'What's up, Kitty?'

She shoots me a withering look, as if to say, 'Don't speak to me, dog shelter cast-off,' then bends and licks her paw.

Kitty has a 'thing' about animals from shelters, apparently. Rico explained it all to me one day, but I am still not sure I understand. Something about shelter animals being *common*, whatever that means. But I do understand the way Kitty treats me, which is like someone utterly and irretrievably beneath my notice.

Meanwhile, I respond to her coldness in the only way I know how, by wagging my tail harder, smiling harder, and occasionally chasing her up a tree.

'She's got a thorn in her paw,' Rico explains, looking at his sister in a worried way. 'A really nasty one. In deep too.'

I shrug, not seeing the problem. 'So pull it out.'

'Stupid mutt,' Kitty spits at me, 'do you think I haven't tried?' She returns to licking her paw, her movements almost savage now. '*Pull it out*,' she mimics me, putting on a high-pitched voice, like I'm still a wet-behind-the-ears puppy, then adds sarcastically, 'Wow, great thinking, Bertie. You should be a vet when you grow up.'

Ouch.

Undeterred, I wag my tail a little more. 'So let me see, then.'

'Get lost!'

Pepper runs in a circle round us. It's another habit of hers. Like breaking into our garden without an invitation.

I'm going to have to have a chat with the poodle about that soon. Her frequent visits were obviously not a problem when there were only cats in residence here, and Rico was the draw she could not resist. You can't blame a compass for pointing north, as Mr Minton used to say whenever Jethro, Biscuit and I chased after the bitches on heat in the park. But I'm feeling my status now as Household Dog, and it's just not on, I decide, to have some other dog wandering in and out of my garden without asking permission.

Admittedly, I'm a touch uncomfortable with the idea of this impending dog-to-dog chat. I grew up thinking of Jethro as the Alpha male, and me as only one step ahead of Biscuit in terms of dominating behaviour. So this will be me stepping up to my new position of Alpha.

On the other hand, I'm looking forward to seeing Pepper's face when I tell her things have changed. She is not going to believe it, for a start. And once she *does* believe it, she's not going to like it much. Bertie the beagle, the newcomer, the shelter animal, the pint-sized pooch, asserting his right to hold this domain without threat of invasion from next door's uppity poodle?

Well, if Pepper doesn't like it, that's too bad.

My garden, my rules.

I just hope she doesn't get rough over it. She is alarmingly tall.

Maybe this thorn could help me.

Squaring my shoulders in an Alpha dog fashion, I tip my head to one side and say, 'Sorry, no can do.'

Kitty frowns at me, pausing in her licking. 'Sorry?'

'Can't get lost. Not here, anyway.' I glance about the Greens' garden. 'Think I've sniffed every spot in this garden now. Every tree, every bush, every blade of grass. Chances of me getting lost here are nil, I'm afraid.'

'Ha ha, very funny,' she hisses.

Pepper barks.

She flashes the poodle a cross look, then continues licking and sucking on her hurt paw.

'Look, trust me, I can get thorns out,' I tell them. 'It's kind of a skill of mine.'

Rico looks at me with interest. 'You've done it before? Performed a deep thorn extraction? I mean, on someone else's paw. Not just your own.'

'Oh yes,' I lie cheerfully. 'Dozens of times. They used to call me the Thorn Doctor at my old home. I was in demand after country rambles, I can tell you.'

'Seriously?'

'Why would I lie about something like that?'

Pepper barks again. She's quite a vocal dog, I've noticed. I suppose it saves on the effort of conversation, since she can just fill any embarrassing silence with a yap or a bark.

Kitty raises her head again to glare at me. Her glowing yellow eyes narrow to the point of near closing as she studies my innocent face.

'He's lying,' she says at last, showing genuine perspicacity. 'Spouting total nonsense. As usual.'

I trot forward to show willing, to within easy scratching distance of her claws, and wag my tail a little faster to show her I'm friendly and there will be none of that chasing up a tree business today.

'Come on, I won't bite,' I say, trying to sound encouraging. 'Let me see it, at least. This deadly thing, this impossible-to-remove thorn. Bet I can take it out for you. What harm is there in showing me?'

Rico purrs and nudges slowly round his sister's back, dipping his head to stroke his fur against hers. 'Show him, Sis.'

Kitty closes her eyes briefly, considering the matter. Then she reopens them, fixing me with a venomous look. 'Very well. But no touching. No licking. No sniffing even, do you understand?' She pauses. 'And no . . . no *breathing*.'

'Not sure Bertina can manage the no breathing bit,' Pepper says helpfully.

I growl.

'Oops, I meant B,' she tells me cheekily.

Kitty looks at the poodle too.

Pepper swings her head and encounters the tabby cat's glare. She swallows and backs away, her fluffy tail bobble swaying nervously. 'Sorry. I'll just . . . watch. From over here. And keep quiet.'

I sit and wait, still wagging my tail.

Kitty thinks about it some more, taking her time, not letting anyone hurry her. Then, slowly and with great dignity, she extends her hurt paw towards me.

'Go on, then,' she says. 'Take a look. But only a look.'

Here goes.

I lean in cautiously.

Her eyes do not move from mine, as if to indicate that at any second she may change her mind about all this unnatural dog–cat cooperation, and scratch my nose to shreds.

Her paw does look quite inflamed. My nose wrinkles at the smell too. Cat odour. Not as bad as my first day here, which means I must be getting used to it. But it's still not exactly my favourite smell.

No sniffing, she said. And clearly meant it. But that's hardly practical, is it? I can't make a proper assessment of the situation without using my nose. It's my most sensitive part. Though I'd be happy not to sniff Kitty if I could avoid it, given her pungent catty aroma. But can I?

With one careful eye on her claws, currently sheathed in that velvety paw, I edge a little further forwards, nose-first.

'No sniffing,' she reminds me silkily.

I consider the dark padded underside of her outstretched paw. There's the tip of the thorn. Driven in deep, with a hint of tangy blood round the entry wound.

'Just a tiny sniff?' I ask mildly. 'A little one?'

'No.'

But my nose quivers, already shifting into pre-sniff mode, and she hisses, all the fur suddenly rising on her back.

'Look,' I say calmly, taking a step backwards, 'you want that thorn removed, Kitty, you're going to have to let me come much closer. And not just sniffing either. Touching will definitely have to happen too.'

'Forget it, mutt.'

'Then enjoy having that thing in your paw for the rest of your life.' I hesitate, then add, 'Or wait until it's infected and Granny Margaret spots it. Because as soon as she sees you limping, she'll probably take you to . . . the vet.'

The vet.

The black circles in the centre of Kitty's eyes double in size. Her fur stays up, but she seems reduced to speechlessness by the mention of her old enemy, gazing at me in horror.

Rico shifts uneasily. 'The vet? I don't like the sound of that, Sis.'

Pepper barks her agreement.

'So what's it to be?' I press her, and wag my tail again. 'Let me take out the thorn, or get an infection and risk a trip to the vet?'

Friendly, friendly, always friendly. That's me, that's Bertie the beagle. And I want to stay friendly, even when laying down the law or forcing a situation to its resolution. I certainly don't want to be a Jethro-style Alpha, all brute force and bad teeth. I want to become a Bertie Alpha, which is . . .

Well, I'm not sure exactly what kind of Alpha I am yet. But my tail does seem to enjoy wagging, so I guess I should keep on with that for as long as possible.

Kitty's mouth scrunches up. Like she's sucking on a mouse's tail. 'Oh, be my guest,' she spits, and extends her paw again. 'Do it, if you can. Take the thorn out. Then we'll see how empty your boasting is.'

I take a deep breath, and nose at her paw.

I'm not exactly lying, of course. I've seen this done. In fact, it's Molly who has the skill at removing thorns.

My clever sister must have drawn at least a dozen thorns and splinters – once even a metal tack – out of hurting paws over the years, not just mine but the others' paws as well. And I have seen her do it, up close, when she took a splinter out of my own hind paw. So I know the basics. Licking all over first, to make sure it's good and clean. Then head to one side, teeth closing round the edge of the embedded object. All very neat, very careful. And then one quick jerk back.

But do I have her skill?

Or her undoubted precision and gentleness?

Only one way to find out, I think.

Reluctantly, I halt the wagging of my tail. No unnecessary movements from now on. Then I sniff the tormented paw pad.

Kitty hisses softly between her teeth, like steam from a kettle spout.

I ignore her this time, and sniff again. The smell alone tells me a great deal. I back up and consider the paw. OK, I understand the problem now. It's a bramble thorn, and a particularly nasty one. Thick at the blunt end, which leaves me guessing at the length being half that of one of Kitty's claws, and of a similar width. Only it's gone in at an angle, not straight. Which is making it near impossible for Kitty to remove by sucking hard, as she normally might.

'I'm going to have to lick it first,' I tell Kitty, hoping to avoid a claw-spagged face by warning her in advance. 'No way round it.'

I lick it quickly and lightly.

Faugh. Cat taste.

Kitty bunches up her body and emits the most disturbing high-pitched whine I have ever heard a cat make. It's so unnerving, in fact, it makes my own hackles rise of their own volition.

Rico says tentatively, 'Steady now, Sis. The dog's only trying to help.'

Another cheerful bark of assent from the poodle. Who is watching proceedings from a safe distance, I note, halfway between the side fence and the fountain.

I wish I could join her.

Hurriedly, before the claws come out and my nose is destroyed, I angle my head sideways and go straight in, lips pulled back, teeth bared.

The high-pitched whine becomes a grim and threatening wail, a terrible note that just seems to rise and rise, never falling. It's worse than one of those car alarms that go off in the middle of the night and sound like an insane supernatural creature whisking up and down the street outside, screaming at the humans. Worse because it's right next to my highly sensitive ears, and I have no way of stopping it except by extracting this thorn and getting the hell out of there as fast as possible.

My teeth close round the slightly protruding end of the thorn. But I have to shift them around a bit, trying to get a better purchase on the slippery thing.

I can taste cat blood in my mouth now.

Gross.

Interesting too, but still gross.

I decide everything is good to go, and fix my teeth firmly round the thorn end. I test it, just a tiny sideways nudge, and already I can feel it loosening.

The pitch of Kitty's wail increases in intensity.

GOOD GRIEF!

One. Two. Three.

I jerk my head back fast, keeping my teeth fixed rigidly round the thorn, and it shoots out with me.

'He's done it!' Rico exclaims.

I hear the surprise in his voice. Obviously the mellow tabby has much to learn about me, the new Bertie, the stoic Alpha dog . . .

Kitty shrieks in pain, and all her claws spring out at once, razor-sharp scythes of death that just miss me as I scramble backwards.

'That hurt!'

Don't bother to thank me, I think.

I spit the offending thorn onto the grass. Gross.

Pepper bounces up and down, gives several excited barks, then prances back to Rico and thumps him with her fluffy head.

There's an awkward silence.

Kitty examines her paw, which is bleeding slightly. She gives it a quick licking, then turns to the path that meanders through the centre of the garden and tries a few halting steps across the paving stones.

She's still limping. But now the thorn has gone, it's clear she is no longer in terrible pain.

Kitty stops, then looks back at me with obvious reluctance. Her face is inscrutable. 'Thank you,' she manages to say.

I wag my tail. 'You are very welcome.'

Rico turns his yellow gaze on me. 'Hey.'

'Hey?'

'The Paw Print Club,' he says.

Kitty looks over at us. Her expression does not change. 'The paw print what?'

'Club,' Rico explains, his look inspired.

'I still don't know what that is,' his sister says.

'A club is a group of friends who like to meet up and . . . Well, it's a group that does things together. It's a mellow place to be. You know, in the club.'

'So?'

'So we should form a club. Join together, make a group. The Paw Print Club.' He holds up one paw. 'Because we all have them, after all. Dogs and cats, yes. But we have paws in common. It's a way of expressing solidarity.'

Kitty narrows her eyes at him. 'Have you been at the catnip again?'

I sit, staring at Rico as though he's suddenly sprouted wings. Like the 'angel' Granny M placed on top of the Christmas tree with great ceremony this morning.

'The Paw Print Club,' I repeat. 'I like it.'

'And to make it official,' Rico adds, 'we should swear right now to stick together and always stand up for each other. No matter what.'

Pepper barks her approval. 'No matter what,' she says after me, then twists her muscular body round in a tight circle. 'Yes, I'll swear. Please let me join. I know I live next door, but I want to be in the club too.'

She reminds me a little of Biscuit when she gets excited.

Biscuit with a tail bobble.

'I'll swear,' I say, and hold up my paw. I'm delighted with the idea. Not just the thought of belonging to a club, but that my new friends actually want me to join. To be one of them. It's like belonging to a proper family again. 'Count me in.'

Rico looks at Kitty.

She is licking her hurt paw, and only looks up at the marked silence, the fur on her back still ruffled. 'What?'

Pepper says pointedly, 'You have to swear too. Or you're not in the club.'

She shrugs delicately, and continues licking her paw. 'I'm not really a joining sort of person. I like to be left alone.'

Her brother gets up and walks slowly round her, purring. 'Come on, Sis.'

'No.'

'We need you,' he points out. 'We can't have the club without you.'

'I don't see why not.'

My tail is wagging violently. 'Come on, Kitty. You're the smartest here. If you don't join, we might as well forget it.'

Rico nudges her chin, rubbing himself past her. 'Need you, Sis.'

'Oh . . .' She makes an unladylike noise, then drops her paw to the stone. When she lifts it again, there's a tiny reddened mark left behind. 'Very well.'

The four of us stand in a rough circle, looking at each other, then dab our paws together. Rico says, 'I swear to belong to the Paw Print Club,' and we all repeat the words after him, 'and to stick together and look after each other. By our four paws.'

After we have finished swearing the oath, I bark loudly, and chase my own tail with excitement. 'Great idea, Rico. The Paw Print Club. It's happening.'

Suddenly the air does not feel quite so chilly any more.

Pepper and I run side by side to the fountain and back, listening to the sound of Granny M's Christmas music drifting out from the kitchen along with the spicy, delicious smell of her baking.

'So what do we do now?' Kitty asks.

I am not sure, and say so.

Rico yawns again. 'Sorry, that was amazing. But far too much excitement for me. I'll think about it while I'm asleep,' he tells us, apparently oblivious to the fact that he can't, and drifts away towards the house.

Watching him go, clearly disappointed that he's leaving already, Pepper sits abruptly and scratches her rump. 'Erm, I'll have to think about it too.' She prances back towards the gap in the fence, sniffing the air, head held high. 'I can smell something tasty cooking. Sorry, sorry, catch you all later.'

'So much for that,' Kitty hisses, and slinks away into the bushes without making any further contribution to the discussion.

Which leaves me alone. Great first club meeting, I think wryly.

I guess it's up to me, then.

Pleased to have something new and interesting to think about, I sit down on the damp grass and pant, my tongue lolling.

The first thing that comes into my head is Molly, of course. But seeing my sister again is a dream that will never come true. It's futile to keep obsessing about how we were parted, and blaming myself for not holding our little family together at the Mintons'.

I have a second chance now, a chance to put my past mistakes right. But to do that, I need to think of the future, and put my personal misery aside. Think about the group instead, the four of us here, my new family.

The Paw Print Club.

❧ THIRTEEN ❧

'I need ground almonds,' Granny M says, popping her head round the door to the living room. She looks pointedly at Mr Green, who has been reading his newspaper on the sofa next to me and Sam, who is watching television.

Mr Green lowers his newspaper. 'Right now?'

'I'm afraid so.' She smiles at him coaxingly. 'Could you pop out for some? I'm baking for Alzheimer's.'

'Alzheimer's?'

'The charity.' She runs a floury hand through her hair without thinking, though since her hair is white, it makes no difference. 'I said I'd help out. The local branch have got a cake stall at the garden centre tomorrow. A pop-up.'

'A what?'

'It means a one-off, I think. Pops up somewhere, then pops off again. All a bit impromptu.' She smiles at Sam absent-mindedly. 'Enjoying your Saturday morning, darling? Oh, I do love this film. One of those space adventure thingies, isn't it? The one they keep remaking. *Star War*.'

'*Star Wars*, Granny. Not Star War.'

She frowns. 'Rather nice weather though. For television watching.'

'It's been raining all morning.'

'That's true. But look, the sun's come out now.' They all look across at the big window that overlooks the driveway and street. The sun, which had shone out very briefly from behind a dark cloud as she was talking, disappears again. The world darkens. 'Well, it's stopped raining, at any rate. Maybe you should turn off the telly and go with your father to the shops. Get some fresh air.'

Sam's chin drops onto his chest. 'I'm comfy here.'

'You could walk the dog.'

I sit up, ears alert.

'He's comfy too.'

I am comfortable, I can't deny that. But that doesn't mean I am too comfortable to consider going for a walk. Actually, it's hard to imagine any circumstances under which I would feel too comfortable to go for a walk.

I scratch my ear, but nothing occurs to me.

Granny M hesitates, rubbing her hands on her apron, then looks pleadingly over Sam's head at his father.

'John?'

'If Sam doesn't want to come, then why force the issue? It's a good film and he's enjoying it. I was enjoying it too.'

I look up at Mr Green in surprise. Was he? That's a pretty impressive skill, watching the television through a newspaper. Humans are amazing.

Granny M does not say anything, but I see concern in her eyes.

'Come on, Bertie,' Mr Green says, throwing his newspaper aside and lurching to his feet. 'Granny M is baking for Alzheimer's, so it's time for the two of us to go shopping.'

I give a short bark.

Shopping isn't really my thing. But to get to the super-market, we have to pass the entrance to the canal path. And I know Mr Green likes to pop down there sometimes, out of sight, to have a cigarette. I know what they are, because Mrs Minton had a bad-tempered next-door neighbour for a while who smoked and occasionally tossed the butts over the garden wall. We would all gather round and sniff them, because even though cigarettes do not smell very appetising, unusual smells are simply too interesting to ignore.

Mr Green never smokes at the house. I do not think Granny M knows about his little walks along the canal path with me and a cigarette. Human noses are not as good at detecting smells as dog noses. Otherwise she would know as soon as he walked back into the house.

Sam does not say goodbye to me, though he watches as his father struggles to clip my lead on while I dance about on my hind paws, barking.

'Bertie, for goodness sake, hold still.'

Is he kidding?

If he doesn't want me to get this excited, he really shouldn't get the lead out. No lead, no hysteria. It's that simple. Though 'walkies' can have a similar effect on most dogs, I've noticed. It used to reduce Biscuit to a quivering mass of dog flab, and send even ladylike Tina into a yapping fit that had Mrs Minton clapping both hands over her ears. But Mr Green must have owned a dog before, because he almost never uses the W word. Not with me, at any rate. Presumably he knows its powerful and mysterious effect on the canine species.

'Better get some more jars of mincemeat,' Granny M says at the door, and bends to pat my head. 'If you will keep feeding mince pies to Bertie, I'll have to make another batch.'

'I don't feed them to him,' Mr Green says defensively. 'Bertie steals them. When I'm not looking.'

'Then stop leaving them unattended on the arm of the sofa. Mince pies are full of spices, it's bad for him to eat them.' Her voice sharpens with accusation. 'Especially so many.'

Mr Green looks down at me. 'See the trouble you've got me into, Bertie?'

I pant unrepentantly, dragging on the lead. Time to go, isn't it? Anyway, what do they expect? Granny M's homemade mince pies are indeed spicy, but they are delicious too. Her pastry is better even than Mrs Minton's. Which makes it even more strange that Mr Green does not seem to like them, and always waits for her to leave the room before feeding them to me.

It's cold outside. Sure enough, he stops just before the bridge over the canal, and leads me down a series of muddy steps onto the icy path below.

'Our little secret,' Mr Green says to me with a wink, and lights a cigarette in the chilly shadow of the bridge.

I nose around the undergrowth at his feet, sniffing the rubbish. But all the discarded food down here is hard and frosty, the really exciting smells long gone. And the stink from his cigarette swamps everything.

A narrow canal boat goes past and I watch with interest. One thick-set man in a buttoned-up waterproof coat, collar turned up, steering the boat, his breath steaming. He raises a hand in friendly greeting to Mr Green, but does not even look at me.

The water ripples behind the boat as it vanishes round the next bend in the canal, then gradually stills again.

Mr Green takes another puff on his cigarette.

I sit and look up at him, bored.

'I quit smoking when we got married,' he tells me, looking guiltily at the cigarette. 'Jenny persuaded me to stop. But since she died, I . . .'

Mr Green falls silent for a moment.

'Someone at work offered me a cigarette after an office party, and I bought a pack, meaning to pay them back, and now . . .' He takes another puff. 'Stupid, really. I only smoke a few a week, and I don't even like the taste. But I can't see the point in giving up. I mean, why bother? Jenny's not here to see me smoking. Not any more.'

I bark, politely.

He looks down at me. Then drops the cigarette and grinds it into the icy mud. 'Yes, you're right. Filthy habit.' He sighs, and leads me further along the path. 'Come on, then. A quick walk to the pub sign and back, then on to the supermarket for Granny M's ground almonds and mincemeat. And I will give up smoking soon, I promise. Just . . . not yet.'

At the supermarket, Mr Green ties me to a post near the sliding entrance doors and the rows of trolleys.

'Stay,' he says in that stern voice that he believes makes some kind of difference to me. Then he vanishes inside the store.

Another dog is already tied to the post. A female Dalmatian with muddy legs.

We look at each other assessingly. She pants and wags her tail speculatively. I wag my own in response. She wags hers harder. I try to match her speed, but can't quite manage it, so give up the attempt. There was a Dalmatian at the dog shelter, though only briefly; a nice family picked him up about two days after he came in. I think he could wag his tail at about ninety miles per hour.

I decide to introduce myself, since we could be spending as long as half an hour in each other's company. 'Hello, I'm Bertie.'

'Spotty.'

I make a face. 'Ouch.'

'Oh, I don't mind,' she says cheerfully. 'My mother's name was Spotty too. And her mother's before her. It's a family tradition.'

There's a large glossy board next to us that keeps changing its picture every thirty seconds or so. Like a television screen, except the picture is static. Pictures of items for sale inside the supermarket, I guess.

Every time it changes, Spotty makes a sudden jerking motion and backs awkwardly, front legs dipping, like she's trying to duck out of her collar.

'It's automatic,' I tell her helpfully.

'I don't like it.'

'It can't hurt you.'

'I know, I know, it's just . . .'

The picture changes. She does the jerking thing again.

'Sorry.'

I raise my eyebrows. 'Hey, whatever turns you on.'

There's a metal bowl of water next to the post. It smells a bit iffy, but I decide to risk it. I'm thirsty after our walk along the canal.

Faugh.

The water is freezing cold and tastes metallic. It goes the wrong way up my delicate nose. I shake my muzzle, sneeze twice, then apologise to Spotty.

'Did I get any on you?'

She wrinkles her nose up but pretends that I didn't. 'Of course not.' Very polite dogs, Dalmatians.

Suddenly, I stiffen at a distant sound. My heart begins to race, my ears straining, my whole body on full alert, but I am unsure why. Then I hear it again. A sweet, familiar sound, and one I never thought to hear again in my life.

Surely that cannot be . . .?

Then I hear it again, and know for certain what I've heard.

My sister's bark.

I turn at once, running to the full length of my lead and jerking back, impossibly tethered to the post.

Molly.

Every dog has a bark all their own, just as each human voice sounds different. And I would recognise my sister's bark anywhere. I've been hearing it since we were pups, playing rough and tumble on the kitchen floor, and I know it as well as my own.

'Over here, over here!' she is shouting.

My heart leaps.

I bark back, as loud as I can, 'I hear you. I hear you.'

Passers-by frown at me but I ignore them.

'Where are you?' I raise my head and bark, surprising myself with my own deep-throated baying. 'Can you see me?'

Her bark is muffled now, like someone has just forced her inside a car. She continues to bark though, strong and persistent. Molly has definitely seen me. She knows I am here. Look at me, look at me, that bark is telling me over and over again. Then her bark begins to fade as the car she's in moves away, somewhere out of sight, manoeuvring slowly through the supermarket car park towards the exit.

But which car is it?

Spotty turns her back on the sliding picture display, staring at me instead. 'Erm, Bertie? I don't like to interrupt a jolly good bark, but is something the matter?' Her brows arch upwards as I continue to bark hysterically, my front legs outstretched, my chest puffed up with the effort. 'You seem a little . . . on edge.'

'That bark, do you hear it?' I strain at the lead, staring around the busy car park with frantic eyes. 'It's my sister.'

The Dalmatian watches me, a little perplexed by my behaviour, not really understanding. 'Oh right, that's . . . nice.'

But where exactly is she?

'We were separated at the dog shelter. Back in the autumn. I haven't seen her since. Listen, that's her bark again.' My ears locate her position at last, and my head turns, hunting to my right. 'Molly?'

A car swings into view.

It's a small blue car with shiny windows that reflect the wintry sunlight, half-dazzling me as it passes. But I recognise the driver and drag hard against my lead, barking and barking.

'Molly?'

Sure enough, it's the pinched-looking woman at the wheel, the one who took Molly from the shelter. She looks even more stern and tight-lipped than I remember, though I expect the manic barking in her ear has not improved her mood.

Then I see Molly.

She's standing up in the back of the car, both front paws on the window frame, staring at me and barking madly.

For that split-second, we look back at each other, same soft brown head, same splodgy ears, same quivering nose, and I see the joy and desperation in her eyes, the same as in mine. Then the car swings on and past me, past the supermarket entrance, past the zebra crossing, and out onto the main road.

'Molly!' My throat is hoarse with barking, my neck and shoulders sore from dragging on the lead, but I can't seem to stop. 'Molly!'

Suddenly a hand grabs my collar, jerking me backwards, and my deep bark becomes a high-pitched yelp.

'What on earth?'

It's Mr Green, and he sounds furious. Hard to blame him, really. I know I'm behaving badly, and I do try hard to stop barking. But I can't.

'You bad dog, Bertie,' he exclaims, releasing my lead from the post. 'Be quiet. Do you hear me? Be quiet right now.'

He turns to apologise to Spotty's owner, an angry young woman who is dragging the interested Dalmatian away and complaining about me at the top of her voice.

'I'm so sorry,' he tells her, looking flustered and red in the face. 'Bertie's not normally this naughty. I can't think what's got into him.'

Spotty adds a reassuring bark to the general confusion. 'Hope you find your sister,' she shouts back at me, then vanishes into the crowd of shoppers and trolleys outside the supermarket entrance.

Out on the main road, I see a bright flash of blue. The pinch-faced woman heading home, no doubt. With my sister a prisoner in the back of her car.

Mr Green is looking over his shoulder at the angry young woman. He swears under his breath, clearly not very happy with me. Moving his shopping bag awkwardly to his other hand, he lets the lead go slack for a few seconds.

I bound forward, surprising him.

'What the hell?'

The lead snaps out of his hand, and I keep running, free at last, ears streaming back along my head. I hear Mr Green yelling my name, but do not stop, dodging cars in the busy car park, ignoring the hooting horns and squeal of tyres. For the first time in my life, I know exactly where I'm going.

After Molly.

❧ FOURTEEN ❧

I force my way through spiny bushes on the edge of the supermarket car park, and out onto the frosty pavement beyond. A kid shouts some nonsense at me through a car window, but I don't look at him. The cars are moving slowly on this side, but faster the other way. Was Molly's owner going that way too?

I skid to a halt on the edge of the pavement, staring up and down the road.

I look for a small blue car.

But it's next to impossible to know which car is Molly's. There are so many cars on this road, including blue cars, all moving slowly, either queuing to get into the supermarket for Christmas shopping or heading back into town with a car full of food and presents. Their exhausts smoke on the cold air; the heavy stink of fuel is everywhere. I see cars with Christmas trees just like ours crammed into the back, and excited children with flushed faces and bright eyes, staring down at me from steamed-up car windows.

A large woman carrying heavy bags stops and stares at me. 'Hello, little doggy,' she says, rather breathlessly. 'You're cute. Are you supposed to be running about loose?'

She spots my trailing lead and puts down one of her shopping bags, making a grab for me. But I dart between her legs instead, knocking her bag over in my hurry.

I hear an ominous crack, like something made of glass has just broken. A bottle?

'Hey, look what you've done!'

She runs after me and tries to stamp on my lead, but I evade her easily. As I dash away, I hear several tins rolling across the pavement and into the gutter.

Oops.

My ears prickle.

What was that? Can I hear Molly again?

Suddenly, a big truck moves past, and I catch a glimpse of a small blue car through the gap it leaves behind. And a dog, staring at me out of the back window, still barking.

Then the traffic moves on, and I can't see the car any more. Molly!

I ignore the woman's shouts behind me and trot on faster in the direction of town, my nose quivering, my face practically stuck to the pavement. I need to remember where I'm going, otherwise I'll become hopelessly lost. And the best way to remember is to learn the smells as I go along.

I run across a narrow lane and begin to pass houses with no front gardens. Doors blackened by street dirt. I can smell other dogs here too, such rich and intriguing scents. The urge to stop and sniff every lamp-post and rubbish bin is almost overpowering.

But I focus on Molly. This could be my one and only chance to find my sister.

'Bertie?'

I hesitate, and slow to a walk, almost stopping. Because I know that voice. Somewhere behind me, Mr Green is still in pursuit. Presumably still carrying Granny M's ground almonds and jars of mincemeat. And he's not in great shape, so he's probably panting and gasping and red-cheeked too.

I glance round.

He's not far behind me.

I expect Mr Green and I are going to have a long and uncomfortable 'chat' when he eventually catches up with me. A chat that will involve all those human words that make Granny M tut and shake her head in disapproval.

I don't turn round, though I feel guilty for running away from him. He's my owner. And this comes under the heading of unacceptable behaviour for a dog; refusing to come back when an owner calls you. Mr Green will have a perfect excuse for taking me back to the dog shelter after this. Then Sam will have no warm furry body to hug when he secretly cries himself to sleep at night. And Granny M will have no one to talk to when she's alone in her kitchen, baking and remembering her daughter, Jenny. And Mr Green will no longer have an excuse to get out of the house and talk about his dead wife when nobody's listening except me.

The Green family need me. No doubt about that.

But right now Molly needs me more.

I wonder about my sister's bad leg. The one that has left her with a permanent limp, and a nasty ache in the winter that only goes away after long hours of licking. How has she been coping on her own with the pinch-faced woman? Poor

Molly must be in constant pain in this bitter weather, and I can't imagine her new owner has even noticed. She has the grim face of someone who is always impatient and uncaring. She probably drags Molly along on the lead and orders her to hurry up when she's limping. And does not know how to take care of her sore leg.

I can't bear the thought of my sister miserable and in pain. I must rescue her.

Mr Green has seen me looking back at him. He stops and whistles hard, two fingers in his mouth. 'Bertie, heel!'

He does not look very happy.

I start running again, my frantic gaze sweeping the main road ahead. I seem to be nearing the side road where Mr Green turns off when he comes to the supermarket in his car. Traffic is moving very slowly on both sides of the road, which is working in my favour. I listen hard, and can just hear the faint sound of Molly's barking up ahead. But there's too much traffic for me to be able to see her or the car.

'Bertie!' Mr Green is running after me again now. He sounds out of breath. 'Get back here, you naughty dog!'

I pause at the edge of the pavement, and consider the dangerous choice of trying to cross the main road. The traffic is so thick, the chances of being hit by a car are very high. But if I can somehow slip unscathed through these rows of slow-moving cars, I would at least be on the same side as Molly's car.

Then a miracle happens.

The small blue car turns across the traffic queue and down the same side road that Mr Green always takes. Directly ahead of me.

The car speeds up as it vanishes, and the muffled sound of my sister's bark fades away.

I stop dead, staring hard at the space where the car had been seconds before. That was definitely Molly I could see in the back of the car, leaping up at the windows, trying to catch a final glimpse of me as the car disappeared down the side road.

'Molly!'

She's gone, and it's unlikely I will be able to catch up with her owner's car now that she's left the traffic queue on the main road.

But I can scarcely believe my luck. Because my chances of finding Molly again have just improved massively. Perhaps the pinch-faced woman lives down that road. Perhaps she even lives near the Greens. It's not certain, of course. But it's better news than if she had continued to drive straight on and headed further back into town. Then there would have been little hope of finding Molly again, except by another chance sighting like today's. Not in the vast, bristling forest of houses and shops and buildings that lie between the Greens' house and town.

As far as I know, that side road leads to the small block of local shops where Mr Green goes sometimes for his newspaper and cigarettes, and the leafy network of streets where the Greens have their house, and the large park at the end. Still a vast area to search, admittedly. But if Molly is living down there somewhere with the pinch-faced woman, I'm going to find them. However long it takes.

First though, I need to know where the woman turns off before she reaches the park at the end of the road.

I leap forward again, but a hand grabs my collar.

'Gotcha.'

I twist and yelp, and bark wildly to be free, but to no avail. Mr Green has caught me again, and this time he's not going to let go.

'What do you mean by it, eh?' He tilts my chin and looks down into my face. I stare past him at the grey sky, unable to meet his accusing gaze. 'This is a very busy road. You could have been killed. Hit by a car.' He pauses, then adds hoarsely, 'What would that have done to Sam? To lose both his mother *and* his dog?'

I wag my tail feebly.

His mouth tightens. The stern note in his voice makes me quake. 'I expected better of you, Bertie.'

He releases my chin and I hang my head, feeling horrible and small.

I expected better of myself.

I have disappointed my owner and, worst of all, I can't explain why.

The walk back home is cold and miserable. More of a trudge than a walk, in fact, with me trailing behind and Mr Green jerking my lead every now and then to keep me moving.

'Come on, Bertie,' he says irritably.

I cast him a quick glance, but continue to hang back. I want to trot by my owner's side as usual, head up, alert to all-comers, obedient and responsive. Yet how can I? I have to slink low to sniff the ground for Molly's scent, and turn my head to look everywhere for the small blue car. Every side street, every driveway, every passing vehicle. It seems my luck has run out though. I see plenty of blue cars on the way home.

None of them are the right one.

When we reach the house, I creep into my basket next to the range with my tail between my legs, ears flat to my head, not even interested in the bowl of dried food Granny M has put down for me.

Kitty is sitting on one of the kitchen cabinets. She gazes down at me with a look of surprise mingled with feline satisfaction. 'In trouble, Bertie?'

'It was a misunderstanding.'

She licks one paw disdainfully. 'It always is.'

I curl up, turning my back on her, and lie shivering while Mr Green tells Granny M and Sam how I ran away from him, and refused to come back when he called, and what a bad dog I am.

I feel awful, and not just because of the exclamations of horror and accusing looks being thrown in my direction by the Greens.

For a few precious seconds today, I found Molly. Looked into my sister's eyes. Knew she had seen and recognised me too.

And now I've lost her all over again.

❧ FIFTEEN ❧

'Bertina! Bertina!'

It's Pepper, and she sounds urgent.

I do not look up at her cry, however. Bertie, I'm thinking irritably. Besides, I am far too busy staring at a frost-edged blade of grass two inches in front of my chin. A whole day has passed since I saw Molly, and I am finding it hard to feel much interest in anything. All I can think about is how I have failed her.

'Bertina, we want to help,' Pepper tells me urgently, wriggling through the gap in the fence to invade our garden again.

Help?

I roll my eyes in the direction of the poodle, but cannot find the energy to respond, feeling too dejected. How on earth can the dog next door help me? She can't even stop her owners from shaving her butt.

It's hard to feel optimistic, especially about my chances of finding Molly, having been grounded after my 'bad behaviour' in running away at the supermarket. I have been going over the possibilities in my head. But the only option I can see is to run away again. Which I really do not want to do. It might tip my already irate owner over the edge, and then

I would end up back in the dog shelter. Where my chances of finding Molly again would be zero.

'No walks until after Christmas,' Mr Green told me yesterday, much to Sam's dismay. 'You need to earn my trust again. If you are a good dog, maybe we'll take you out on Boxing Day.'

'But, Dad, that's a whole week,' Sam exclaimed.

'I don't care,' his father said firmly. 'Bertie has to learn to behave himself. Or we can't keep him.'

Sam, of course, stormed off to his room in tears at this decision, slamming his bedroom door so hard the whole house shook.

And Granny M had a 'quiet word' with Mr Green, which ended with him leaving the house and not coming back for several hours.

And it was all my fault.

So I have been lying miserably in the back garden today, listening to the dreary, endless trickle of water into the icy pool below the fountain. And now the poodle has appeared to disturb my grim thoughts. Under other circumstances, I might have concluded she wanted a game. Tag, perhaps. We do play that sometimes when the weather is not so cold. But today the sun is hidden behind dark clouds and it feels like it's going to rain later. And I am not in the mood for a game, as any casual observer could guess from the way my chin is buried deep between my paws.

'Kitty told me what happened yesterday,' Pepper continues, and tosses her top bobble with an air of violent passion. 'I think it's just dreadful. Being separated from your sister like that. You must be distraught.'

I say nothing.

I am not sure that *distraught* is a word I would ever use to describe myself. Beagles are not much given to being distraught, as a rule. All the same, I am curious to hear what Pepper has to say.

Kitty jumps down from the fence and comes mincing over the frosty grass to hear what is being said, her expression one of acute discomfort. She hates cold weather.

'You could at least make an effort to look interested, Bertie,' she says. 'We've been talking about you, and Pepper thinks she knows what you need.'

To be left alone, perhaps?

It seems unlikely that my friends are going to let me lie here in brooding solitude any longer though. I sigh and sit up instead. My bottom was getting chilly anyway.

Rico, who has been hiding rather ineffectually in a leafless shrub, pushes his way out through the bare branches and strolls after his sister.

'Yes, she wants to help you,' Rico agrees. 'And I think it's a good idea. We're all in the Paw Print Club now, remember? And members of the club should stick together. Help each other out.'

The bait is too much for me.

'Help how?'

Pepper bounds up and down the cold lawn, looking slightly hysterical. Her normal expression, in other words. 'By finding your sister, of course, Bertina.'

I tilt my head to one side, considering her. Is she serious?

'OK, I'll bite.' I see Pepper's eyes widen and add hurriedly, 'I mean, go on, I'm listening. And please, call me Bertie. If you can bring yourself to do it.'

'I thought you didn't mind Bertina so much?'

'That was then. Now I mind.'

'Oh.' The poodle struggles with this for a moment, then makes the necessary mental adjustment. 'Well, Be-rt-ie, you're grounded, but I'm not. I can still go walkies.'

I don't want to, but find myself wagging my tail mindlessly at the mere mention of the word, *walkies*.

Then I realise Pepper is also wagging her tail bobble.

Pure conditioning. We can't help doing it.

I only hope the cats haven't noticed.

'I still don't see —'

'I can keep an eye out for Molly on my walks,' she points out triumphantly. 'All I need from you is a proper description of your sister, and . . . and some idea what she smells like.'

Kitty stares. 'What she *smells* like?'

'Of course.' Pepper sticks her nose to the ground and her bobble-tipped tail in the air, and parades up and down in front of us in that precarious position. 'I'll have to locate her scent first. How else am I supposed to find her?'

I feel rather more excited as I consider the possibilities.

'But hold on,' I say, 'doesn't your owner always w . . . take you the same way?'

I am careful to avoid the trigger word, *walk*.

Pepper smirks. 'Usually, yes. But he's a soft touch, so easy to manipulate. A little nudge here, a little drag on the lead there, and he laughs and says, *you want to go that way today, Pepper?* And obliges.'

'So you can go a different way every day?'

'If necessary.'

'And check all the houses on each street.'

'Exactly.'

Rico sits up straight, looking impressed. 'In other words, if a beagle so much as barks in one of those houses—'

'Or leaves her scent in the front garden,' Kitty adds.

'Or leaves her scent in the front garden,' her brother repeats, nodding, 'or even on the pavement outside, then Pepper is going to be able to find her.'

Pepper gives a short, approving bark.

I think about it. 'It does sound like a great plan. But there are all the back gardens to cover as well.'

Rico looks perplexed.

'That woman who took Molly from the dog shelter,' I explain, 'she's the kind who might keep a dog out the back. In a kennel, maybe. Or even an outbuilding.'

'How awful.' Pepper is horrified. 'This woman, can she really be that bad?'

'She looks it.'

I describe the woman's stern demeanour and pinched face, and the brutal way she took my sister away from me that day, without even giving us the chance to say goodbye to each other, and they sit round me in a group, listening and not saying anything. I can see from her poignant head tilt that Pepper is moved and appalled. But the cats seem less affected by my story. Perhaps because they have less experience of the powerlessness of collars and leads, and how much we rely as dogs on the good nature of our owners.

'So what do you suggest?' Pepper asks, her nose wrinkling.

'I'm not sure.'

'Because my owner is quite easy-going, but I think even he would draw the line at me dashing into other people's back gardens and poking about in their outbuildings.'

I look at the cats.

'You and Rico are free to wander wherever you choose,' I point out.

Kitty meets my gaze with an unreadable expression, then cleans meticulously behind one ear with a wetted paw. 'So?'

'So while Pepper's checking out the fronts of the houses . . .'

'We can search the back gardens,' Rico concludes, and nibbles speculatively on a squashed-looking blade of grass. 'Hmm. Not a bad idea.'

Kitty turns her head and fixes him with an outraged stare. 'Not a bad . . . Excuse me?'

Her brother hesitates, no doubt a little concerned by the ferocity in her eyes. I'm not finding it an exactly comfortable expression either. It makes me not want to turn my back on her. That kind of look.

I decide to intervene.

'What I think Rico means to say is,' I begin, while keeping a careful distance from her paws, 'that you two, being cats, are uniquely skilled in such demanding activities.' Her eyes narrow, her claws begin to show, and I hurriedly elaborate. 'You know ... High-level espionage, tracking, search-and-rescue, peering through first-floor windows. All that cat stuff.'

'Hmm,' Kitty murmurs, watching me suspiciously.

She does seem vaguely mollified by my flattering description of feline tracking skills. Her tail is still whisking angrily though. Never a reassuring thing with a cat.

Pepper runs back from investigating an old cracked plate that Granny Margaret put down yesterday for the cats, containing some leftover tuna fish from their supper. There's nothing lickable on the china plate – I already checked – but it's clear she enjoyed making doubly sure.

'So, when are we going to put this plan into action?' she asks excitedly, wagging and bouncing, all legs and bobbles. 'I can't wait.'

I muse. 'When's your next walkies?'

'Not until tomorrow. You missed today's.' She looks disappointed. 'I suppose that means the cats are going to get first crack at this.'

Kitty turns her yellow gaze on the poodle. 'So?'

'Erm ...' Pepper eyes that whisking cat's tail for a few seconds, her long muzzle swaying from side to side with its sinuous movement, and then quickly backtracks. 'That's actually quite a good idea, isn't it?' Wrong answer. The tail speeds up. 'No, what am I saying? It's a *really* good idea. The best, in fact. Definitely what we should do. Cats first. Dogs second.'

Kitty's eyes flash. 'Hmm,' she murmurs again, but her tail rests still at last.

The dangerous moment has passed.

'Tonight, then?' I suggest.

Rico nods. 'We'll stay out after dinner. Start scoping out the back gardens.' He looks at his sister. 'Together or separately?'

'We stay together,' Kitty decides, then sniffs the air in both directions, up and down the block, on the alert for any delicious cooking smells in our vicinity. It's the right time of year for tasty leftovers, as we all know. People having guests to stay and throwing parties. No domestic pets go hungry at Christmas, not in my experience. 'That way, if we find any scraps, you can keep watch while I eat them.'

'Sure thing, Sis,' Rico agrees, docile as ever.

'So you're looking for a beagle that looks more or less exactly like me,' I point out, probably unnecessarily, but I don't want to miss this opportunity to search for my sister by proxy, 'only with a bad leg'.

'If your sister Molly is out there,' Kitty says with icy confidence, 'we'll find her.' Then she leans back, cocks one hind leg in the air at a perilous angle, and licks her bottom. 'Trust me.'

Pepper and I look at each other, a little disconcerted.

Cats.

Suddenly, the back door opens and Sam comes running across the frosty grass towards us. He has a football, and kicks it energetically in my direction.

'Fetch, Bertie!'

Without even thinking, I run after the football, fall over my own paws in my haste, try an enthusiastic header, accidentally knock the ball under some low-growing bushes, and then have to spend several minutes retrieving it.

Not really my game, football. Give me a chewy tennis ball any day.

Thankfully, Sam does not seem to notice my incompetence.

'Hey, Pepper!' he says, somehow cheerful again after his row with his dad, and stops to stroke the poodle. He seems fascinated by the dog's curly white fur, grinning as the frizzy bobble on the end of her upright tail waves furiously back and forth. 'Do you want to play football with me and Bertie?'

Pepper barks.

Sam gets the football back and dribbles it towards us.

I lower myself to the ground and pretend-growl.

Sam is smiling, but his face is flushed, and close up, I can see that his eyes look a bit shiny. Like he's been crying again.

Another argument with his dad?

'Fetch!' he shouts again, and kicks the football violently down the garden for Pepper and me to chase. It bounces off an old stone statue half-buried in grass beneath the trees, and he cheers. 'Goal!'

There is no sign of the cats.

I suppose ball games are not their thing.

But I am more cheerful now than I was this morning. I was miserable earlier, grounded and in disgrace with my humans, and convinced that I would never see Molly again. Now though, entirely thanks to Pepper and the cats, we have a plan in place to search for her. Not just wishful thinking and daydreams, either. A plan that has a very real chance of succeeding.

Assuming that Molly really does live around here.

I push the fear away.

Today is not a day to be pessimistic. Today is for hope.

Sam gets the football back after a slight tussle with Pepper, who does not quite understand the concept of relinquishing the ball once she's got it, and dribbles it round between the trees. We give chase, nosing at the cold, wet ball, then running after it as Sam kicks it further.

'Goal!' he shouts again, rather prematurely, raising his arms in the air in a victory salute as he gives the football another enormous kick.

It flies through the air, back towards the house.

Too far, too high.

There's a sudden, ominous crack.

'Oops,' Pepper exclaims, slowing in her headlong pursuit.

Sam stares, drawing in his breath.

I stop and glance back at the boy. Then see where the football has come to land. Oh, this is not very good. The football has slammed into one of Granny M's cold frames on the patio. And broken the glass. And rolled away across the patio, right in front of the back door. So there can be no doubt what just happened.

The back door opens abruptly.

Granny M comes out in her house slippers, staring down at the football first, then at me, Sam and Pepper, all of us frozen in fear on the lawn. Then her head turns and she surveys the damage to her cold frame.

'Oh, Sam,' she murmurs, and shakes her head.

He does not react.

'Better come here, Sam,' she says clearly, looking at him.

At this, his face crumples, and he runs in the opposite direction, back towards the trees at the end of the garden.

I hesitate, unsure whether to follow him or wait for Granny Margaret. She's looking frail these days, I think. Probably not getting enough sleep.

I heard her in the night again, pacing about upstairs. Sometimes she comes down to the kitchen when she can't sleep, and sits with me into the early hours, reading a book or staring at nothing. It's obvious the old lady is not happy. But it does not matter how much I wag my tail, or lie beside her during the long, cold stretches of the night, I cannot seem to cheer her up.

'Sorry, I'd better . . . erm . . .' Pepper gives a low whimper, and slips away, squeezing through the gap in the fence and disappearing back towards her own house.

So much for solidarity, I think drily, watching the white flash of the poodle on the other side of the fence.

Granny Margaret is looking worried. 'Sam,' she calls after him several times, raising her voice, but I can tell she's not going to pursue the boy.

She sighs, and then looks down at me instead.

'Find him, Bertie,' she says softly. 'There's a good dog.'

I give a short bark, and trot down the garden after him, my nose to the ground. Not that I need to sniff him out. I saw which way Sam went. Besides, he's fairly predictable when trying to hide from the grown-ups. It's always the big sycamore that he climbs, nestling in among the bare lower branches, his back to the trunk, out of sight from the house. His dad is always telling him off for climbing the trees in their garden, saying he could fall and hurt himself. But Sam never pays any attention.

Sure enough, he's up in the sycamore again, cradled in the branches.

I sit down below him, and wag my tail. When he does not look down, I start to whimper, then bark sharply.

'Go away, Bertie,' he tells me, his voice choked.

He's crying, I realise.

I jump up at the trunk, leaning on it with both front paws, and bark louder.

'I don't want to play,' he insists tearfully, then sniffs. 'I told you, go back to Granny. I'm not in the mood.'

But I ignore him and keep barking.

Eventually Sam leans down and glares at me from behind his sleeve, his eyes red and puffy, his face damp with tears. 'Oh, Bertie!'

I sit and wag my tail harder.

Sam laughs reluctantly, then slowly lets himself down out of the branches. He crouches next to me, and strokes my head. 'Is she cross with me? I bet she is. She's only just cleaned all those frames, and I broke one.' He sniffs, and wipes his face on his sleeve. 'I heard the crack.'

I nuzzle my head into his hand.

'Dad's going to yell at me for this, you see if he doesn't.' He closes his eyes. 'I didn't mean to kick the ball so hard. Now I've ruined everything again.'

I look up at him, and he sits beside me, his back to the trunk. 'And it's almost Christmas. That's meant to be, like, the best time of the year. When everyone's happy. You know, with loads of presents, and Christmas cake, and tasty food everywhere.'

I bark politely.

He strokes my ears. 'Yeah, you like cake, don't you?' He sighs. 'Sometimes I wish I was a dog, Bertie. Life would be so simple then.'

Simple?

I think of Molly, of how desolate I feel without her, of the guilt of having been the reason we were taken to the dog shelter in the first place, and I find it hard to keep wagging my tail.

He doesn't really understand what life is like for a dog, I think, a little sadly. No voice, no power; no way to explain when we're hurting inside. But I keep panting gently, leaning against his small, warm body, just being there for him. Because Sam is only young. Still a puppy, really. That's why Granny M sent me down the garden after him, I'm sure. So he wouldn't be alone when he was upset.

'I miss Mum,' he says suddenly, and wipes his face with his sleeve again. Then gulps hard. 'I miss you, Mummy. I miss you so much. Why did you have to go away?' He starts to cry. 'Please come back. Please, please . . .'

Suddenly, I hear a twig crack, and look round. Granny M has crept up on us and is standing a short distance away, looking very sad too. She is wrapped in a thick shawl against the cold, her long hair clipped up on the back of her head, delicate white strands escaping everywhere, lying against her papery throat.

'Darling boy,' she says, her voice cracking. She holds out her arms, beckoning him. 'Come here. It doesn't matter about the cold frame.'

Sam scrambles to his feet, looking guilty. 'I'm sorry.'

'It was an accident,' she insists, taking another step towards him. 'Honestly, Sam, I'm not cross. You can certainly kick a ball though, that's for sure.' Her smile is lopsided. 'But you're missing your mum, aren't you? It's only natural, at this time of year.'

I look up at the boy, wagging my tail, sure her reassurance will comfort him.

But it seems to be having the opposite effect.

'No, I'm not . . . m . . . missing Mum,' Sam tells her thickly, stammering. He rubs his eyes, then stamps past her. 'Just leave me alone. I want to be left alone.' His voice is fierce as he runs back towards the house. 'You don't understand. None of you understand.'

I run a little way after him, confused and uncertain, but he vanishes into the house.

I stop and look back at Granny M.

She does not move at first, staring down at the frosty ground. Then she walks slowly back to the house in the wake of her grandson, her expression pained.

I walk beside her, watching her face.

She looks down at me. 'You know, he was such a lovely boy before . . . before Jenny passed on. Always laughing and joking, not a care in the world. I wish I could make him that happy again.' She sighs, and reaches down to rub my ears. 'You're a good dog, Bertie. And I know you did your best.'

Granny M shakes her head, straightening to look sadly at the house. The back door has been left wide open. The Christmas lights around the kitchen windows blink on and off in a steady rhythm. The sound of carols floats out into the chilly air, with nobody listening to them.

'But what that boy really needs is his mother. And nothing on this earth is going to bring her back.'

❧ SIXTEEN ❧

To my disappointment, the cats appear at the back door the next morning with nothing to report from their night-time scouting.

'We searched up and down this block and the next,' Rico tells me wearily once Granny M has let him and Kitty back inside, and he has lapped up half a saucer of milk. 'Spent most of the night hunting for any trace of Molly.' He sighs. 'Nothing.'

I nod. 'Well, thanks for trying.'

Kitty curls up in a corner by the range without even speaking to me, and is soon fast asleep.

Rico makes a face, then joins her. 'Sorry.'

The two cats have done the best they could. And I really appreciate their hard work. It's clear they're both exhausted. But it's hard not to let my disappointment show. I had hoped to hear much better news. Maybe even to discover where Molly is living.

Instead, I'm exactly where I was yesterday.

Nowhere, in other words.

I can't even summon much more than a feeble tail wag when Mr Green abruptly decides we are going fishing by the river. 'Not the canal,' he tells Sam grandly over breakfast. 'But the river. Very different.'

'It's freezing out there,' Sam protests.

'Nonsense, it's lovely weather. Besides, you'll soon warm up once we're by the river and the rods are set up. Nothing like a fishing expedition at Christmas to get the blood pumping.' He mock-punches his son's shoulder. 'Come on, man up. It's fishing. The great tradition. Man against fish. Man against the elements.'

'But I'll catch cold, standing about by the river all day.' He looks at Granny M, who has drifted into the kitchen to hear their conversation, her apron on again, wearing a pair of yellow rubber gloves. 'Won't I, Gran?'

Granny M bites her lip, clearly unwilling to interfere between father and son. But she seems unable to resist Sam's look of entreaty.

'It is a bit chilly today, John.'

'Then Sam can run upstairs and grab an extra sweater while I find the rods,' Mr Green says firmly, then nods to his son. 'Off you trot. Hat and scarf too, please. We are going fishing.' When Sam looks back at him mulishly, he hesitates. 'Look, you really enjoyed yourself that time before, when me and . . . and your mum took you fishing. You would have been about seven. Do you remember?'

Sam shrugs, then stamps out of the kitchen. 'I'll get another sweater.'

His dad closes his eyes briefly. 'Sam is such hard work at the moment. There's no pleasing him.' Then he notices Granny M's rubber gloves. 'What on earth . . .?'

'I've been mopping out the downstairs toilet. We may have guests drop in over Christmas, you never know. It would be nice to get everything spick and span.'

175

'Can I help?'

'Oh, it's no trouble. And it helps take my mind off . . .' She pauses, looking at him anxiously.

'Off what?'

'I am getting a bit worried about Sam,' she admits at last. 'He seems very fragile, with Christmas coming up. It's always hard at this time of year, when . . . Go easy with him, won't you? Try not to argue.'

'If he behaves himself, there'll be no need for any arguments.'

Granny M's brows pleat together. 'John,' she begins, laying a rubber-gloved hand on his sleeve, then stops, seeing his sudden stillness. She hesitates, then forces a smile. 'Have a good time.'

'Would you like to come too?'

Her eyes widen, suddenly incredulous. 'With only a few days left to Christmas? I'm far too busy, I'm afraid.' She bustles back to the downstairs toilet, adding, 'I'm in charge of Christmas Eve meals for the homeless this year, don't forget. And there's another batch of mince pies to bake once this clean-up's done.'

'Please don't bother on my account,' Mr Green calls after her, and awkwardly pats the slight round of his belly. 'Too many mince pies already.'

But she's gone.

He glances down at me. 'Could you manage another batch of mince pies, Bertie?'

I wag my tail.

'I thought so. Greedy guzzler.' He rummages in the cupboard under the stairs for his fishing tackle, while I stand about, still wagging my tail hopefully. When he pays no attention, I bark. He looks round at me through the forest of mops, brooms and vacuum cleaners under the stairs, then grins. 'Yes, all right. You can come too, Bertie. But only as long as you agree to sit quietly and not scare the fish away.'

I give another few barks of excitement, and turn a quick, neat circle, rucking up the hall runner.

Backing out of the low cupboard with the tackle he has collected, Mr Green casts me and the rucked-up rug an ironic look. 'Is that your idea of sitting quietly?'

I grin as he turns, and sit down abruptly.

Right in his path.

Mr Green trips over me, drops his armful of fishing tackle, and almost headbutts the coat stand.

'Bertie,' he roars, in a voice that signals punishment.

Oops.

I dash up the stairs, and thrust my way forcibly into Sam's room. He is dragging a second sweater down over his head. 'What the . . .?' he says.

Jumping onto his narrow bed, I burrow under his duvet and hide there among the crumpled sheets, my rump quivering, my tail tucked between my legs.

A moment later, a hand plucks the duvet away. Sam stares down at me, perplexed. 'Have you been naughty again, Bertie?'

I tilt my head to one side, giving him what Molly used to call my 'winning smile', then wag my tail apologetically.

Sam laughs. 'You are a very silly dog. Still, I'm glad it's not just me who keeps getting into trouble with Dad.'

I roll on my back, all four paws in the air, and he tickles me.

Ah, this is the life.

'Hurry up, Sam, for goodness' sake,' Mr Green suddenly calls up the stairs, making Sam jump, 'and bring that dog down with you. Foolish animal almost knocked me out just now. And he's supposed to be grounded. But we'd better take him with us to the river. He'll only make a nuisance of himself by getting under Granny M's feet if we leave him at home.'

I wag my tail cheerfully.

'And don't bring your iPad,' his father adds. 'It's you, me, and the fish today. Understand?'

'Yes, Dad,' Sam chants dutifully, then makes a face at me. 'Pity you didn't knock him out for real,' he mutters.

He drags down the sweater properly, then searches through his lower drawers for a suitable woolly hat and scarf. I watch him and let my tongue loll out, enjoying this adventure immensely. He's only a small boy, but with two sweaters on, he looks enormous. Especially round the middle. Like he's the one who's been eating all the pies.

'I swear, Bertie, one of these days . . .'

Sam pulls a torch out of his bottom drawer, flicks it on and stares down into the thin beam of light. Then switches it off and shoves it under all the clothes again.

'I keep remembering that day when Mum and Dad took me fishing along the river. There's this massive tree there.

An old oak, with a hollow. That's where Mum and Dad first kissed, they said. We had such a great time that day. Mum kept laughing and . . .'

He stops, suddenly very sombre.

I sit up and look at him curiously, my head to one side.

'It was my fault,' he says, his voice choking. 'Gran says it wasn't, but I know better. I was there, she wasn't. If Mum hadn't tired herself out, coming to watch me play that football match that day, she'd have been stronger. Strong enough to fight the cancer.'

I whine, concerned that the boy has misunderstood.

He picks out a hat and scarf from the drawer, adding mysteriously, 'I don't like the idea of upsetting Gran though. She's old, and old people get upset really easily. They worry about things, you know? And I don't want her to worry.' He gives a heavy sigh, and closes the drawer again with an effort. 'Not about me.'

I am upset by what he's saying. Something seems seriously wrong. But I'm unsure how to cheer him up. So I follow the boy downstairs and out to the car, determined to keep wagging my tail as we set off on our fishing expedition. The sky looks more cold and grey than it did before, and I'm aware of an uneasy feeling in my tummy. Though it could just be indigestion; I did wolf my breakfast down rather speedily this morning, head down in the dish, aware of cats circling at the periphery of my vision.

I don't like the idea of upsetting Gran though.

Upsetting her by doing what, exactly? I watch him for clues, but can't guess what grim deed Sam is contemplating.

From the way he's talking though, I suspect it's going to make Granny M very unhappy indeed.

Not to mention his dad.

The river is not that far from the house, it turns out. Only a few twists and turns further out from the town centre, then a short run along a country road, passing a few farms and isolated buildings. We could have walked it in about an hour, perhaps. But I suppose Mr Green decided it was too cold for us to walk so far. Or there was too much fishing tackle to carry. Or he's too lazy to be bothered.

Personally, I like a nice long walk.

As long as someone can be persuaded to carry me when my legs start hurting.

'Here we go. Remember this place?' Mr Green parks on a gravelly track not far from the river, which I can see shining through thin, bowed reeds along the waterside. 'Now, Sam, you can carry the bucket of bait. It shouldn't be too heavy for you. I'll bring the rods and tackle. And the flask.'

There are a few other people dotted along the river, sitting wrapped up warmly with rods dipped towards the water.

'Where are we going to sit?' Sam asks, sounding miserable before he's even started.

Mr Green points the way through the window, then shuts off the engine. The sun is out today but the wind is still cold, with occasional sharp gusts, a typical midwinter's day.

I don't mind the weather. I run back and forth on the back seat, wagging my tail frantically. This is going to be fun.

F.U.N.

There are ducks on the river.

Three depressed-looking ducks, and a swan, to be precise.

I jump out of the back as soon as the car door opens, and run up and down the river bank, barking hysterically at the wildfowl.

'I'm going to eat you, I'm going to eat you,' I yell at the ducks, who paddle swiftly away down the river, looking alarmed as well as depressed now. I bark at the swan, who hisses and stretches his wings. 'And you too. Probably.'

'Shut up,' Mr Green tells me, and throws a Wellington boot at my head.

I yelp, and sit dazed for a moment, my ears ringing.

That wasn't very nice.

'I knew he would do this,' Mr Green mutters, and comes limping over to collect his boot, shooting me an irritable look as he bends to pick it up. 'Sorry if that was a shock. But you mustn't bark, Bertie.'

'Dad!'

Hopping about as he attempts to put on his other Wellington boot, Mr Green glances at Sam, and shrugs. 'First rule of fishing, Son. No barking dogs. The fish hear a barking dog and they swim away. Then we'll never catch anything.'

Sam crouches to rub my ears. 'Sorry, Bertie. Probably best though if you keep quiet from now on. I don't know if you've noticed, but Dad is kind of obsessive about fishing.'

I say nothing.

I sit and look at Mr Green instead.

It's a long, baleful stare.

Mr Green gets the tackle and rods out of the boot of the car, tucks a folded deckchair under one arm, then hands the bucket of bait to Sam. As he locks up the car, he spots me still staring at him, and sighs.

'All right, I'm sorry,' he says again. 'I'm sorry I threw a boot at you, Bertie. Really sorry, okay? But you have to understand, fish are shy. And one thing they really don't like is the sound of barking.' He hesitates, then adds winningly, 'I brought biscuits.'

I think about it for a few more seconds, then decide to forgive him. As long as there are biscuits in my immediate future.

I run towards him, nose in the air, wondering which pocket the promised biscuits are in, and he bends to pat my rump, his armful of rods clattering awkwardly together as he nearly drops them again.

'There's a good boy.' He swears, clutching at the rods as they slip, then apologises to Sam, who is looking up and down the river bank with a nostalgic air. 'Sorry, I didn't mean to say that.'

Sam turns back, grinning. 'It's okay, Dad. I've heard worse at school.'

'You have?'

'Some of the boys swear.'

'None of your friends, I hope.'

He makes a face. 'I told you, I don't have any friends.'

Mr Green struggles with the complicated mess of rods. 'No? What about that nice girl you were talking to after chess club last month?'

'Harriet?' Sam's voice is practically a squeak, he seems so embarrassed. 'No, no, she's just . . . Someone in my class.' He hurries forward as his dad drops one of the rods. 'Look, why don't you let me carry some of those?' He helps his dad with the fishing gear, grinning when his dad swears again under his breath. 'Right, where shall we set up?'

I follow them to the water, watching with satisfaction as father and son discuss the best spot along the river to fish from. Perhaps Mr Green knows what he's doing after all. This morning, Sam was depressed about me being grounded, and his gran's cracked cold frame, and his dad being generally grumpy. Plus, the memory of his mum has been haunting him more than usual recently. It's obvious Sam still thinks he's to blame for her death, and the weight of that guilt has been keeping his spirits low.

Now though, the boy is smiling and animated as he trots along the bank, pointing out good level places to set up a deckchair, or deeper pools away from the river current where the fish may be lurking.

Perhaps things are going to improve for him this Christmas, after all.

I want Sam to be happy again. I want them all to be happy, the Greens. When people are unhappy every day, there's this atmosphere that builds up around them. Like everything's damp and dark and gloomy, and struggling to feel happy again is just . . . well, pointless. I don't know how else to describe it except that it's like a smell. Only a horrible smell, not an interesting one. A smell that warns you to keep clear. Like the smell inside the waiting room at the vet's surgery. Fear and sweaty paws. That smell.

But every now and then, the sun breaks through, and they smile.

What I want is for every day to be a smile.

We wander along the river bank together for a while, admiring the river, looking for a good spot for the deckchair.

'Look!' Sam exclaims, pointing at a large tree set back a short distance from the water's edge. 'Mum's special oak. The one with the hollow. Mum put me up there once, to shelter from the rain.'

Mr Green stops, staring at the huge, gnarled trunk, draped in ivy. Then he nods. 'That's right, Sam. Well remembered.'

'Mum said you and her . . .' Sam looks embarrassed.

'First kissed under that tree.' Mr Green manages a smile. 'A long, long time ago. You weren't even a twinkle in my eye, then.'

'I'm pretty sure I was *never* a twinkle, Dad,' Sam says firmly, scrambling up the trunk to peer into the hollow that nestles between the lowest branches. It does look like a cosy spot to hide from the rain, I think, and watch with pride as he jumps back down with seemingly little effort.

My human is very good at climbing!

'Oh yes you were,' his dad says, grinning. 'Trust me, I remember.'

'Was not.' Sam mock-punches him in the arm.

Mr Green gently bounces a fishing rod on his son's head. 'Was so,' he insists. 'Now, come on, where are we going to set up camp?'

As his father walks ahead, Sam stops to rub a hand longingly across the rough tree trunk, then turns to me. 'I wish you could have known my mum, Bertie. She was amazing. And she loved this place. So I love it too.' He smiles. 'At least, this is where I remember being happiest.'

I wag my tail to show that I understand.

Eventually, Sam and Mr Green choose a good spot for the deckchair, and both begin to bait their rods with maggots. I nose into the bucket, fascinated by the wriggling little bugs. But Mr Green says, 'Bertie' in his warning tone, so I leave the bucket alone. Instead, I thread my way through the legs of the deckchair a few times to get a feel for the grass. The ground is cold and damp, but the river smells interesting, and I think rabbits must come here too, because there's a strong rabbity smell.

I do like rabbits. Those little white bobtails, flashing at top speed across the grass. Like a cheeky invitation to chase them.

No rabbit-chasing today, I tell myself sternly.

I got away with the barking earlier. It was an impulse, and a mistake, and my humans seemed to recognise that. But I don't think Mr Green would be very happy if I started chasing up and down the river bank, and I don't want to put him in a bad mood again.

Tempting, though.

Mr Green settles into the deckchair. Much squeaking and creaking. Sam throws down a coarse blanket and sits cross-legged on that at his side. I curl up under the deckchair and stare at the water rolling past. We sit in silence and wait for the fish to bite. It's quite a long wait, as it turns out. Several dreary hours, in fact. I doze for a while, dreaming of rabbits and chasing them endlessly through long grass.

When I wake up, the world is exactly as I left it, except that my legs have gone stiff.

I stretch out under the deckchair, groaning slightly.

'Maybe it's a bit cold for them today,' Mr Green suggests.

Sam sighs, and pokes the wriggling maggot pot with a stick. 'We haven't had a bite in ages. Should we put more bait in?'

'Not yet, don't want to over-do it.' Mr Green unscrews the top of his flask and pours out a cup of Granny M's home-made tomato soup for each of them. 'There you go, Sam. Something hot to warm you up.'

Sam is ecstatic. 'My favourite,' he says, sniffing enthusiastically at his soup.

I too sniff the air. Not sure I like the sound of tomato soup. But I wouldn't say no to a snack. My favourite would be rabbit stew, I think wistfully.

Didn't Mr Green mention biscuits?

I nudge his leg under the pretence of stretching out my paws, and give a meaningful little whimper.

Sam glances down at me, then up at his dad. 'Bertie's been so good,' he points out.

That's the spirit, I think.

'Perhaps he should have something to eat,' he continues.

Before I can object, he's dribbled a little steaming tomato soup onto the grass beside the deckchair. Never one to say no to a snack, at least in broad terms, I get up and sniff at the soup patch. My nose twitches. Tomato. Ewww. But there's a creamy tang going on there too, so I give it a little lick.

I yelp at the heat.

'Oops, too hot for him,' Sam says, biting his lip. He leans over and strokes my ears. 'Sorry, Bertie.'

I wag my tail as a thank-you for his concern, then trot out into misty sunshine to lick some grass, trying to soothe my tongue. I remind myself not to try soup again before it's cold.

At least my young master seems much happier now. I have to admit, I did get rather worried by Sam's comments before we left the house. I was beginning to think I should find some way of communicating the problem to Granny M.

But this trip to the river, having good times with his dad, bonding over old memories, all seem to have lightened the boy's mood.

Mr Green reaches into his coat pocket and pulls out a biscuit. I jump up at his knee, licking him ecstatically. He laughs and tosses it onto the grass under his chair. 'There you go, boy. Good dog.'

Now we're talking. I run back to the shade under his deckchair and enjoy the tasty biscuit, looking about myself as I eat. Crunch, crunch, crunch . . .

Suddenly, my jaws freeze in mid-crunch.

There's a dog bounding towards us across the grass. A big, big dog. A German Shepherd, by the look of its large barrel-like chest and pointy ears. And a few hundred feet in front of it, zigzagging hysterically, is a little brown rabbit.

My brain clicks into some kind of dream state. There's a jerk, and a tremendous thud, and the world tilts on its axis. My eyes cloud over. My paws move swiftly and of their own accord. My ears track minute flickering noises over the grass, the drumming of furry feet across loose, muddy soil. My nose quivers in ecstasy.

The sweet taste of the biscuit, still lingering in my mouth, pales into insignificance beside the delicious, bone-crunching gorgeousness of this creature with the little white bobtail.

I can think of only one thing now.

Rabbit.

❧ SEVENTEEN ❧

For the next few moments, I completely lose my under-standing of where I am and what I'm doing. I don't hear Mr Green shouting, or Sam tugging on my collar and being partially dragged along with my reckless momentum. It's a kind of chase-madness. Me and the big dog, both intent on only one goal. The same goal. The same rabbit. Have to get the rabbit. There is nothing else in life worth having. And it ends in a loud splash, and the icy shock of water, and me paddling like hell towards shore, all four paws going at once.

'Bertie?'

Sam is standing on the bank, staring at me, his hands on his hips.

Oops.

The bank is muddy. Somehow I manage to clamber out of the water though, and shake myself all over.

'Bertie!' Sam gives another shriek and runs away, wiping water from his face.

I stare around, a little dizzy, my fur dripping, not entirely sure what just happened. The other dog must have slunk back to its owner, I realise, hearing a distant whistle from some other angler.

Of the rabbit, there is no sign.

And why is Mr Green lying on his side on the ground, still wrapped up in the tipped-over deckchair, staring at me with bulging eyes?

Humans are so odd sometimes.

'Come here, you!'

I evade Sam's attempt to capture me, and run over to his dad instead, intending to sniff about for the remains of that biscuit.

But when I venture too close, Mr Green reaches out and grabs me by the collar. He's still lying on the ground in a sea of wriggling maggots. In fact, it looks as though, when I dashed madly out after the rabbit, the deckchair tipped over, and he fell on top of the open bucket of bait, and now . . .

'Bertie,' he roars, his face very flushed. 'You bad, bad dog. I swear, after Christmas, I'm taking you straight back to the shelter.'

Sam bursts into tears. 'You can't. He's our dog now. He belongs to us. And he didn't mean it. You saw what happened. It was an accident.'

'It's always an accident with Bertie.'

'Because you never give him a chance.' Sam stares at him, tears running down his cheeks. 'Just like you never give me a chance either.'

Mr Green releases my collar. 'Sam . . .'

'You hate him.'

'No, I don't.' The deep colour is fading from Mr Green's face now. He knocks a maggot away from his mouth. 'Calm down now. I didn't mean it.'

'Yes, you did. You hate Bertie, and you hate me too. Because I chose him. Because I'm always making mistakes too.' His voice chokes in his throat. 'So it's all my fault whenever Bertie does something wrong.'

Mr Green scrambles to his feet, and rights the fallen deckchair. 'That's not true. Look, I shouldn't have said that about the dog shelter. I was angry, that's all. He sent me flying. And such a little dog too.'

Sam drags his rod out of the water. 'Forget it. I don't want to go fishing any more.'

'Sam, for goodness' sake —'

'I want to go home.' He stamps back towards the car. 'At least there I can sit in my bedroom. I don't have to spend time with you.'

Mr Green stands there, his shoulders slumped, watching as his son reaches the locked car and waits beside it. For a moment I think he is going to drag him back. Then he sighs and begins to collect up the fishing gear.

Worried that I have behaved dreadfully and made matters a thousand times worse between father and son, I run about the riverbank and wag my tail. *Wag, wag, wag*. That's my way of saying sorry. Only I'm not sure Mr Green is really aware of that. Or if he is, he probably does not much care if I'm sorry or not.

He shoots me a glance at last, shooing me away from the heap of wriggling maggots. 'You can be such a pest at times, Bertie,' he says, and I hang my head at that accusing tone, shuffling out of his way. 'But my son obviously loves you. Unconditionally, no matter what you do. I wish I could get

Sam to love me like that too. The same way I love him. The same way his granny loves him.'

I sit to listen, watching him fold up the deckchair and stick it under his arm.

'I wish I had your easy knack with him. I try to find the words, to show Sam how deeply I feel, but I just can't seem to do anything right these days.'

I whimper.

'I don't want to keep being so hard on Sam,' he mutters. 'I hate that look on his face when he's done something wrong and I have to tell him off. But I need to hold the family together. To keep a sense of structure in his life, of boundaries he needs to respect . . . Jenny did it so well, without upsetting him. I realise that now.'

Mr Green bends to pick up the last of the rods, and then straightens, his eyes unhappy as he stares at Sam, still waiting next to the car. 'If only Jenny . . .' His voice cracks with emotion at her name. 'Oh, Bertie, I miss her so much. It's this constant pain, gnawing away at me inside. And I want to talk to Sam about it. Tell him I understand how he feels, because I feel exactly the same way too. To share my memories of his mum, that sense of loss now she's gone. But whenever I try . . .'

Then he shakes his head, looking miserable. 'What's the use? When you've lost someone, that's it. There's no point living in the past.' He looks down at me, tears in his eyes. 'Is there?'

I tip my head further over, looking at him sadly. I can feel his pain, but do not know how to comfort him.

He sighs. 'Come on, Sam's waiting for us.'

I trot after Mr Green as he heads for the car, but my heart is aching. I am suddenly worried that my plans for a future with Molly again have been built on foolish daydreams.

When you've lost someone, that's it. There's no point living in the past.

I lost Molly at the shelter.

Then I found her, and lost her again, in the same moment.

Is there any point hoping I can somehow find my sister again, and this time, hold on for good? After all, she was always the sensible one. And even she may have given up on me by now.

Things seem to be taking a turn for the worse when we return to the house.

As Mr Green pulls up the drive, I see two cats waiting for me. Kitty is on next door's wall, pretending to be the stone statue of a cat. Her brother sits on the gravel drive, tail curled neatly round his front paws.

There's something ominous about the way they are staring at us.

'Oh for goodness' sake . . .' Faced with an immovable cat Mr Green hesitates, then reluctantly beeps his horn.

Rico eyes his owner with mild disdain, then gets up and moves slowly and with dignity onto the lawn.

Given that last night's expedition was a bust, I am surprised to see them up and about already. I had assumed

Kitty at least would sleep all day. But she is looking perfectly alert. Maybe even a little smug. And Rico looks uncharacteristically wired. Like someone has plugged him into an electric socket. He actually runs towards me as Sam opens the back door and I bound out over the lawn.

'Catch anything?' Rico asks when I reach him.

I shake my damp fur, still uncomfortable after my impromptu dip in the river. 'Apart from a cold?'

Sam passes us on his way inside the house, his lip stuck out and trembling, the fishing rod trailing after him.

'Hey, careful with that,' his dad calls after him. 'That's expensive equipment.'

Sam does not even appear to hear him.

I give a little groan, helpless in the face of their mutual stupidity. If only I could get those two to sit down together for a proper chat. I'm sure they would stop arguing if they understood how bad both of them feel about the death of Sam's mother. But of course they are both too wrapped up in their own pain to risk a conversation about it.

'What's up with those two?' Rico asks, perplexed. 'I thought it was meant to be a fun trip out?'

'There was a rabbit.'

Kitty jumps down from next door's wall, licking her lips. 'Sounds tasty. Did you bring any of it back?'

'It got away.'

'Typical useless dog.' She sniffs the air. 'No fish, either?'

'Sorry.'

Rico stretches, looking disappointed. 'I'm starving. All this walking and hunting . . . We ought to get extra rations.'

'Have you two been out again?' I ask.

Kitty purrs, weaving around her brother. 'You want the good news or the bad news first?'

'Erm . . .' I cock my head to one side, considering the question. It's surprisingly tricky. 'The good news, I guess.' I hesitate. 'No, wait. The bad.' She draws breath, and I change my mind again. 'Hang on. The good news. Yes, definitely the good news first.'

Kitty arches her brows. 'Sure now?'

I say nothing, but wait.

Rico grins, watching me. 'We found Molly.'

'Good news? Damn, that's the best news I've ever heard in my life.' I bark wildly, and run in a tight circle, chasing my own tail and ignoring Mr Green's startled look as he carries the fishing rods past me. 'I knew it, I knew it. I knew we'd be able to find her together if we put our skills to . . .'

Kitty waits.

I slow down, looking at them both. 'So what's the bad news?'

'That woman she's with,' Rico says carefully, 'the one you described, the woman with the nasty, pinched face . . .'

'Yes?'

'We don't think she's a very good person.'

I have no time to discover what Rico means by that worrying pronouncement, as Granny M comes to the front door then, calling me in to be rubbed with a clean towel and given a tasty bowl of dog meat in gravy. Normally this kind of pampering would be eminently acceptable to me. But I'm itching to hear the rest of the cats' report, and so I make a nuisance of myself again, wriggling impatiently as I'm towelled dry, and making even the old lady murmur 'Bertie' under her breath, shaking her head.

The cats follow me in and watch from high vantage points around the kitchen as I shrug off the towel, and scoff down my food so quickly I barely taste it. Which is a shame, because what remains on my chin afterwards is tangy and delicious.

Then we all beg to be let out into the garden.

Granny M stops by the back door, gazing at us each in turn, her brows furrowed. She turns to Mr Green, who has been making himself a sandwich. 'If I didn't know better, John, I'd say these three were up to something.' Her hand rests on the handle as she studies us, one after the other. 'I expect they can hear something we can't, that's all. One of those high-frequency sounds that only animals can hear.'

He makes some assenting noise, his mouth full of sandwich.

She glances at him. 'You haven't made a sandwich for Sam, have you?'

He shakes his head, still munching.

'Good,' she says, 'because I'm doing a beef stew for supper. With herby dumplings. It's in the slow cooker at the moment.' She hesitates, looking at him shrewdly. 'Sam didn't look too happy when he came back. He's gone straight up to his room and barely spoke to me. No evidence of any fish caught, either. I take it the fishing trip didn't go as planned?'

Mr Green makes a face.

'Oh dear,' she says sadly, but does not press the matter.

I scratch at the glass.

'Yes, all right,' she says, laughing, and opens the door for me.

I trot outside, and the cats follow me.

'Behave yourselves,' she tells us, then shuts the door after us to keep the heat in. But I can see her still watching us through the glass, curious and amused.

We gather outside in the thickening air, and within a few seconds Pepper is there, slipping through the gap in the fence, a white ghost in the dusk.

'Have you heard the news?' she asks at once, looking at me with compassion.

'Some of it.'

'The cats came and told me as soon as they got back,' she says proudly, and tosses her curly top knot. 'They wanted to go back, see if they could get into the house. I told them not to do anything, but to wait for you. I hope that wasn't interfering. It wasn't, was it?'

'No, that was useful.'

'You see?' She shoots Kitty an accusing look. 'I'm not an air-brain. Whatever some people may think.'

I begin to shiver, still a little damp despite the towelling I received from Granny M.

It's a cold night, the air sharp with frost.

Normally I would rather be lying in my cosy basket beside the range on a chilly evening like this. But I barely notice the cold, turning at once to Kitty and Rico for more news of my sister.

'So come on,' I say urgently, 'you saw her? You actually saw Molly?' When Rico nods, I say, 'Tell me everything. Right from the beginning. Don't leave anything out.'

'We started at the supermarket today. Found a spot in the trolley bay and hid there. Since hanging round the back gardens proved pointless last night,' Rico tells me.

'Good idea.'

'We got lucky. After an hour, she showed up.'

'The pinch-faced woman?'

'That's right,' Rico said, 'and she wasn't alone. There was a beagle with her. That's how we were sure it was the right woman.'

Kitty has been licking her paw and cleaning behind her ears, but at this she stops and looks at me. 'Your sister is a smaller version of you, isn't she? It's quite uncanny, the resemblance between you.'

'Go on.'

Rico says, 'You told us she kept your sister in the car when you saw her at the supermarket before.'

I nod impatiently.

'Well, this time she brought Molly out of the car and tied her up outside the entrance door.' Rico looks pleased with himself. 'That was a stroke of luck. So I left Kitty to watch my back, and slipped out of the trolley bay to speak to her.'

My heart leaps. 'You actually spoke to her?'

198

'Oh yes.'

'Tell me,' I prompt him.

'I said, are you Molly? And she said, yes. And I said, are you Bertie's sister? And again she said, yes. But she looked pretty amazed. Because . . .' Rico pauses, then cleans his whiskers thoughtfully, 'well, because a cat was speaking to her. And I guess she's not used to that.'

I grin broadly. 'Go on,' I say again.

'I wasn't sure how long her owner would be inside. So I told her as briefly as I could everything you had told us, and all about the Greens, and the Paw Print Club, and how we had promised to help you find her, and she . . .'

Rico pauses, looking awkward.

'What is it?' I demand, a little worried now. 'What did Molly say?'

He shakes his head, then says, 'She howled.'

There's a short silence.

I feel awful, but can't bring myself to admit it. I know all three of them are staring at me, waiting for me to say something. So I mutter, 'Go on,' again, and suppress a little whimper of unhappiness.

Molly, howling in a public place?

It doesn't sound much like my self-possessed sister.

Which means only one thing. It's obvious she has been treated abominably by the pinch-faced woman, and was so overcome by Rico's explanation that she was reduced to primitive howling, right there outside the supermarket. I dare not consider too closely what might have happened to her at that woman's hands. It would reduce me to howling too, and then Granny M really will suspect something is going on out here.

But what has been done to my beloved sister now that I am no longer there to protect her? Has she been starved? Beaten? Locked up in some dark, dirty hole? I want to rush over the wall and down the street right now, to track down the awful pinch-faced woman and . . .

Well, I know a dog must never attack a human. It's one of the first laws we learn, and the last to be relinquished in a life-and-death situation. But I'm so furious now, my mind and heart churning with wild and dangerous emotions, that it's a good job she's not standing in front of me here. Because it would be very hard not to at least growl and snarl and bare my teeth, and let that pinch-faced woman know exactly how I feel about her cruelty to my sister.

'So what happened then?'

Kitty sharpens her claws on the stone path. 'We followed them home. It wasn't hard. They live a few blocks from us, in a little house set back from the road.' She makes a face. 'She stopped at several houses on her way back. Houses with old people in them. Rang the doorbell, left Molly outside, went in for a chat, and then came out a short time later with . . . something in a basket.'

'What kind of something?'

Kitty looks uninterested. 'You asked us to find Molly. Not look in her owner's basket.'

'Every time she came out of these houses, her basket looked heavier,' Rico said helpfully. 'Maybe they were giving her food.'

'Old people, giving her food? That doesn't seem right,' I say.

'Then what?'

I think for a moment, then growl under my breath. 'Maybe she's a thief. Pretends to go into their houses for a chat, then steals something while they're not looking, and pops it in her basket.'

Pepper barks crossly. 'What a nasty human.'

Kitty looks impressed. 'She sounds rather clever.'

'What she sounds is wicked.' I reply to Pepper with an equally angry bark. 'And I don't intend to let her get away with it.'

Pepper nods enthusiastically, and wags her tail bobble.

Kitty seems less happy about my pronouncement. Her eyes glow yellow in the gloaming, and her whiskers quiver. 'I hope you don't mean we need to go back to her house.'

'That's exactly what needs to happen.'

'But there's a male dog right next door. We didn't see him, but we could hear and smell him. Deep, chesty bark. Real stinky too. I refused to go any nearer than the street. Because of the unpleasant smell.'

I look at Rico. 'You couldn't get inside the house?'

He shakes his head. 'Sorry. The woman slammed the front door, and that was it. Kitty kept guard, and I walked along the fence and into the back garden. But there were no windows open round the back either.' He pauses, head on one side. 'There is a conservatory though.'

I turn in a slow circle, listening to the familiar noises of the gathering dusk. The sound of a dog barking excitedly

201

somewhere in the distance, and another replying slightly further away. Traffic on the main road, someone beeping their horn. The tinny voices from next door's television, set on high. Christmas carols in Granny M's kitchen, filling the whole house with deep, jolly voices and floating out into the garden.

Somewhere out there is my sister.

Close by.

In terrible jeopardy.

'I'm not spending Christmas without Molly,' I say suddenly. 'Or at least, not without having seen her again properly, spoken to her, let her know I haven't forgotten about her.'

Kitty stares. 'But the smelly dog—'

'I don't care if there are a thousand massive guard dogs waiting on her lawn,' I tell her, 'and they all smell like rotting fish. I'm getting to see Molly again, and try to get out of that place. Tonight.'

Pepper squeaks, 'Tonight?'

'I'm not leaving my sister under the pinch-faced woman's roof another night. Not now I know where she lives. I'd never forgive myself. It's going to be difficult though. Probably dangerous too. But it will all be worth it if I can get Molly back.'

I look from Rico to Kitty to Pepper. 'Who's with me?'

❀ EIGHTEEN ❀

I spend the evening curled up on Sam's bed while he colours in a home-made Christmas card. After the row with his dad at the river, the boy has a sad and desperate look, which I find worrying. But I know the young are resilient, so I'm hoping he will feel better in the morning. It is almost Christmas, after all, and that always has a wonderful, transformative effect on humans. Even grumpy Mr Minton was kinder to us dogs on Christmas Day.

When Sam has finished his card, he shows it to me. There's a picture of a Christmas tree on the front, with colourful presents underneath it, and shining baubles on the branches, just like the one downstairs.

For his gran, I wonder?

But then he opens the card and reads it aloud to me. 'Happy Christmas, Mum. I miss you, and life is horrible without you. Please . . .' His voice breaks, and he rubs a hand across reddened eyes. 'Please come back to me, even if it's only in a dream. I still love you, your son, Sam. Kiss, kiss, kiss . . .'

He shows me all the kisses he's drawn beneath his name, that stretch on right to the edge of the card, and onto the other side.

'What do you think, Bertie? Would Mum like it?'

I wag my tail.

Then he throws down the card, and sobs, 'What's the use? My mother's dead. She'll never see it. Mum, oh Mum, I'm so sorry.'

I whimper, then crawl closer and snuggle into his side, wagging my tail ineffectually. He tries to push me away, still sobbing.

'Not . . . not now, Bertie.'

Quickly, I lick the boy's hand, and he jerks it away with a muffled groan. I sit up and watch him, distressed now. How can I comfort this child? I'm not his mother. Though she can't comfort him either. Like he says, she's gone for ever.

What Sam needs right now is his dad.

But I saw the way Mr Green looked when we came home from the fishing trip. Like he too is locked into his own dark world of misery and loss.

If only there was some way to bring father and son together, and make them see that they could comfort each other. But what can I do? I'm a dog, not a human. I'm just an animal they've adopted, and one who's always causing trouble too. I don't have the words they would understand. All I can do is watch and hope and wag my tail.

In other words, fixing this grief may be beyond even my skills.

❀   ❀   ❀

The small gold clock on the mantel in the living room chimes, and then strikes the hour. I have been waiting for it since midnight, lying alert and restless in my basket. My ears perk up and I listen hard. Definitely one bong only, which, as Pepper explained to the cats before we came back inside, means it must be one o'clock in the morning.

That's our signal. Time to get ready.

I jump up and scrabble about with my paw along the floor beside the warm range. There's often a sticky black deposit there, a kind of goo that dribbles down from the oven above, and although Granny M mops the kitchen floor most days, her eyesight is not good and she often misses the sticky stuff. Besides, for the past few weeks, she's been too busy with Christmas preparations to worry about the odd spot under the oven.

Which is perfect for my plans.

Once my paw is coated with the black, tar-like deposit, I rub both sides of my muzzle and draw a streak over my head, then jump up to study my reflection in the glass of the back door.

I look like a character from one of these war films Mr Green likes to watch. Dirty black streaks on my cheeks and nose.

Commando Bertie, at your service.

Not bad.

Rico strolls in from the living room. 'One o'clock. As agreed.'

I hear a rustle from the top of the fridge, then Kitty jumps down to join us. She yawns and stretches laboriously. 'About time too. I was getting bored.'

'I hope Pepper hasn't forgotten.'

'She'll remember,' I reassure Rico, who is looking anxious. I know he only agreed to come on this mission so he could spend extra time with the poodle. 'And if she doesn't, I can always bark outside her house until she remembers.'

'Of course.'

I shake my head. A cat obsessed with a poodle.

It's beyond weird.

But who am I to judge? I had a thing for Tina once, back when I was a young and impressionable pup, and she's a greyhound, which makes her part-horse if you ask me.

'Camouflage?' I offer them both my paw, still coated with sooty deposits, and Kitty sniffs at it, then recoils. 'I know it's a bit smelly,' I tell her, 'but you should try some. It will help us blend into the dark. Become invisible.'

'I'm a night-hunter,' she points out, looking offended. Her tail whisks furiously. 'Everything about me is naturally designed to blend into the dark. I don't need stinky goo to achieve invisibility, thanks.'

I shrug, and look at Rico. 'Goo?'

'Noo.'

'Suit yourself.'

Undeterred, I smear more black stickiness on my face to hide the white splodges nature gave me. I'm not sure what the white splodges are designed to do. Make me look like a beagle, I suppose. Which they manage to do very successfully. Tonight though, I want to look mean and invisible. Or as close to that as a beagle can achieve.

Afterwards, I wipe my dirty paw on my blanket. 'I need all the help I can get.'

'We didn't like to comment.' Kitty's smile is wicked.

'Right,' I tell them, putting my shoulders back and puffing out my chest, 'if you're both ready, then it's show-time.'

'I'm ready,' Kitty remarks.

'Ready,' Rico agrees.

I jump up to check my reflection one more time. Pure hero.

'OK, here we go.'

I nod to Rico, who jumps up onto the kitchen surface, pads lightly along until he reaches the sink, skirts the edge, then stops at the window.

Kitty waits, licks a paw, then jumps up effortlessly to join him. Straight onto the narrow rim of the sink.

Show-off.

Rico wrestles with the broken window catch. Kitty watches, then puts a shoulder to the glass once the catch lifts. Together they heave the glass open.

'Done,' Kitty says with evident satisfaction.

Now it's my turn.

I had expected to need either to jump quite a distance – not easy, with my short legs – or push my basket across the kitchen floor, then use it as a step up. But to my delight, Granny Margaret left a sealed box of tins and packets on the floor earlier in the day, right beside the kitchen cupboards. 'For the Christmas appeal,' she had told Mr Green mysteriously, and he had nodded without looking up

207

from his newspaper. It's a little higher than my head, which means it's the perfect height for our purpose.

I launch myself at the Christmas appeal box, and manage to scramble onto the top, hauling myself up in an undignified manner that has both cats sniggering.

From there, it's a simple leap onto the kitchen surface. I bang my head on the toaster, give a muted yelp, then somehow tumble into the sink. Luckily it was drained some hours before, so my paws and bottom get damp, but otherwise no harm done.

Kitty snakes out of the partially open window, and drops silently into the bushes below. Rico glances at me, then follows her.

I hesitate, suddenly wondering if I'll actually fit through the narrow kitchen window. But I squeeze my head and ears out, then my shoulders, shivering in the cold air. So far, so good. The ground below is dark. I can smell the cats, and hear them rustling, but my eyes have not yet adjusted. I almost back out, suddenly frightened. What if I get lost and can never find the house again, and Sam is left all alone? Am I making everything worse by trying to rescue my sister?

'Oh, do hurry up,' Kitty says from below, and now I can see her two eyes glowing in the dark.

Awkwardly, I let myself slide out, paws first, scrabbling at the wall, crash through the scratchy branches of a shrub, and end up in an embarrassing heap under a bush.

Ouch.

Rico nudges me. 'You still alive?'

I clamber up, and give myself an exploratory shake. Everything seems to be intact. 'Absolutely,' I say, with more bravado than I feel, and head straight for the lawn. 'Come on, let's do this.'

It's a break-out.

Halfway across the frosty lawn, I stop and wait for the cats to catch up.

Rico grins. 'This is fun.'

Then all three of us set off running again, tearing down the garden. Soon we are lost in the shadows under the trees. I look back once as we head for next door's fence, but can't see the back door any more. There's a half-moon above the house, ghostly in the chill air. And Pepper is waiting for us by the gap in the fence.

'You got out OK then,' I say to her.

She nods and glances over her shoulder, clearly a little nervous.

Her owner is staggering down the garden path in wellies, waving a misty torch beam from side to side, whistling and calling, 'Pepper? Pepper?' in a cracked voice. 'Where are you, Pepper? Here, girl!'

'Better be quick,' she tells us, 'before he spots me.'

I check, doing a quick head-count, but we're all there. Even Kitty, whose eyes are gleaming gold as the torch beam heads our way.

'Right,' I say, 'which way?'

'Follow me,' Pepper says hurriedly, and we all pile through the gap in the fence and run across her untidy back garden. 'Through here.'

I duck my head and wriggle after her through a ragged hole in the hedge. There's wire netting halfway through. I

209

get my paw caught in it, but Pepper grabs hold of the edge in her teeth and drags it down, freeing me.

'Thanks,' I say, a little breathless.

Then I burst out the other side, and tumble down a grassy bank with a jolt. We're in a narrow lane. No street lights, no cars. But I can see the main road up ahead, brighter than the surrounding streets, with the sounds of occasional passing cars.

'We did it.' I bump the poodle's shoulder. 'Thank you, Pepper. Doing this for me, putting yourself on the line . . . It means the world.' I look round at the two cats. 'You too. I'm really grateful for your help.'

Pepper nods, looking shy. 'No problem, Bertie. That's why we formed the Paw Print Club, isn't it? To help each other out. Now come on, we don't have all night to find your sister.'

The four of us start to run along the lane together, side by side.

We don't have all night to find your sister.

Before this moment, it was just a plan. What I hoped to do if everything went my way. But now she's said that, now we've broken out and are running free, it all suddenly feels real. My heart races and I can hardly prevent myself from throwing back my head and baying at the moon with pure, unadulterated joy. I do love my humans, but I love my sister too.

I'm going to see Molly again tonight. And if this all goes without a hitch, I'll be back home before the Greens even notice I've gone.

❧ NINETEEN ❧

We run through the cold, dark streets on the edge of town, countryside smells assailing us from one side, the soft glow of the town centre on the other, lighting up the sky for several miles.

'This way,' Kitty says when Pepper hesitates at a crossing. 'We have to cross the road.'

Luckily there is no traffic at this time of night.

It's chilly, but I don't feel it, my paws moving swiftly, my blood running free and hot, like I'm chasing a rabbit or seeing off an intruder.

'Not far now,' Rico announces eventually.

'How was her leg?' I ask him.

'Whose leg?'

'Molly's.'

Rico looks at me blankly.

Briefly, I explain about Molly's bad leg. How I caused that dreadful accident with the truck when we were young pups, and how ever since, my poor sister has walked with a pronounced limp.

Rico seems mystified. 'I didn't notice her limping, to be honest.'

Kitty stops suddenly, and I almost bump into her.

211

'This is it,' she says pointedly, and nods towards the darkened house to our left. 'This is where Molly lives.'

My heart leaps with excitement as I creep to the gate and study the house where my sister lives. The others watch me, and I realise they are waiting for instructions.

'Right,' I say, 'first of all, we need to discover where Molly sleeps.'

I just hope the house is not impenetrable. Otherwise our mission could be over before it's properly begun. I sniff the air.

'Kitty, you've got the best nose here. What's your best guess as to Molly's current location? Front or rear?'

The tabby looks pleased to have been asked. She gathers herself, then springs up onto the top of the fence and balances along the top a few feet, nose in the air.

'Rear,' she decides in the end.

I turn to her brother. 'Rico, you said you went round there earlier while Kitty stood guard. What's access like to the rear of the house?'

'There's a fence blocking off the back path, and an iron gate that seemed to be kept locked.'

'Flush with the ground?'

Rico shakes his head. 'There's a narrow space between the bottom of the gate and the ground.'

'Could Pepper squeeze under there? Or me?'

'Maybe you,' he decides. 'Not Pepper though.' He glances at the poodle apologetically. 'Sorry. It's nothing personal. Bertie's just a lot shorter than you.'

Pepper waves her white tail bobble encouragingly. 'Apology accepted.'

212

'Okay,' I say, thinking fast. 'Pepper, I'll need you on guard duty. Could you watch the front of the house for us, and give three short barks if you see any lights come on inside?'

She nods. 'Sure.'

'Kitty,' I say, 'I know you're not keen on the smell of next door's dog – and, frankly, I don't blame you, he is a smelly brute – but could you overcome that just for tonight, and see if you can climb up there?'

I nod towards the front of the house, where the low, single-storey garage meets the rest of the house. I can see a ledge there, and the frosted window above it has been left slightly open. Perhaps a toilet?

She makes a face. 'You want me to go inside?'

'Just to see if you can locate Molly.' I think of the stern-looking woman, and feel suddenly uneasy. 'Actually, no. Forget it. It's too dangerous.'

Her yellow eyes narrow. 'Too dangerous?' Kitty jumps down from the fence. 'Watch and learn, little beagle.'

She sets off at a trot towards the dark house.

'Kitty, be careful,' her brother calls after her, his tone anxious.

'Okay, Rico,' I say briskly, 'now it's down to you and me. Show me this gate. And no miaowing. We can't risk being heard.'

I glance up as we pass the garage. Kitty is already on the ledge, positioning herself for the best chance to slip in through the open window above. It's going to be a tight fit though. And at a sharp angle too.

'Cats have nine lives, don't they?' I ask Rico under my breath.

'So they say.'

The gate is made of metal bars, too tightly spaced to squeeze through, and incredibly low to the ground. Rico slips underneath by arching his back in the most fantastical way, like he's made of rubber.

I'm not made of rubber.

'Come on,' he says, from the other side, looking at me through the bars.

I suck in my breath, lower myself to the ground and roll onto my side, then drag myself along in an undignified shuffle, until my head has cleared the bottom of the gate. Restless and eager to see Molly again, I run ahead of the cat into the shadows of the back garden.

'That must be the conservatory.' I can see it ahead, a faint gleam illuminating the floor and furniture, like there's a light on somewhere inside the house. 'Looks like the pinch-faced woman might still be awake.' I glance back at the dark looming mass of the garage wall. Everything is still silent. 'I hope Kitty got inside safely.'

'I imagine she did.'

'You have a lot of faith in your sister, don't you?'

He shrugs, looking vaguely amused and not even remotely worried for his sibling. 'There was a ledge and an open window, Bertie. That's not exactly a challenge to the average cat. And Kitty is not an average cat.'

We creep closer to the conservatory.

Suddenly I see movement inside. A dark shape hurrying across the room, tail held high. It's Kitty. She looks out through the conservatory door, eyes wide.

'There,' I say to Rico.

He bounds to the door as though they've been parted for months, not a few minutes, and the two cats stare at each other through the glass, purring.

Then a larger shape appears behind her.

My heart jolts.

I know that head, tipped to one side, tail wagging curiously, the familiar white-splodged face staring back at me.

'Molly!'

❦ TWENTY ❦

It's like seeing a reflection of myself in the glass, but a fraction shorter and with eyes that sparkle as I smile into them.

'Molly, I can't believe it's you.'

She rubs her muzzle on the glass panel, half-frowning, and I realise she can't hear me. Not properly. Not through the door.

'I'm so sorry,' I tell her, and hope my expression says the rest. 'I tried to find you earlier. But it's been difficult to get out. I was grounded.'

Molly tips her head further over, a question in her eyes.

'I got into trouble.'

Her eyes narrow, and her ears perk up.

'Trouble,' I repeat, as loudly as I dare. I make some straining and choking actions, to indicate that I couldn't get away. 'I was . . . naughty.'

She turns to Kitty, and there's a hurried conversation that we can't hear on this side of the glass. Then Kitty runs out of the room.

Presumably she's on her way back to us with a message.

Being a cat, Kitty can just leap out through that small window, the same way she got into the house. But Molly is larger and rather less skilled at scaling high walls. So she is stuck where she is until I can think of some way to get her out of the pinch-faced woman's house. And I am stuck on this side, unable to communicate properly.

Except through a cat.

Life is full of these rich ironies . . .

'I got out tonight, but they keep me locked up most nights.' I pat the glass. 'Like this. No way out.'

She nods as though she understands.

Then my sister places her paw on the glass too, right over mine.

We stare into each other's eyes.

I think of all the times in my childhood when I was naughty, and Molly told me off, and we squabbled and fought. And all the times her poorly leg ached, and I comforted her, and we lay together, warm under the kitchen table at the Mintons'.

No wonder Molly howled when the cats told her I was out there, somewhere nearby, desperately looking for her. I have never been one to get all misty-eyed, but I feel like howling right now. We're so close and yet so far. Only this thin sheet of glass between us. But it might as well be a huge stone wall or field after field of empty countryside. I can see her but we can't hear or embrace each other. So I'm no closer to getting my sister back.

'I'm going to get you out of here,' I try to reassure her, though I know she probably can't hear what I'm saying. But maybe she can understand the look in my eyes. 'I just . . . I just haven't figured out yet how to do that.'

She must be able to read my mind. Because she suddenly tips her head back and howls. Like I've died.

Which I may do if we get caught here.

'No, don't cry, Molly,' I tell her urgently. Tapping my paw against hers through the glass. 'Please don't.'

Though I'm so close to howling myself; it's hard not to tip my own throat back and join in with her long, sad howl.

'Rico?' Kitty appears on the roof above us. She runs along the guttering, then jumps down, landing heavily on the grass. When she joins us at the conservatory door, she's out of breath. 'She says there's no way for her to get out.'

'Evidently,' I say.

'She said not to bother. Not tonight.'

Molly is still howling. A light goes on inside the house somewhere.

Rico's eyes gleam, and he backs away from the conservatory. 'Erm, I don't want to hurry your reunion, Bertie. But it looks like a human is coming.'

'Yes,' Kitty agrees. 'Time to get back home.' She rubs herself against my rump, and I flick her deliberately with my tail. She turns, hissing. 'Ow, watch it, you hairy lump.'

'I'm staying right here.'

Rico looks horrified. 'That's not what we agreed.'

Out the front, we hear the muffled sound of a dog barking. Three short barks, to be precise. The alarm call.

'That's Pepper,' Rico mutters, staring at me as we hear the three short barks repeated. 'Uh-oh. Not good. Definitely sounds like trouble. I think we'd better leave, Bertie.' He hesitates, and when I do not move, adds uncertainly, 'Erm, *now*.'

'You go.'

Kitty scratches my rump with her claws. 'Move it,' she growls. 'Back under the gate. That's an order. We're finished here.'

I look back at Molly.

My sister's face is miserable. But she slides her paw down the glass, and drops it to the floor. Then she's backing away, shaking her head.

The light is growing brighter inside the house. I can see a tall, wavering shadow on the wall at the back of the conservatory. The pinch-faced woman making her way slowly through the downstairs of the house, heading for the conservatory, for my sister . . .

'Come on, Bertie,' Rico whispers, already out of sight in the shadows, heading back towards the gate. 'If someone sees Pepper out the front, they might try to grab her collar, or . . . or call the dog catcher. You don't want that, do you?'

I can't seem to breathe properly, staring at Molly.

'We're the Paw Print Club,' he reminds me unhappily. 'We stick together. We don't leave other members to get caught.'

Kitty is still nearby, waiting. She glares at me too with huge, baleful eyes. 'Look, your sister says she'll try to get outside after dark. Like we did. I told her we'd come back. Same time tomorrow.'

The door to the conservatory is pushed open, and I see the pinch-faced woman there in the doorway. Tall, angular, in a loose-fitting dressing gown, her hair sticking up, staring down at Molly with a shocked face.

How can I leave her now? To be told off? To be punished, perhaps?

Torn, I can't seem to move.

But I know what Molly would say if she was outside with us. And it would not be 'Stay'.

The woman is stumbling across the conservatory now, staring wide-eyed into the dark garden as though she can see us standing here. Ghosts in her garden.

'Bertie, quick!' Kitty hisses.

I give up.

I turn and run for the gate, aware of the cats alongside me, and squeeze under the gate so hurriedly that I feel the cold metal graze my shoulder. Pepper meets us at the gate, nervous and prancing about with a wildly agitated tail bobble, and we run down the street together. Heading home. Back to our daily lives of kind humans and comfortable baskets and tasty dinners.

I feel like I've failed my sister.

Again.

But there's a larger sliver of hope in my heart now. Because I've seen her, and our paws almost touched, if it hadn't been for the glass between us. And she's told Kitty she will try to break out, like we did, and then we could be reunited properly, tails wagging, running together down the street.

Tomorrow night.

I have to hang on to that, and hope I'm not grounded for ever after tonight's escapade.

We round the corner, running wildly, paws barely touching the icy pavements, and Pepper slams into a lamp-post.

We all stop.

Rico turns back to her as the poodle recovers, then staggers on a short distance, but unsteady on her paws, her expression dazed. 'You hurt, Pepper?'

'Oh, only my . . . brain.' She shakes her head, then gives a startled little bark and lopes on again, gathering speed. 'Crazy.'

I allow myself a quick grin before following at a trot.

We did it.

The Paw Print Club did it.

We broke out of our houses and found Molly. And tomorrow night, we'll be back in her quiet street. Only with a proper plan this time, and even more determined to rescue her from the pinch-faced woman.

'Crazy.'

The streets are empty, and we make it home without incident. It's still dark. Pepper goes to lie down outside her back door, exhausted by our adventure, and Rico trails thoughtfully after her. Kitty gives me a glance, then climbs a tree and disappears along its branches.

The house stands dark and quiet.

I sit outside the kitchen door, feeling shivery now that I'm no longer moving, and peer up at the sky. There's a long while until dawn, by my reckoning. And nowhere comfortable to lie. My paws feel sore from all the running on hard roads, and my shoulder aches where I squeezed under the metal gate. I start to wish I was inside, curled up in my basket beside the warm range.

But then I remember Molly's familiar face on the other side of the glass, her paw held up against mine, and I know it was all worth it.

Just for those precious seconds together.

I pace up and down the frosty patio, trying to keep warm. But the stone is icy under my paws and the air is too sharp; it actually hurts to breathe too deep. Granny M said a few days ago that it might snow this Christmas, and I am inclined to agree. The world does feel very cold. Cold and still. Though maybe that's simply because I am outside in the dark, instead of inside with the humans I have grown to love.

Suddenly, a light comes on in the house.

I sit up straight, staring.

Granny Margaret, wrapped in a vast shawl and wearing a woolly bed cap, puts the kitchen light on, unlocks the back door, and pokes her grey head out.

'Bertie?' she whispers uncertainly.

I give a short bark and run towards her, wagging my tail with ridiculous relief.

'Oh, Bertie,' she says, and throws the door open to let me inside.

I run past her into the warm kitchen, relaxing at last now that I'm back where I belong.

Granny Margaret gazes around, and makes a clucking noise that she uses to summon the cats. But Rico and Kitty are nowhere to be seen, so she shrugs and closes the door.

'Where on earth did you go, you silly dog?' She checks me over. 'What were you up to tonight, Bertie? I came downstairs and found the window open, and all three of you gone.' She strokes my ears. 'I must ask John to fix the catch on that window. You had me worried.'

I wag my tail apologetically and can't quite meet her eyes, feeling guilty.

After she's put some fresh water and dog biscuits down for me, and made herself a cup of tea while I wolf them down, Granny M whistles me to follow her upstairs.

'I know a little boy who needs a friend.' She creaks open his bedroom door, and nods me inside. 'Go on, up you go.'

I jump onto the bed and tread over Sam's sprawled limbs. The boy is asleep, but stirs when I curl up beside him.

'Bertie?' he murmurs sleepily, and puts his arm round me.

Granny M smiles and closes the door.

I lie against his soft body in the darkness, working out how we will go back and rescue Molly tomorrow night. I mean to stay awake as long as possible until I have the perfect plan. But I am warm now and so relieved to be safely home, back with the family where I belong, that I can hardly keep my eyelids open. And before long, my breathing slows and deepens, and begins to match Sam's . . .

❧ TWENTY-ONE ❧

I'm talking excitedly to Pepper and the cats by the fountain the next day, discussing how we will break Molly out, when Mr Green stamps out to the shed and extricates a hefty bag of tools. Then he heads back inside, and a few minutes later we hear him fiddling with the broken catch on the kitchen window.

'What about tonight, Bertie?' Rico asks suddenly, listening with his head turned towards the kitchen. 'If Mr Green mends that window catch, how are we going to get out?'

Pepper stares at the house. 'Oh no.'

I could howl with despair. Granny M did say last night that she would ask him to fix the window. But I had not reckoned on him doing it so soon. 'Molly thinks we're coming for her. She's planning to run away tonight, to be waiting for us when we arrive.' I sit down, suddenly very deflated. 'This is a disaster.'

'I could have told you it would be.' With an eloquent shrug, Kitty jumps up onto the fountain surround to join her brother. She parades along the narrow edge, and bends her head gingerly to sniff at the icy water. 'I don't want to crush your daydreams, Bertie, but perhaps it's time to face facts.'

'Meaning?'

'Your sister has another owner now. You live here. She lives somewhere else. There's no way you can make this work, even if you break her out tonight.'

I feel my temper rise. 'That's just your opinion, and you're entitled to it.'

'Not just *my* opinion. It's what we're all secretly thinking, isn't it?' She looks at each of the others in turn, then sits and curls her tabby-striped tail round her front paws like a question mark. 'You haven't thought this out. As usual. Everything's all guts and heart with you. No brains.'

I give a short angry bark. 'Come down here and say that.'

'So you plan to break your sister out of her home tonight. To help her escape the clutches of that evil woman?'

'That's right.'

'And how do you know she's evil?'

I laugh. 'You saw her.'

'But her house looked quite comfortable. Messy, but in a cosy way. Your sister has her own basket. Fleece-lined. I wouldn't mind one of those myself.' Kitty looks at me in a supercilious manner. 'And she didn't look underfed to me. Or beaten. Or scared.'

'Again, that's just your opinion.'

I suppress my sudden desire to chase the cat up the nearest tree. Kitty is a part of my household now, and she deserves a say, just like everyone else. I simply need to put her straight on a few things, that's all.

'Look,' I say, struggling to sound calm, 'you only saw the pinch-faced woman from a distance. Am I right?'

Kitty shrugs.

'I met that woman in person,' I point out. 'Up close and personal at the dog shelter. Trust me, she was nasty. The type who enjoys making dogs suffer.'

'Very well,' she concedes. 'Let's assume Molly is not in a happy place, and you're going to rescue her. Where is she going to live once she's escaped?'

I hesitate, glancing about the frosty garden. 'Somewhere round here, I guess. Maybe in . . . in the shed.'

'And Mr Green won't notice her there?'

I frown. Damn cat. She's right though, much to my chagrin. This is not something I've thought about very much. Up until now, it seemed enough to focus on getting Molly out of her prison. Not worry about how she would live once she was free.

'Well, if he does,' I say slowly, 'I expect he'll want to adopt her too. Granny M will, for sure. She's an intelligent woman.'

'Oh, I agree,' Kitty says silkily. 'Too intelligent not to pick up the phone and call the dog shelter as soon as she claps eyes on an identical beagle in her back garden. Then the dog shelter will ring the pinch-faced woman, and she'll come straight over and collect Molly the same day.'

I say nothing.

'Then we'll be back where we started,' Kitty finishes, fixing me with her unblinking yellow stare. 'Only now Molly will be in massive trouble with her owner for running away. And all of us will have wasted our time trying to help her. So much for the epic deeds of the Paw Print Club.'

Perhaps it was a mistake not chasing her up the tree. She would have looked amusing trying to finish that sentence while hanging upside-down from a high branch.

Pepper's owner whistles for her at that moment, and the poodle starts violently, looking round at us, clearly distraught. 'I don't want to g . . . go yet,' she stammers. 'I'm one of you. One of the Paw Print Club.'

The whistle comes again. 'Heel, Pepper!'

Rico looks at her. 'You'd better go to him,' he says. 'You don't want to get in trouble. Especially after last night.'

'We'll see you tonight as arranged, Pepper,' I say encouragingly. 'Assuming we can manage to get out.'

She shakes her head mournfully. 'No point. He's put an old lawn roller in front of the hole in the hedge. I tried to move it, but it's too heavy.'

'We'll have to find another way out, then.'

The whistle comes again, this time louder. 'Pepper, come here now!'

Sadly, she nudges us all in turn, head bowed, tail drooping. 'See you later,' she murmurs, then runs back to her owner. He drags her through the narrow gap in the fence, shooting us a cross look. She's obviously in disgrace after her escape last night.

Poor Pepper.

I look back at the patio. Granny M is in the kitchen doorway, shaking a rug as Rico darts past her into the kitchen. She looks sharply at me and Kitty, almost as though she knows what's going on. Which is ridiculous, of course.

But she is a very intelligent woman.

'Do you want a biscuit, Bertie?' she calls suddenly.

227

Definitely intelligent.

I straighten, wagging my tail.

'Huh, that's typical of a dog. The offer of a biscuit and you forget everything else,' Kitty comments, jumping down from the fountain edge to sharpen her claws on an old piece of trellis.

'Actually,' I say, stung by that remark and very much on my dignity, 'I need all the energy I can get. I've got a long night's work ahead.'

She stares. 'You're not seriously going back to Molly's tonight, are you? Without the broken window catch? Without the hole in the hedge?'

I hesitate. Perhaps she's right that I shouldn't attempt it again tonight. Not because of the difficulties of getting out, but because things seem so fragile with the Greens right now. It would be too awful if my need to rescue Molly caused my own family to break down. Everything seems so strained, especially with Christmas coming up.

'Let me think about it,' I tell her, more confidently than I feel. 'I have to find a way. Molly is my flesh and blood. And she's relying on me.'

I trot off towards the house and the promised biscuit. But I know the cat is not exaggerating. It is going to be problematic. Not least because I don't want to upset Granny Margaret or Sam, or even Mr Green, by running away.

I love Molly. But they're my family too now.

❊   ❊   ❊

Sam is in the kitchen, sitting at the table and writing something in a notebook. I run to rub against his dangling legs. He bends to scratch my head, then carries on writing without saying anything.

'Here you go,' Granny Margaret says, and holds out a large, bone-shaped dog biscuit. I take it delicately from her hand, then run back with it to my basket. I can smell its milky deliciousness, and it makes me think of being a puppy again, of cuddles and treats, and games with Molly.

Mr Green finishes with the window, and packs away his tools. 'Ideally, it needs a new catch,' he tells her. 'I'll get one after Christmas. Meanwhile, I've used some wire to make it more secure.'

'What a good idea.'

'I can't imagine how it came open during the night.'

Granny Margaret shrugs, but glances across at me drily as she murmurs, 'Maybe the wind? Or perhaps one of the cats knocked against it.'

Once Mr Green has taken his tools back to the shed, I stare up at the secured window, wondering how on earth I can keep my promise to my sister.

I wish I could tell my humans about Molly, but of course I can't. Perhaps I should wait until after Christmas. Or slip out again tonight, perhaps before they lock the door in the late evening. Then somehow climb over the stone wall on the other side of the garden, and make my way through the back gardens until I hit the road on the far side.

What I can't do is give up. Molly is expecting me to go back for her.

'Goodness, Sam,' Granny M exclaims, glancing at Sam's notebook as she passes the table. Balancing a film-covered plastic box of cookies in each hand, she peers at what he's drawn. 'That doesn't look very ... nice. What are those creatures?'

'Zombies.'

'Oh.' She looks at him dubiously. 'I didn't know you were into those stories.'

He shrugs, and carries on drawing.

'What's that?' she asks, still staring over his shoulder. 'Is that an axe? And that ... Is that a gun?' When he does not say anything, she says, 'I don't think you should be drawing things like that, Sam. They're not appropriate.'

He jumps up, slamming the notebook shut. 'Why can't you mind your own business? It's just a picture, that's all.'

'Sam!'

I glance at the back door, which has been left open despite the cold weather. Mr Green is there, his hands dirty, scraping his boots outside before coming in. He is staring at Sam, surprise in his face. 'Don't let me ever hear you speaking to your grandmother like that again,' he tells his son. 'Apologise at once.'

Sam's lip trembles. 'No.'

'I beg your pardon?'

'Gran's got no right to tell me what I can't draw.' He tucks the notebook under his arm but does not leave the table, glaring back at them both, his face very pale, his eyes red-rimmed. 'I was drawing zombies, that's all. It was a picture, only a bit of fun. Why shouldn't I draw what I like?'

'Apologise,' his father says sternly. 'Right now, or you can forget Christmas.'

Granny M looks horrified. 'Oh, John, no.'

'Don't interfere, Margaret.' Mr Green pulls off his boots, then comes into the kitchen in his socks. He looks furious, a flush in his cheeks. 'I'm sorry but it's important that Sam realises he can't behave badly and get away with it.'

'I'm sure he doesn't think that.'

'Really?' Mr Green swivels his steely gaze round to where I am standing in my basket, crunching on my bone-shaped biscuit as I listen. 'It's like the way he encourages Bertie to misbehave too.'

I swallow hastily, and drop the biscuit.

'That dog needs some proper training. I've said it again and again. But all I hear are excuses.' Mr Green shakes his head. 'I really think we made a mistake with Bertie.'

'No,' Sam says at once.

'We didn't think hard enough about what kind of dog we needed. Beagles are very temperamental dogs. They need strict training, otherwise they can become destructive.'

'That's hardly fair, John.' Granny M shakes her head. 'Bertie isn't destructive. A little bit naughty, perhaps.'

Mr Green runs a hand through his hair, which is standing on end. He would look rather comical, if it wasn't for the frown on his face. He seems very stressed. 'All right, what about the broken window catch?'

'That could have been the cats.'

'Well, however it got broken, it's still a nuisance. Because of that, Bertie escaped while we were asleep and could have been up to all sorts without us knowing anything about it. Pepper escaped too last night, I just heard. The roads can be busy this time of year, even at night. Either of them could have been hit by a car. Plus, I had to spend this morning fixing it so he won't be able to get out again. And I simply can't deal with all this extra worry, Margaret, not on top of . . .' He draws a shaky breath, then finishes, 'On top of everything else.'

'Oh, John,' Granny M says sadly, and I see her gaze drift back to the photograph of Jenny, Sam's mother, on the wall.

'No, I've made up my mind. After Christmas, Bertie has to go.'

When Sam makes an instinctive noise of protest, Mr Green screws up his face. At least he looks upset too, I think, but shrink from the emotion in their faces as I look round at the Greens. Have I caused that?

'Son, I know it's hard to hear. And I'm sorry. But it's not just because the dog keeps causing us headaches. We got your school report yesterday. It's not good. Not good at all. Your school work is suffering. You're spending too much time playing with Bertie in the evenings, and not enough time focused on doing your homework.'

'But if . . . if you take Bertie away, I'll have nothing.' Sam's face is lined with pain. 'Nothing, do you hear me?'

'You'll have me and your grandmother,' his father says sharply, 'and the cats. Kitty and Rico. That was always enough for you before.'

'You can't take him away. You can't, you just can't!' Sam is almost screaming. 'I love Bertie.'

Mr Green sighs, his hands clenched into fists by his side. He looks genuinely torn. 'I'm sorry, really I am. But I can't see how else to deal with this situation.'

Sam breaks from the kitchen and thuds upstairs.

Granny M looks at Mr Green. Her mouth is trembling too, like Sam's was. She must be very upset, I think. 'I know you're trying to do what seems best here. But I want Bertie to stay too.'

'Even with all the trouble he causes?' he demands, looking perplexed.

'Even with that.'

He looks at her helplessly, then shrugs. 'If you think I'm making a mistake, then . . . Look, I'm just trying to do the responsible thing.'

'Sometimes you have to do the irresponsible thing. To stay human.'

He drags on his boots again, looking upset and frustrated. 'I don't even know what that means, Margaret. But I do know Bertie is my responsibility, legally speaking. And if he escapes, I'm to blame for whatever he gets up to while he's roaming wild.' He takes a deep breath. 'Right, I'm going down the garden. Apparently Bertie's a "bad influence" on Pepper, so I've agreed to try closing up that hole in the fence. So Pepper doesn't keep coming into the garden.'

'Well, I have to go out too.'

He frowns. 'Again?'

'I'm in charge of floral arrangements at the church this year. Apparently, there's been a last-minute issue with the holly wreaths.' She nods to the boxes of freshly made gingerbread, which smell delicious. 'Plus I have to drop that gingerbread off at Shirley's first, for the meals-on-wheels festive treats run tomorrow.'

He hesitates, then sighs. 'Fine, you'd better tell Sam to come out into the garden where I can keep an eye on him.'

'Go easy on the boy,' she says softly, then adds, 'Look, I made you a cup of tea. There's a slice of gingerbread too.'

'I'll have it later, thanks.'

He disappears and Granny M shakes her head, her look troubled as she watches him head down the garden.

'Oh, Bertie, that poor man,' she says, and reaches for her coat on the back of the chair. 'He needs to stop trying to control everything and everyone, and look around at the blessings in his life.'

She smiles at me, but it's a thin, world-weary smile. 'Don't worry, I won't let him take you back to the shelter. Just make sure you behave yourself until Christmas is over, and better keep away from Pepper next door too. Promise?' She bends and strokes my ears, then makes a face. 'What on earth? Bertie, you have something horrible and sticky on your head. Hang on.'

I sit patiently while she grabs a wet wipe and cleans the last of the sticky goo off my face from last night's commando outing.

'That's better.'

Then she heads out of the kitchen, juggling her car keys and the two boxes of gorgeous-smelling gingerbread.

I hear her in the hallway, calling up to Sam that his dad wants him outside in the garden. She adds, 'I'll only be out

234

an hour. Then we'll sit down and talk things out. Please try not to worry. Your dad's bark is always worse than his bite.'

Then the front door slams and the house goes quiet.

I won't let him take you back to the shelter.

Is she right?

I can't help worrying, despite Granny Margaret's reassurances.

Sam was so upset too.

Of course Mr Green may be more serious if I do manage to slip out again tonight. Perhaps I should give up on my hope of rescuing Molly before Christmas. This household is already stretched to breaking point without me doing something irresponsible like running away.

But what about Molly?

My sister could be suffering terribly – and here I am, eating this tasty biscuit, lying in my comfortable basket, contemplating leaving Molly for another few days in the clutches of the pinch-faced woman.

I whine sadly to myself, but it doesn't help at all.

If only I could decide what to do for the best. What I need is another council of war. Perhaps I should ask Kitty to organise one for later today. It's hard to admit that I need help, but perhaps it's time I accepted that I'm part of a club now. The Paw Print Club. And what I can't accomplish alone, perhaps I could accomplish with the help of my new friends.

After I've finished crunching the last of my tasty biscuit, I go in search of Sam, and trot upstairs, my tummy full and warm. Outside his bedroom door, I pause, a little confused.

I can hear banging and thudding from inside. Drawers being opened and shut, hurried steps back and forth.

I whimper, and scratch at the door. But it remains closed.

My dog-sense tells me something is horribly wrong.

Then the bedroom door flies open and Sam is there, wrapped up in his coat, hat and scarf, like he's on his way out somewhere. He has a fishing rod in his hand, a bulging rucksack strapped to his back, and his face is streaked with tears. His expression is mulish though. Like he doesn't care what anyone says or does any more, because he has only one thing on his mind.

His face reminds me of my mood last night. Before I found Molly.

'Oh, Bertie,' he says, then drops to his knees at the top of the stairs and embraces me awkwardly. He buries his face in my neck and shoulders. 'Please look after Granny M and . . . and my dad too. My dad doesn't love me, but I love him. And I know you'll look after him for me. Make sure he has a good Christmas. My present for him is the one with . . . with the gold wrapping paper.'

He rubs my ears, then sobs, 'I can rely on you to see Dad gets the right present. Can't I, Bertie?'

I know you'll look after him for me.

I don't understand. What does he mean?

I bark, suddenly very concerned.

'Hush, Bertie, there's no need to worry,' he says as though to reassure me, which is ironic, as I am far from reassured. 'This is for the best, honestly. Dad blames me for what happened to Mum. That's why he's been so bad-tempered recently.' He swallows hard, and wipes his sleeve across his wet face. 'But you'll see, once I've gone, Dad will be much happier. He won't keep shouting. And he won't send you back to the shelter. Not when I'm not here any longer to keep winding him up, and reminding him of . . . of Mum.'

I wag my tail but Sam is no longer looking at me. I watch, perplexed, as the boy treads heavily down the stairs and makes for the front door.

I bark again, this time more urgently, and run down the stairs after him, so fast I almost lose my footing and tumble over my own ears. Sam is not allowed out on his own. I'm fairly certain of that rule, even if the ones that concern me are a bit misty at times.

Tearful, Sam looks back at me. 'I can't take you with me, Bertie,' he says, his voice croaking. 'I don't have enough food for both of us. Besides, you might bark, and give me away. I need to stay hidden.' He opens the door and peers outside. The cold air that rushes in makes me shiver, but he still does not change his mind. 'I'll probably never see you again, Bertie. So this is goodbye. Thank you for . . .'

He can't get the words out, and steps outside instead. The world looks grey and uninviting. Then the front door swings shut behind him.

I stare at the closed door for a few moments in consternation. Then I run into the kitchen, barking frantically. It's empty and the back door is shut too.

I can see Mr Green at the bottom of the garden, his back towards the house, bending over the gap in the fence. I bark and yelp as loudly as I can, but he does not turn. My mind is whirling with fear. I am sure now this cannot be right. What is Sam going to do out there on his own? What will he eat? Where will he sleep? How will he survive, especially when the weather is so cold and cruel? He's still only a child, and he looked so upset when he left, tears running down his face.

Then I remember what Mr Green said about how heavy traffic is around Christmas time, and a new terror strikes me. What if Sam is crying so hard, he does not look where he is going and gets hit by a car?

Oh, this is all my fault.

I run back into the hall, whining and jumping up at the front door. Perhaps I can try running after Sam instead. It's shut tight though and won't budge.

I sit down in front of the front door, throw back my head and howl.

There's no one in the house.

No one to hear me howl.

No one to know that Sam has run away from home.

❧ TWENTY-TWO ❧

It turns out that Sam left a note. Once Mr Green has stopped searching the house and garden, yelling Sam's name until his voice is hoarse, he calls Granny M at the church.

'Sam's gone,' he tells her down the phone, sounding shaken. 'I thought he was just playing a trick on me. But I've looked everywhere, and he's not here. And there was a note on his pillow.' He listens, then shakes his head. 'No, this is serious. He's run away. You need to come home.'

After he's hung up, Mr Green rings the police. Then he searches the house again. Just in case Sam is hiding somewhere. But of course he is not.

'Where's my boy, Dertie?' he asks as I follow him around the house, trying to show him that Sam is no longer here by whining and running back and forth.

I wish I knew where he was.

While he waits for the police to arrive, Mr Green sinks into a chair at the kitchen table and buries his face in his hands. Sometimes he mutters his son's name in a despairing tone, and sometimes I catch the word, 'Jenny.'

I don't know how to comfort the man, so lean against his knee and thump my tail weakly on the floor.

Then the doorbell goes, and Mr Green jumps up with a muttered exclamation. 'Sam?'

He stumbles to the front door, a sudden hope in his face.

Only it's not Sam.

It's the police.

He shows them the note, and the police read it in silence, heads bent over the sheet of paper.

A short while later, the front door flies open, and it's Granny M back again, bustling into the kitchen, breathless and with tears in her eyes too, unable to believe what has happened.

'Oh, John, is he back yet?'

But Mr Green can only shake his head and look grimly at the clock.

The first hours following Sam's departure pass very slowly. The police take his disappearance very seriously indeed; some make important-sounding calls on their mobile phones, and others stand about and nod sympathetically while Mr Green gives them a full description of his son. I wish I could help in some way, but there's nothing I can do except sit unhappily in my basket by the range, watching feet in polished black shoes passing back and forth. Kitty is standing on the kitchen table, being fussed by a policeman with shiny buttons, while a woman police officer takes yet more details from Granny Margaret about Sam's behaviour that day.

'No,' she keeps repeating, her voice unsteady, 'I don't have the faintest idea where Sam could have gone. I would tell you if I knew.'

'Of course, sometimes kids don't actually run away, they hide under the bed or in a wardrobe,' the policewoman says, 'just to make a point, to make Mum and Dad feel guilty. That's why we usually insist on searching the house thoroughly before getting the helicopter out. We found one eight-year-old girl hiding in an attic once. She'd been missed during the initial search.' She smiles wanly. 'The girl was up there a full three days before the family realised.'

Mr Green comes heavily downstairs with yet more police officers, having helped them to search Sam's bedroom again, and the rest of the house. Sure enough, they've taken their time about it, up there over an hour, searching every nook and cranny in every room, behind curtains and inside cupboards. They took a sniffer dog up there with them, an attractive liver spaniel called Sarah, who checked me out as soon as she came into the house, gave me a good sniffing, and has ignored me ever since.

I'm not offended. There's no accounting for taste.

As the police troop into the room, Granny M turns to look at them with a start, nearly knocking her half-drunk cup of tea off the table.

'Whoops,' the woman officer says, and catches it in time, but not before tea sloshes over the table and onto the floor.

Kitty hops sideways to avoid getting tea on her paws, and looks at me eloquently before jumping to the floor.

'What a nuisance that boy is,' the cat says, stalking to the back door – probably to avoid the Spaniel, who is already on her way over for another good sniff-around. 'All this fuss. No one cares when I go missing for a day or two.'

'Yes, but you're a cat,' I point out.

'So?'

I shake my head silently. *Cats*.

Granny M's gaze flashes to Mr Green's face as he enters the kitchen. 'John, did you check the attic?'

Mr Green looks awful. His face is very pale, and his hair is standing on end again, like he's been running his hands through it desperately. 'Yes, of course. We looked everywhere. He's not in the house.'

The policeman nods. 'Your grandson's definitely a runaway. His note makes that clear. I've called it in, and the helicopter should be here soon.'

'I haven't even seen this note yet.' Granny M's voice shakes with emotion. 'Will someone please tell me what it says?'

The policeman with shiny buttons produces the sheet of paper Mr Green gave him earlier. He clears his throat, then reads aloud, 'Dear Dad and Granny Margaret, I don't want you to worry but I have decided it's time to go. I keep doing the wrong thing and causing rows, and I know you will all be much happier without me. Perhaps if I had left home before, Mum would still be alive. I know it was my fault she died.' He pauses, as Mr Green has said a very rude word, then gives a little cough and continues reading. 'I have taken plenty of warm clothes, so I will be fine. Do not come and look for me. Granny Margaret, please give my Christmas turkey and chipolatas to Bertie. Love, Sam.'

'That poor, poor boy.' Granny M weeps into a hanky.

Mr Green looks grim. 'We'll get him back.'

My ears prick up and I shift in my basket, hearing the noisy whirr of a helicopter as it approaches the house.

'But why on earth does Sam think his mum's death was his fault?' Granny M is asking now. 'That's what I can't understand.'

'I don't know.'

'It's just ridiculous, Sam thinking he caused his mum's death in some way. He must be so confused.' She shakes her head sadly. 'Was it me, John? Did I cause this? Did I do something to upset him, maybe?'

'No, of course not.'

'Perhaps I've been so busy with my charity work in the run-up to Christmas, I forgot to think about Sam.'

'I'm sure that's not it,' the policeman says.

But Granny M is not reassured. 'Oh, this is all my fault. I should never have gone to that church meeting today. I knew he was upset over your . . . argument. I should have stayed, comforted him.'

'It wasn't your fault,' Mr Green says flatly. 'It was mine. All mine.' He closes his eyes briefly, a spasm of pain crossing his face. 'I lost my temper over the dog this morning. I raised my voice. I didn't mean what I said about Bertie. But Sam must have thought . . .'

He stops, apparently unable to continue.

'Best not to dwell on the why right now. More helpful to consider the where instead. His favourite haunts, and all that.' The policeman with shiny buttons passes Sam's note to one of the other officers, then checks his watch. 'Coming up to the three-hour mark. No reason to get too concerned at this point, but once it starts getting dark ... Well, runaways usually come back on their own once dusk falls. Especially at this time of year. Christmas Eve tomorrow. Presents to look forward to, and a slap-up meal. But if Sam isn't back by nightfall ...'

He shrugs, and does not continue.

'Oh, this is awful.' Granny M puts a shaking hand to her mouth. 'I wanted this to be such a happy Christmas for him too. Where can he be?'

Awkwardly, Mr Green goes to Granny M and puts a hand on her shoulder. 'Please try not to worry, Margaret,' he says, though I can tell from his voice that he's desperately worried too. I expect he does not want to upset her any further, though even I don't believe him when he adds uneasily, 'As the officer says, Sam's only been gone a few hours. I'm sure the police will ... That is, I'm sure he'll turn up soon.'

'That's the spirit,' the shiny buttons policeman agrees briskly. 'We've mobilised the dogs though, just in case, and you can hear the helicopter up there. A coordinated initial search of the immediate area will take place in ...' Again, he checks his watch. 'The next half hour, I expect.'

I feel so guilty, looking up at the glum faces in the kitchen. This is my fault, nobody else's. It's clear that Sam's departure is down to my bad behaviour recently, and all the rows it's caused among the Greens.

I hang my head in shame. I'm not a puppy; so maybe it's time I stop behaving like one, and start to take responsibility for the consequences of my actions.

First off, I should be looking after the members of my family who are still here. Not loafing about in my comfy basket like this has nothing to do with me. Mr Green is talking to one of the police now, his mouth drawn and pinched. I jump out of the basket and trot over to Granny M instead. She looks a bit lost, and like she needs some proper comforting.

Granny M glances at me as I rub against her legs, then reaches down to stroke my ears. 'Hello, Bertie.'

I wag my tail apologetically. Her voice sounds so shaky.

'I'm sure everything will turn out okay,' the policewoman is telling her. 'We'll find him.'

Granny M straightens, still clutching her hanky, and blows her nose weakly. 'I do hope you're right, officer. It's just so cold out there at this time of year, and I keep imagining young Sam alone in the dark, scared and hungry. I can't help thinking . . . it must be my fault.'

'You mustn't blame yourself,' Mr Green says, his voice rough, uneven. 'You heard what the note said. Sam thinks I . . . That is, he believes that I don't . . .' His voice breaks. 'That I don't love him.'

'You're his father. Sam can't think that!'

'I'm afraid he can, Margaret. I've been too distant these past few months, that's what it is. Thinking about another Christmas without Jenny. Wrapped up in my own misery, constantly remembering . . .' Mr Green looks at the photograph on the wall of his late wife, his eyes full of tears. 'I've let Jenny down. I've let both of them down.'

'John . . .' Granny M holds out a hand, and he takes it compulsively.

'I knew he was unhappy, and didn't make time to sit down with him and deal with it.' Mr Green bites his lip, which is trembling. 'That note, it's broken my bloody heart. To think Sam has been blaming himself all this time for what happened. As if anything was to blame for his mother's death but the cancer that took her from us. No, it's my doing. I should have been there for Sam. Listened to him more. Talked about Jenny. About why she died.' He shakes his head. 'Instead, all I did was shout at him.'

The policewoman looks round at him, suddenly more alert.

She turns to a clean page in her notebook, pen poised as though for more scribbling. 'So the two of you had a row today?' She looks keenly at Mr Green. 'What about, exactly? It sounds like you argued quite often. How bad were these rows?' Her smile seems false now. As though she suspects Mr Green of having chopped up his son and buried him under the patio. 'Sorry to bombard you with questions. But anything you can tell us would be helpful.'

'We argued over . . . Bertie.' Mr Green looks flushed now.

'Bertie?'

'The dog.'

Everyone looks round at me. Including Sarah the spaniel, whose nose twitches suspiciously in my direction. It's an awkward moment.

I wag my tail feebly.

Sarah strains at her lead, panting. 'I knew you were to blame. Soon as I walked in and smelled you.'

Smelled me?

I hear a snigger from the door. Kitty and Rico are out on the patio with the back door open, listening to everything that's being said.

Her handler says her name disapprovingly, 'Sarah,' and the spaniel sits at once, fawning, looking up at him with big eyes.

I knew you were to blame.

I hang my head again, feeling awful.

'Bertie,' the police officer says slowly as she writes my name down in her notebook, then hesitates, frowning. 'With a y?'

Granny M spells my name aloud.

The police begin to discuss plans for a search of the local area. Mr Green sits down with Granny Margaret to write out a list of places within walking distance where Sam might be hiding.

Mr Green stands up and hands the list to one of the police. 'I expect we'll find him in the park. Loads of places to hide in the park. And he always begs to go there with Bertie. Either that, or in the school grounds.'

The police officer with shiny buttons nods sagely. 'We often find younger runaways hiding in the school grounds. They feel safer there. On familiar territory.'

Listening to the humans, I have a sudden brainwave. It feels like an electric shock, it's so powerful. But how to communicate with the humans?

I jump up at Granny M's leg, barking frantically and pawing at her knee.

'Bertie, for goodness' sake!' She pushes me away, her expression shocked. 'Not now, you naughty dog!'

Helplessly, I turn to Mr Green, barking at him too, trying to get him to listen.

He looks down at me, frowning darkly. 'I'm so sorry,' he tells the police. 'He's not usually this noisy. It must be having all these strangers in the house, it's upset him.' He grabs me by the collar and drags me out onto the patio, not unkindly. 'Go on, Bertie. Off you go, have a good run round outside.'

Then he shuts the door.

I jump up at the door, and stare inside, scratching at the glass panel and still barking. But nobody pays any attention to me.

Frustrated, I stop barking and run out onto the damp lawn to find the others. I have to tell someone or I will go mad.

I'm getting really scared for Sam now though. The afternoon is moving towards dusk, the cloudy sky darkening. There's a distinct chill in the air, that feeling again that it might snow soon. I hate to think of Sam outside in this cold weather, frightened and alone. But as I glance up, the helicopter that's been hovering over the house finally swings away and disappears above the rooftops. I have to hope they will find my young master.

But if they don't, what am I going to do about it?

Rico looks at me, his expression troubled. 'What is it, Bertie? What on earth made you start barking like that? Kitty thought you must have started a fight with that police dog.'

I shake my head impatiently. 'I know where Sam's gone.'
'What?'

'They wouldn't listen to me though. They threw me out.'
I chase my tail, round and round, suddenly desperate to get
out there, to find Sam, even if no one else will help me. 'At
least, I think I know where he's hiding. I've got a pretty
good idea, anyway. Which is more than the humans have.
They think he's gone to the park. Or the school.'

'Why would he go there?'

'Exactly.' I bark again, my heart racing. 'He's not stupid.
He knows they'd look for him there straight away.'

'So where has he gone, Bertie?'

'I think he's gone back to where he was the most happy.'

Kitty yawns and looks at me sideways. 'And how would
you know where he was most happy?' she asks, her tone
disbelieving.

'Because he told me once.'

'So where is he, then?' she demands, her eyes narrowing
to yellow slits. She weaves around us, her tail whisking back
and forth. 'Far away? Nearby?'

'We need to call a proper meeting first.' I nod towards the
fence, where Pepper is parading up and down behind the
wooden slats, now that she can no longer slip easily through
the gap. 'You want to talk? Then come on, let's talk where
Pepper can join in.'

Kitty looks disdainful. 'Why?'

'Because we're still part of the Paw Print Club and Pepper
is a founding member, unless you've already forgotten the
oath we swore.' I ignore the cat's snort and run across to the

fence where Pepper is waiting, long white nose pressed between the slats. 'Hey, Pepper. You must be freezing, waiting out here all this time. You should go in, try to warm up. It could be ages yet before they bring him home.'

'That doesn't matter.' Pepper's frantic gaze searches my face. 'Where's Sam hiding, Bertie? Do the humans know yet?'

'They don't have a clue.'

She looks at me shrewdly. 'But you do?'

'Possibly.'

Rico climbs over the fence and balances on the top, looking down at us both. 'Tell us, then. Don't keep us in suspense.'

I think of Sam as I last saw him, standing at the top of the stairs, wrapped up in a thick coat, his rucksack on his shoulders, and a fishing rod in his hand.

'I could be wrong,' I say slowly, 'but I'd guess he's gone to the river.'

Kitty has joined us by the fence. She says nothing but her large, mesmeric eyes fix on my face as she listens.

Pepper looks horrified. 'The *river?*' She barks, as though unable to contain herself. At the kitchen door onto the patio, I see a police officer glance in our direction. 'Are you sure?'

'Not entirely, but it would be a good place to start looking.'

'That's awful.' Pepper whines. 'A river has . . . well, it has water.'

I look at her ironically. 'Yes.'

'Deep water.'

'Yes.'

'Deep water?' Rico shudders, his eyes very wide as he looks from the poodle to me. 'We have to find him, Bertie, and quickly.'

Pepper barks her agreement. 'Sam needs our help. He needs the Paw Print Club. All that deep water . . . What if he doesn't know how to swim? He might drown. On his own by a river. Especially in the dark.'

'And in this bitter weather,' Rico adds.

I nod, beginning to feel very concerned for the boy myself. 'Which makes it all the more important that we find a way to tell them where he is.'

Kitty has been sitting beside us, looking slightly bored. Suddenly she stiffens. 'Hold on, what about tonight?'

I frown. 'Sorry?'

'Tonight.' She stares at me with accusing eyes. 'Don't tell me you've forgotten about Molly?'

A shock wave of guilt ripples through me as I realise what she means. I have indeed forgotten about my sister, faced with the very real possibility of losing my young master. We are supposed to be rescuing her tonight from the pinch-faced woman. But I haven't even thought about her for the past few hours.

My sister's need to escape that awful household is pressing. But she can wait another day or two, surely? She could be suffering terribly at the hands of the pinch-faced woman, it's true. But Sam's situation is potentially life-threatening. It's getting dark. The temperature will plummet over the next few hours. He can't wait. Not even while I try to rescue my sister.

Besides, with all these police officers milling about the house, and Mr Green and the old lady in such a terrible state, how can I contemplate upsetting my owners further by running away again?

'Bertie?'

I meet Kitty's stare. 'You're right, I . . . I'd forgotten. Can you help me out?'

Her eyes widen and she flicks the tip of her tail as though cross. But she does not tell me to get lost.

'I need you to go and speak to Molly,' I say. 'You know the way. Get back into the pinch-faced woman's house if you can, without being seen, and tell Molly what's happened. That we have to postpone her rescue.'

'I hope she'll understand,' Kitty says slowly.

'Of course she will,' I say with utter conviction. 'Sam has to come first. He's only young and could be in terrible danger.'

I hurry back into the house, wagging my tail with new enthusiasm now that I have something to contribute to the search.

To my disappointment, Sarah the spaniel has vanished. Gone sniffing somewhere, I imagine. She had a good nose for it, I have to admit. Though she did not seem to think much of me. I suppose beagles aren't her thing. Too frisky, probably.

The humans are all still gathered about the kitchen table, poring over a map alongside the list of places where Sam could have gone. I sit and listen, then bark every time they suggest looking in the wrong place. It's not a brilliant plan but it's the best I can do. To my frustration though, they ignore me at first, then the police officers start to shoot me irritated looks. I don't want to behave like a nuisance again, but if they rescue Sam it will be worth it.

Even Mr Green turns round at one point and tells me to, 'Get back to your basket!'

I run to my basket, and sit there obediently, still wagging my tail, still listening to their conversation.

'So,' Mr Green says wearily, 'your officers have already searched here, here, and here, and in the vicinity of the supermarket, with no sign of him anywhere.'

'That's right.'

'How about the park?'

'Well— '

'WOOF! WOOF! WOOF!'

They all turn to glare at me. The officer narrows his eyes at me, then turns back to his work, tapping the sheet of place names again.

Reluctantly, I fall silent, as my barking does not seem to be working. All I'm doing is making everyone cross.

'Next up will be the park, in answer to your first question. We have a search team standing by if he's not back by the time night falls. And if he's not in the park, there's always the churchyard. I've already got someone there, doing a preliminary sweep around the graves.'

Granny M clutches her pearls. 'The churchyard?'

'Very popular with runaways too, after the park and the school.'

'Oh my goodness,' she says faintly.

'And given what you've said about his unhappiness over your daughter's death . . .'

Mr Green walks to the window and stares out at the darkening sky, but says nothing. His shoulders are hunched though, and his face is haggard. It's clear he loves his son more than anything else in the world, and is frantic to get him back. I just wish poor Sam understood that, and was not alone out there in the cold, thinking himself unloved and unwanted.

Watching her son-in-law with a look of foreboding, Granny M asks the policeman tentatively, 'And if Sam's not at the park or at the school or in the churchyard? What then? It's Christmas Eve tomorrow.'

The officer smiles. 'Which makes it all the more likely he'll make his own way home tonight. Look, I don't want you to worry, Margaret. Even if he doesn't turn up on the doorstep soon, I'm confident we'll have found him within a few hours.'

Not if you don't search along the river, I think, starting to fret again.

'WOOF! WOOF! WOOF!'

'Bertie, be quiet!' snaps Mr Green, spinning round to glare at me.

The officer with the shiny buttons straightens, also looking round at me. 'I'm sorry, but perhaps you could find somewhere else for the dog to sit? Maybe another room? Or outside, if it's not too cold?' He pauses, turning back to his work. 'Just until this is over.'

Granny M looks up at him in shock. 'Over?'

'I mean, until we find Sam,' he reassures her.

She nods, then gets up unsteadily. 'Come along, Bertie. I'll take up upstairs. You can sleep on my bed.'

I stare at her in shock.

They're going to shut me away behind a closed door.

I can't let that happen.

I run into the hall and jump up at the front door, pawing at the wood hard enough to leave scratch marks. 'WOOF! WOOF! WOOF!'

'Bertie?'

Mr Green and Granny M have both followed me to the door, staring in amazement. Some of the police officers also pile into the hall after them, watching with a mixture of curiosity and disgust as I bark as though my life depends on it. They probably think I've gone mad and need to be taken to the vet.

I just hope I'm not foaming at the mouth too. That would be unfortunate.

But why on earth is nobody catching on yet to the fact that I'm trying to tell them where Sam is? They can't seriously think I'm rabid. Why do they imagine I'm jumping up and down like I'm crazed, if I don't have something important to show them?

Humans.

I don't understand how they think.

But then, I suppose they don't understand how I think either.

Mr Green tries to grab my collar but I resist, still barking furiously and scratching at the front door.

'What on earth—' he demands.

'He wants Sam back,' Granny M says suddenly, and blows her nose noisily. Her voice is thick with tears. 'He knows that his master has run away. Look at that. Ah, poor little dog. He must be so distressed.'

Yes, I think, whining and staring at her desperately. I know that Sam has run away, and I also know where he's gone. Or at least I have my suspicions.

But she does not understand.

Granny M strokes my head, so that I am forced to settle down rather than risk hurting her, then grabs my collar. 'Come on, Bertie,' she says, and drags me towards the stairs. 'Time to go upstairs.'

'Allow me,' the officer with shiny buttons says firmly. He scoops me up in his arms and carries me upstairs. 'Your bedroom, did you say?'

'Thank you,' Granny M calls up after us, relief in her voice. 'Second door on the right.'

The officer pushes open the door to Granny M's bedroom, deposits me on the bed with no attempt at gentleness, then lowers his face to mine, glaring into my eyes. His shiny buttons look very large, this close. 'My late mother-in-law had a beagle just like you,' he tells me. 'I didn't much like him, either. Soon as she was dead, off he went to the vet.'

I resist the urge to close my teeth around one of those large, shiny buttons on his coat and pull.

'Do we understand each other?' he whispers.

I do not wag my tail.

'Good,' he says, with satisfaction, as though I have spoken, and straightens up, adjusting his immaculate black uniform. 'Now, my friend, you are going to sit here quietly. No more barking. No more scratching at the door. No more whining. We've got a serious job to do downstairs, and you are only getting in the way. Understand?' He backs to the door, watching me steadily the whole way. 'There's a good doggy.'

My heart racing, I leap off the bed and charge the door, determined to make my escape.

He jumps outside and slams it shut in my face. Then laughs.

No!

I hear him going downstairs.

He has no idea what he's done. But that consideration does not help me calm down. Sam is out there, friendless and probably very scared by now, and it seems I'm the only one with a really good idea where he might be hiding. Just let me at those shiny buttons, I think, raging silently at the policeman's perfidy. Two minutes, that's all I'd need.

I look around, smelling lavender and rosewater and talcum powder, Granny M's familiar scents. The bedroom is already getting dark, though the curtains are still open. I jump up on the bed again and stare desperately at the gloomy sky, trying to decide how much longer until nightfall.

Not long enough.

Sam is out there now, cold and alone in the gathering darkness. And if he hears a helicopter searching for him along the river bank later this evening, he's too smart to be standing out in the open where it can spot him.

They're not going to find him in time. Sam's going to spend the night outside. He could freeze to death in this weather.

And it's all my fault for not stopping him from running away.

❧ TWENTY-THREE ❧

It's a truly dreadful night. Even worse than the first night I spent after Molly had been taken from me. I lie by the door, despite the cold draught, my nose on my outstretched paws, unable to sleep for worrying. I am listening to the sound of feet in the hallway below, police coming and going, cars starting up and moving away, other vehicles arriving, and every now and then the distant roar of the helicopter circling the town. But I am also thinking. Thinking about Sam, and Molly, and how my bad behaviour seems to affect those I love. And I make a promise to the darkness, to be better behaved in future and to think of others before myself.

I just hope it's a promise I can keep to Sam. That he is going to be discovered and brought home safely. Because it's obvious the police have not yet managed to find him.

Granny M does not come upstairs until the early hours of the morning, after I have long since given up hope of being released. I hear the creaking step, then the door opens, slowly pushing me back like I'm a draught excluder.

'Oh Bertie,' she gasps, staring down at me. 'I had forgotten all about you. Poor thing. You've been upstairs on your own for hours.' She fumbles for the light switch and I sit up, a little stiff and cold, but still able to wag my tail. 'You must need to go outside.'

I hear someone below in the hall. 'I'll take him out. You go to bed.'

'All right.'

She does look very tired, her face more lined than usual, her mouth turned down. She bends to stroke my head, and I lick her hand.

'Still no sign of Sam,' she murmurs. 'You miss him too, don't you? The police say there's going to be a proper search of the whole town tomorrow. Hundreds have volunteered to join the search, many of them parents at the school. So good of them to offer to give up their time, and on Christmas Eve too. People are so very kind.'

'Bertie?'

I barely recognise the voice, it's so changed. But it's Mr Green, waiting downstairs in the hall to let me into the garden. He sounds dead inside, I think with foreboding. Like he's already given up on the thought of ever seeing his son again. I expect he's just exhausted though. From what little I could hear through the closed bedroom door, Mr Green has been traipsing round the town on foot most of the night, looking for Sam despite the cold and the dark. Though he ought to get some sleep soon, or he'll collapse.

It seems Granny M is thinking much the same thing.

She sighs, then straightens. 'Go on, boy, time to go outside. I need to lie down for an hour or two, before the police come back again.' She sighs. 'Not that I'll be able to sleep a wink. Not with my grandson out there in the cold.'

I wag my tail. I know exactly how she feels.

I trot down to Mr Green, glad to be moving about again after hours stuck in that small bedroom. He gives me a speaking look, as though to say he has not yet forgiven me for barking so loudly while he was trying to talk to the police, then lets me out of the back door. The officers have all gone. But they will be back first thing in the morning, by the sound of it.

'Go on, Bertie,' Mr Green tells me wearily, glancing up at the sky. He shivers, then goes back inside and pulls the door partially shut. His voice is full of sorrow, all his earlier frustrations buried deep under his fear for Sam. 'Good dog.'

It's still dark outside, but not pitch-black. More that cold, clear grey that comes just before dawn on a winter's morning.

When I've finished, I run about the lawn, smelling strange feet everywhere. The police must have searched the garden too. Makes sense, of course. I head for the trees, eager to see if the gap in the fence has been closed up. But I find no gap. Only several large blocks of wood blocking the hole where we squeezed through into Pepper's garden.

I crane my neck round to peer through the fence slats at Pepper's house, but it's silent and dark.

All asleep, I guess.

Rico is waiting for me at the bottom of the garden. His tail is whisking about wildly and he looks genuinely worried, which is unusual. He is normally so laid-back, something has clearly upset him. 'Bertie, at last. Where on earth have you been?'

'Locked in Granny Margaret's bedroom.'

The cat stares.

'It's a long story,' I say drily. 'Look, I'm sorry I wasn't around. Where's Kitty? Did she see Molly? What's been happening?'

Rico makes an odd hissing, yowling noise under his breath, like he's in pain. 'I don't know, I don't know.'

'Calm down.' I sit, watching him. 'Take a breath. Now tell me what the problem is.'

'It's Kitty.'

I meet his tormented gaze. 'Go on.'

'I walked with her to the pinch-faced woman's house. The window was partly open again, so she slipped in through it. I waited by the gate.' His ears flatten and he growls, so loud that I glance back at the house, worried that Mr Green will come out to see what's going on. 'She never came back.'

'What?'

'I waited for ages, but then I saw the window had been shut from the inside. So she couldn't get back out. I had to give up in the end. I thought it was better to come back and tell you what had happened. Only you weren't here either. And Pepper's locked up inside her house.' He lowers himself to the ground, his fur standing on end as though he's been in a fight. 'It's been awful. There was no one to talk to, and I didn't know what to do. The pinch-faced woman must have caught her.'

'Possibly.'

'Kitty could be dead,' he bursts out hysterically.

I am thinking hard. 'No, don't think like that. That woman is mean and cruel, obviously. You can see it in her face. But she's not a cat-killer.'

'How do you know?'

I have to calm him down. 'Because . . . I just do, that's all.' I nuzzle against the cat, worried by how cold he is. 'You're freezing.'

'No, I'm fine. Just a bit chilly, that's all.'

'You're sure?'

'Bertie, I'm covered in fur.'

'Good point.'

'What about Kitty? She's trapped in that house.'

'Okay, look, you need to trust me. I'm sure Kitty will get out again eventually. But she could be hurt. Or . . . or too upset to find her way back.' I hear Mr Green whistle for me, and glance over my shoulder, torn. I want to respond, to be a good dog. But I need Rico to hear me out first. 'Can you go back to that woman's house and see if you can spot Kitty inside? Don't risk capture. But just be there for her, in case she gets out.'

He nods slowly. 'For how long?'

'For as long as it takes. Which, knowing Kitty's ingenuity, shouldn't be too long.'

Rico hesitates, then blinks. 'Right.' His ears slowly straighten again, and his body posture relaxes. 'I guess I'll catch you later then. Time for the Paw Print Club to get involved again.' He pauses. 'Any news of Sam?'

I shake my head, miserably. 'I wish there was.'

'It's all going wrong,' he mutters.

'Don't say that,' I say with difficulty. I don't feel much more confident than Rico, but I can see he needs to be reassured. I push my shoulders back, lift my head and inject some optimism into my voice. 'Things are going to work out just fine, you'll see. Now come on, it's nearly dawn. Once the humans are awake, I'm going to do everything in my power to get them to the river. Meanwhile, you go and see if you can contact Kitty. Make sure she knows you're still waiting for her.'

He nods, and starts to run back into the trees. Then he stops and looks back at me. 'If I don't make it back, will you tell Pepper that I . . .'

'Chin up, Rico.' I give him a short, encouraging bark. 'You'll make it back.'

Rico takes a deep breath, then miaows back. 'See you later then, Bertie. Good luck.'

'Good luck, Rico.'

I bound back across the lawn to where Mr Green is waiting at the back door. He looks down at me.

'I would ask what on earth you were up to out there,' he says, his voice thick with exhaustion. 'But I'm beginning to know better. Come on, I've put some food down for you. I think you missed dinner last night.'

My tummy rumbles as I head for my heaped food bowl by the range. Too right I missed dinner. But how could I eat earlier when I was so fearful for Sam? Now at least I have a plan, and with some luck, it might just work out.

'Was it my fault, Bertie?' Mr Green asks suddenly. He closes the back door and turns to look directly at me, his eyes mournful. 'Did I chase Sam away, forgetting to make time for him, brushing his fears aside, always arguing with him?' He sounds close to breaking point. 'You and he are so close, he must have said something to you about . . . About me, about wanting to run away.'

I try to wag my tail, but this time it simply refuses to wag. Perhaps because I share his unhappiness over Sam's disappearance, and find it hard to understand how we all missed the signs. The boy's note pointed to his secret fear that he had caused his mother's death. I ought to have done more to keep his spirits up, and to push him and his dad closer together. But instead I was selfish, and behaved like a pest . . .

Well, at least I can try to comfort Mr Green now.

I force my sad tail to wag, and run to Mr Green, whining softly.

He looks down at me, and does not respond.

I jump up on my hind paws and dance round in a circle, acting the clown to make him laugh.

He watches my silly antics for a moment, then his eyes soften, crinkling round the edges. 'Oh, Bertie,' he says, a catch in his voice, then crouches to stroke me. 'I'm so glad you're still here. I should never have threatened to send you back to the shelter. That was an awful thing to say.' He keeps stroking me, his hand rhythmic on my spine. 'You're a good dog, aren't you? Good and loyal and warm-hearted. I wish I'd seen that before. But everything has been so hectic lately. And with Christmas coming, I miss Jenny so much it hurts.'

I drop back to four paws and wag my tail, panting gently at the exertion of my little dance. It's good to feel his hand stroking between my floppy ears and along my back. It's the first time Mr Green has shown me this level of affection, and it changes everything between us. I feel the love emanating from him, and send it right back with my dog-sense, keeping my eyes on his face, trying to apologise for all the little accidents, to show him how loyal and loving I want to be for the Greens.

It seems to be working too, from the way his face is relaxing.

'Go on,' he says at last, straightening up. 'Have some food, Bertie. I know you must be starving by now.'

'I don't know what I'm going to do if we don't get Sam back,' Mr Green murmurs, as I'm tucking hungrily into my dinner. He still sounds tired, but the terrible emptiness has gone from his voice. 'I'm trying to be strong, for your mother's sake at least, but I don't think I can bear another . . .' When he pauses, I look back up at him, puzzled. That's when I realise he is talking to the photograph of his dead wife. He finishes sadly on the word, 'Loss.'

I gulp down my mouthful, staring from him to the photograph. Gravy drips from my chin and I do not even bother to lick it up.

He thinks Sam may be dead. That the boy will never come back.

From the living room, I hear the clock striking the hour. It will be dawn soon. The signs are already there, a soft light creeping inexorably across the sky.

Suddenly, for the first time since Sam left, I'm no longer worried but frightened. What if Mr Green is right and we don't find him in time?

I don't think I could bear another loss either.

A few hours later, the police return with several cars and vans, and traipse in and out of the house, talking loudly, chatting on their radios, spreading maps over the kitchen table, and making 'fortifying' cups of tea for an exhausted-looking Granny M. Outside, the sky is light again, and the world is busy, people going out shopping for Christmas Eve, neighbours dropping by to wish the Greens all the best in their search for young Sam, the postman dropping by parcels, and the telephone constantly ringing.

Nobody has remembered to switch the Christmas lights on since the day before yesterday. The tree stands dead and unlit in the deserted living room.

I sniff around the shiny presents, still unsure what to do but determined to get the humans' attention somehow. Every now and then, I come across a wrapped present that smells of Sam, and my heart leaps a little, then sinks again.

One of the presents that smells of him is wrapped with extra-shiny paper. Suddenly I remember what Sam said to me before he ran away.

I can rely on you to see Dad gets the right present. Can't I, Bertie?

I whine sadly to myself.

Sam has to come home safely, and in time to give his dad his Christmas present. He just has to. The alternative is too horrible to consider. And it seems increasingly likely that I am the only one who can get him back.

But when I slip back into the crowded kitchen, to my dismay the police are talking yet again about a search in the wrong place.

'We had a sighting early this morning,' the policeman with shiny buttons is telling the Greens, 'over near the canal. A boy answering Sam's description was seen walking along the towpath just before dawn. So we're going to concentrate our search there.'

Granny M nods slowly. She looks very grey-faced after a sleepless night. 'Can we come along?'

'Margaret, no.' Mr Green looks horrified. 'It's too cold out today. I'll go instead. And someone needs to be here. Just in case Sam comes back on his own.'

She sighs. 'But I feel so useless, just sitting about in my kitchen, doing nothing. With all my neighbours offering to look for him, and on Christmas Eve too. It doesn't seem right.'

A policewoman smiles at her. 'You have some wonderful neighbours. There were dozens of them waiting outside when I arrived, all determined to join the search.'

Lying quietly at Granny M's feet, I listen to their conversation.

What was the other thing Sam said to me before he ran away?

I need to stay hidden.

There's nowhere to hide down near the canal. Only a few

bushes along the towpath. But at the river there's that special tree, the one with a hollow. The one where his mum and dad first kissed. The one he showed me proudly when we went fishing there together. The tree that always reminds him of his mum.

A large oak with a hollow like that would make a cosy shelter for a boy his age, perhaps somewhere to keep wrapped up and warm, out of the cold and scary dark.

Granny M finishes her second cup of tea and shakes her head at an offer of a third. 'No, thank you.' She glances at me, and I jump up at once, wagging my tail enthusiastically. 'Bertie needs to be walked.'

'I'll do it,' a young police officer says.

My heart sinks.

But to my relief, Granny M smiles at the young man, then refuses politely.

'I could do with the fresh air, to be honest.' She makes her weary way across to where my lead is hanging up. 'Come on, Bertie. Ten minutes' walkies. Then everyone's going off to search for Sam again. Maybe I could bake while I'm waiting. Bake something for . . . for Sam's return.'

Mr Green seems to be having some difficulty talking again. 'That's . . . that's a lovely idea, Margaret. Thank you.' His eyes look rather red this morning. 'I'll be out looking for him again soon too.'

Meanwhile, I am ecstatic.

This is my best chance. My chance to make a difference. My chance to show them all where Sam is hiding. Or at least where I hope he's hiding.

269

I turn in circles and hop about as she tries to attach the lead, barely able to contain my excitement. My tail is wagging back and forth so violently, it hits a policeman in the leg and he swears loudly. It's the man with shiny buttons. I glance back at him as she leads me to the front door, and see his face all cross and bunched-up like he wants to kick my bottom.

I guess that's what Mrs Minton used to call, 'Karma.'

When Granny M opens the door, we are confronted by all the wonderful neighbours the police officer mentioned. Many of them are standing on the Greens' front lawn in sturdy boots, thick coats or waterproofs, wrapped up with hats and woolly scarfs, and armed with walking sticks. All ages, all sizes, from young kids running about the lawn to older people who look like they could hardly make it to the end of the street, let alone all the way to the canal and back.

Oh,' Granny M says blankly.

'Good morning, Margaret,' one of the old men says, touching his cap. 'Don't you and John worry, we'll find your grandson and have him home with you in good time for Christmas Day.'

'Thank you, Mr T . . . Terry,' she stammers, then gazes about in amazement. 'Oh, hello, Mrs Perkins. Mr . . . erm, Mr Colley too. How kind of you to come along. And Miss Chakrabarti, isn't it? From the library?'

She shakes her head, leading me gingerly between the assembled crowd, suddenly looking very small and old beside all these robust friends and neighbours in their walking gear. 'Goodness, so many of you. And up so early in the morning. You're all very generous. I . . . I don't know what to say.'

'Merry Christmas?' a teenager calls out shyly.

'Oh yes, thank you, dear.' Granny M puts a shaking hand to her mouth, tears in her eyes. 'Thank you all. Thank you so much. And yes, Merry Christmas.'

'We'll bring Sam home,' Miss Chakrabarti assures her.

'Thank you.' Margaret hesitates. 'I want to help too, but John thinks someone should stay home in case Sam comes home.'

Miss Chakrabarti smiles. 'Of course. That's a good idea.'

'I need to walk Bertie now. But I won't be long.'

They move aside for her, calling out Christmas greetings, and she hurries through the rest of the crowd, head down, tears falling down her cheeks now.

'Please don't upset yourself, Margaret,' one woman says as we pass, touching Granny M's sleeve in a brief gesture of comfort. I recognise her as one of the ladies who comes round sometimes to help out with Margaret's charity work. 'He'll be home for Christmas Day, I'm sure.'

I trot beside Granny M, light-pawed on the cold pavement, turning heads as usual with my distinctive splodgy ears and back markings, my tail wagging exuberantly. Granny M fumbles for a handkerchief in her coat pocket, and dries her tear-stained cheeks. Then she blows her nose and pushes the hanky back into her pocket.

'What generous friends I have, Bertie,' she murmurs, glancing down at me, and then shakes her head wonderingly. 'Giving up their spare time to look for my grandson.

And at Christmas too. What can I have done to deserve such lovely neighbours, Bertie? The police are very good, of course. But all these other people . . . I really don't know how we would manage without their help.'

A moment later we reach the alley that goes towards the park.

Granny M begins to turn down the alley, and I dig in my heels suddenly, shoulders down, tail flat to the ground, and resist.

'Bertie, don't be naughty, dear.' She tugs on the lead. 'This way.'

I growl and tug her the other way, further on along the street that leads to the main road, the way that eventually leads to the river.

'Bertie, come to heel,' she tells me, jerking on the lead, and makes a sobbing noise. 'Bertie, please behave for once, there's a good dog. You know it's this way. Down the alley.'

But I refuse, and in fact start to back away, dragging her a few feet further along the street.

'Oh, no, this way!'

She's tearful again now. I hate doing this to her. But this is the best and only way I can explain to her where Sam is hiding.

She drags me back, and I yelp, then jump up and down, barking wildly.

'WOOF! WOOF! WOOF!'

The crowd outside the Greens' house have been watching this little dance, clearly bemused. One of them comes running over. It's the woman she called Miss Chakrabarti, the lady from the library.

'What is it?' the young woman asks. 'Can I help? Is your dog misbehaving?'

'He won't go down the alley to the park,' Granny M explains, and shakes her head, looking flustered. 'I don't know what's got into him. Bertie usually loves the park.'

I drag desperately on the leash, trying to shift her.

Miss Chakrabarti watches me a moment, hands on hips. Then she says slowly, 'Well, I could be wrong, but I think he wants you to go that way today.' Then she frowns. 'Do you think he might . . .'

'Might what?'

'Is it possible he knows where Sam is?'

I bark, thrilled that someone seems to understand at last what I'm trying to communicate.

'WOOF! WOOF! WOOF!'

Then I start to back up again, dragging poor old Granny M along with me, my whole body pulling against her.

Granny M stares, then takes a deep breath. 'Well, I suppose it's possible.' She gives up trying to restrain me and starts to follow me instead. 'I feel silly, doing this. But he is quite a clever dog.' I pull harder, wagging my tail fiercely, and she speeds up, breathing harder. 'Go on, then. Take us to Sam, if you think you know where he is.'

'Let me hold him for you,' Miss Chakrabarti says helpfully, and takes the straining lead from Granny M. Her eyes widen as I pull her along too, head down, intent on getting my message through. 'Gosh, he's pretty strong, isn't he? And determined. I wouldn't want him to pull you over!'

She turns and waves back to some of her acquaintances in the crowd.

'Hey, we think the dog might know something!'

Several run over at once, looking excited, then others catch up with them, then a few more. There's Pepper's owner in his raincoat and flat cap, Sadiq from the youth club where Granny M volunteers once a week, always-friendly Mr Bradley from across the road, wheeling his little boy in a buggy today, and even young Harriet who helps her mum deliver the newspapers at the weekends, and many more I don't recognise, but who greet Margaret by name, smiling and patting her on the shoulder.

Poor Granny M looks quite dazed by all their reassurances.

But it's exactly the audience I need. Suddenly I'm dragging Miss Chakrabarti along the street, followed by Granny Margaret and a whole crowd of friends and neighbours.

'What does he know?' Harriet calls out, excitedly.

Mr Bradley pushes his buggy hurriedly along behind Miss Chakrabarti. 'What's happening? Has Bertie found Sam's scent?'

'I'm not sure,' Miss Chakrabarti tells him, panting as I drag her along. 'But it's possible. Dogs can track people anywhere, I think.'

'That's right,' Sadiq volunteers, sounding very confident, 'and he's a beagle. They're meant to be brilliant at finding things. Good noses, you know?'

Harriet asks, 'Can I hold his lead for a bit?'

'Better not,' Mr Bradley tells her, not unkindly, 'you might not be able to hold him. Look at the way he's powering along!'

And Granny M's voice above the others, calling out from behind, 'Good boy, Bertie. Find Sam. Show us where he is. I know you can do it.'

Cars hoot as we pass, more people tag along, then some police officers appear and start following me too, asking Miss Chakrabarti questions and seeming astonished by what she's saying.

'Are you sure about this?' one policeman demands, a little breathless as he catches up with the front of the pack.

Granny M sounds impatient. 'Of course not. But it's worth trying, isn't it? And he is a clever dog. Our clever Bertie.'

The officer gets on his radio, and soon a police car pulls alongside us, and Mr Green jumps out to join us, along with the older police officer with the shiny buttons.

'Margaret?'

Granny M sounds a little breathless too. 'Oh, John, thank goodness. We're following Bertie. Miss Chakrabarti thinks he may know where Sam is.'

'The police told me, but I couldn't quite believe —'

'I know it sounds unlikely. But perhaps we ought to have more faith in the little chap. Look at his legs go! He's obviously very keen to take us somewhere. Let's find out where.'

'But the police have organised a search party.'

'This is a search party too. Our own search party.' She hesitates. 'And Bertie's leading it.'

For a moment he says nothing, and I half expect him to persuade Granny M and Miss Chakrabarti against walking any further. It must seem very odd to anyone watching us, all these humans following a beagle along the road.

But to my surprise Mr Green reaches through to pat my head in an affectionate way. 'All right, Bertie,' he says approvingly. 'You keep going. I just hope . . .' Again, I hear that little crack in his voice. 'I hope you know where to find my boy.' He adds, 'You look tired though, Margaret. Are you okay to keep walking?'

'I'm fine, don't fuss.'

Mr Green falls in beside her. He lowers his voice. 'All the same, this is very . . . unexpected. Do you think Bertie really knows where Sam is?'

'I think *Bertie* thinks he knows. He and Sam have been close lately, remember. So let's trust him for once.' It sounds like she's smiling. 'Humans don't have a monopoly on wisdom. Sometimes animals know more than us.'

So now I have Mr Green and Granny M and Miss Chakrabarti behind me, and all the neighbours, and the police, and dozens of others behind them, and a police car rolling slowly alongside us while we stay by the road.

Townspeople stare from cars and front gardens and driveways, and cats on fences hiss as we pass, and dogs bark wildly, and a few of them even run after us too, and I'm at the front of this Christmas circus, splodgy ears flapping along the pavement, head down, shoulders braced, dragging all of them after me like they're on a rope.

We walk for ages. Well, it seems like a long way to me.

Down the street, up the main road, across the busy junction, with the police flagging down cars so we can all cross safely, through the industrial estate, and over the rough grasslands at the back towards the river. And the humans keep walking too, following my lead, ignoring the cold, chatting together, laughing, cheering, shouting out my name, encouraging me, like a vast rippling pack at my back.

I feel like the most important dog in the world.

Finally I can smell the river, its thick unmistakeable scent on the air, and suddenly I'm barking again, barking at the top of my voice, dragging harder than ever on the lead.

Because I smell something else too.

❦ TWENTY-FOUR ❦

I drag them over to a thicket of trees not far from the river bank, my nose snuffling along the rough ground the whole way, utterly focused on tracking my young master. I can smell Sam. At least I feel sure I can. Little sniffs of scent that seem achingly familiar. Yet I can't see the boy anywhere.

My heart plummets. What if I've made a mistake?

What if Sam's not here after all?

Or he's there, but . . .

I can't bear to consider that possibility.

'He's stopping,' Miss Chakrabarti says, sounding excited.

As I come to a halt beside the oak with the hollow, she stops too, still holding my lead and whispering little words of encouragement.

I look up, sniffing the gnarled old trunk. That's his scent, for sure.

To my dismay, Sam is not in the hollow of the oak. I look about, but the place is cold and desolate. No sign of him anywhere.

So what have I been following? A phantom scent? Or perhaps it's his scent, but from last time we were here at the river. Perhaps in my hope and enthusiasm I have miscalculated how long this scent was laid down.

Behind us, Mr Green stops, and Granny M alongside him, supported by his arm. And young Harriet who sometimes helps deliver the newspapers with her mum, Sadiq who volunteers at the youth club, Mr Bradley with his son in a buggy, smiley Stephanie with her pug, Chaplin, and all the others beyond them; the ones I know and those I don't, the assembled walkers slowing as they arrive, one by one, at the empty riverbank.

There's a long awkward moment of silence. Everyone stares first at the cold flowing river, then at the other bank. The whole place looks tranquil but definitely uninhabited.

Mr Green is looking around himself too. He turns on his heel, surveying the parking area, the trees, the water.

'Is this where Bertie was leading us all this time? To the river?' He pauses. 'There's nothing here.'

I can hear bitter disappointment in his voice.

'Oh dear,' Granny M mutters.

They look at me, and I hang my head. I was so sure . . .

I am so deflated that I don't even see Sam step out from behind one of the trees.

'There he is!' someone cries.

Mr Green exclaims, 'Sam!'

I look up, my heart racing.

It's Sam, all right.

Still wrapped in his coat, gloved and scarved, and with his woolly hat slightly askew, he looks cold and shaken and deeply unhappy.

But he's alive, and seems unhurt.

279

I bound forward so powerfully at the sight, I snap the lead out of Miss Chakrabarti's hand. Side by side with Mr Green, I run across the frosty grass, barking joyfully.

Sam stares.

Not just at me, but at his father and grandmother, and Miss Chakrabarti, and the police, and all his neighbours and friends, some with excited dogs, some with walking sticks, and the dozens of people who have simply tagged along behind us on the way out of town, wondering what was going on and where we were all going.

'Bertie,' he gasps, and sinks to his knees as I reach him first. The boy embraces me, crying and gulping into my shoulder. His chilled body shakes as he adds brokenly, 'I thought I'd never see you again.'

A few seconds later, Mr Green is there too, hugging his son, in tears as well. 'Oh, Sam,' he keeps saying, 'Sam, my boy, you're alive.'

'I'm so sorry, Dad.'

'No need to apologise, Sam,' his dad says, holding him so tight I wonder the boy can even breathe.

Granny M sobs with delight. 'Sam, my darling, I do love you,' she tells him at once, tears falling down her cheeks without her bothering to wipe them away. 'You know that, don't you? I probably haven't said it enough, and I should have done.' She looks so happy to see her grandson; it's as though all her dreams have come true at once. It's hard to remember how ashen Granny M looked this morning, how full of despair, seeing her joyous smile now. 'Come here, let me hold you.'

She hugs him too, the two grown-ups leaning into the boy together in a comforting triangle. Luckily, no one seems to mind that I am capering about between their legs like a mad thing, ecstatic to have my young master back.

'I'm sorry, Gran,' Sam tells her too, his voice muffled against her coat. 'It was stupid of me to run away.'

Mr Green's hat has fallen off, I notice, and his hair is standing on end. 'You don't need to say anything, Sam. We've missed you so badly.' He hugs his son again, then releases him reluctantly. 'My goodness, you're freezing. Let's get you home, son, and into a warm bath.'

'No, I . . . I have to say something first.'

Sam looks round at everyone as they encircle him; the police, his neighbours, the people who followed along as we tracked him, his father and his grandmother.

'Dad, Granny M,' Sam says, and swallows hard, then rubs his sleeve across his reddened eyes. 'I know Mum's death was all my fault.'

Granny Margaret looks horrified. 'No, no, it wasn't.'

'Yes, it was.'

His father shakes his head at once. 'No, what you put in your note, Sam, it simply isn't true. You have to believe us.'

'No, it was that football match,' Sam insists. 'I nagged her to come and watch me play, even though I knew she was sick. I was so selfish. I didn't care what might happen. Then she went into hospital, and . . . and she never came out again. The nurses said she wasn't strong enough to fight any more.'

He sobs, staring at his dad with fresh tears running down his cheeks. 'Because of me . . . I made her come out to that football match instead of resting. And she had no strength left.'

'Sam, no.'

'I killed her. I killed Mum.'

'Wait.' His father grabs Sam as the boy twists away, and holds him tightly. 'Listen, you've got it wrong. That football match . . . Your mum told me how proud she was of you, that it was one of her most treasured memories, watching you play that day. Being able to get there, to stand and watch the match.' He is crying again now. 'I should have told you this before, made it clearer what happened. Your mum loved you very much, Sam. But she had cancer. And sometimes when the cancer is really bad, there's nothing the doctors and nurses can do. That's what happened to your mum. She was sick a long time before then, and she knew time was short. That's why she wanted to spend as much time as possible with you.'

Sam pulls back. 'So —'

'Her going into hospital was nothing to do with getting tired at that football match. It wasn't your fault. You made her last days out of hospital worth living, Sam. She told me that before . . .' He pauses. 'Don't ever think of that time as anything but very, very special.'

'I didn't realise,' Sam says in a small voice.

'Because I didn't talk to you properly afterwards. As I should have done. I was so busy thinking about my own feelings, my own grief, that I wasn't able to see how much pain you were in too.' His dad hugs him again, compulsively. 'I'm so sorry, Sam. All this has been my fault, I understand that now. But I'm going to make it up to you, I promise.'

'It's okay,' Sam begins, but his dad interrupts.

'No, it's not okay,' Mr Green insists, his tone emotional. 'I wasn't sure how to deal with our grief, and I got my parenting the wrong way round. I thought it was important to show you that daily life hadn't changed for you, that there was continuity. Basically, that you couldn't play up and get away with it. But somewhere in there, I was far too hard on you. I forgot to tell you how much I love you. How proud I am of your strength and resilience since . . . since your mum died.'

'Oh, Dad.' Sam buries his face in his dad's shoulder.

I bark and try to jump up at my owners, to join in the hugging, but Miss Chakrabarti makes a grab for my lead. I dance quickly away, happy to be free for once.

'Now, Bertie,' she says, grinning. 'They don't need you getting in the way right now. Though you were very clever to find Sam for us.'

Harriet pats my back as I squeeze past her. She has a lovely smile, I realise. 'Thank you, Bertie. I'm glad Sam isn't lost any more. I like him.'

I wag my tail happily.

All around us, everyone seems to be hugging now. Neighbours are shaking hands and laughing. Total strangers are spontaneously embracing and only afterwards introducing themselves. People shout out, 'Merry Christmas!' and 'Well done, Bertie!', others wishing Sam all the best, raising their voices to be heard above the sound of the crowd.

Mr Bradley lifts his child out of the buggy, holding him up to see what's happening. 'Look, it's Sam. We found him. Or rather, Bertie did.'

Suddenly I hear something that tugs at my heart. A dog, barking. But when I look round, my tail still wagging, I can't see anything but legs and feet. There are still people all around us, though they stepped discreetly back while Sam and his dad and Granny M were talking. So it's hard to get a clear view. Yet I can hear a dog barking somewhere near the river.

A dog who sounds like . . .

Before I can formulate my thought, Granny M appears.

She bends to rub the top of my head, and I glance up at her, distracted. 'There you are, Bertie. You are a very good dog. In fact, I think you're forgiven for all the trouble you've caused lately.' She smiles, glancing at her watch. 'And there's still time to visit the butcher before they close for Christmas, and find a juicy bone for your lunch tomorrow.'

A juicy bone? I grin, and my mouth waters with anticipation.

There's that bark again.

Perplexed, I weave past Granny M and Miss Chakrabarti, who are chatting animatedly now, and Pepper's owner, who has removed his flat cap and is scratching his head at what has happened, and the policeman with the shiny buttons, who is busy on his radio, his expression also one of astonished relief. I suppose he must be telling the police helicopter to return to base, and his officers to call off their search of the town, and the dog-handlers that a beagle has found him instead.

I bet that will annoy Sarah, the police sniffer spaniel.

Under other circumstances, I might have grinned at that thought. But I have no time. Instead I keep running. My lead trails behind me like an extra-long tail, and though several people try to grab it, I am too quick for them.

'Hey,' Sadiq shouts, spotting me, 'where are you going?'

I like Sadiq but I can't stop for him. I have a more urgent mission. I begin to run through the crowd, looking around myself all the time.

The bark is getting louder.

It's so familiar. The fur on my back rises and prickles.

I run among the people, searching wildly, my nose to the ground, ignoring their shouts and exclamations and laughter, and suddenly there she is.

'Molly!'

She's barking, jumping up and down, grinning, and on the other end of her lead is the pinch-faced woman. But the woman is not frowning sternly.

She's smiling.

'Oh my goodness,' the woman says, her voice quite friendly, not hoarse and grim as I imagined, 'another beagle, and you look just like my Molly.'

Molly and I stand together, tails wagging joyously, rubbing noses and revelling in the warm press of fur and familiar smell.

'Molly, I've missed you so much!'

'Bertie.' My sister can't seem to stop grinning. 'I must be dreaming. I can't believe I've actually found you again.'

I breathe in her wonderful scent. My sister, and she's really here, standing right beside me, leaning into me as I am leaning into her. To me, Molly smells like family, a glorious scent that reminds me of puppyhood and good times and our only dimly remembered mother. And we're back together at last.

It's the best moment of my life.

'You're not dreaming, Molly,' I assure her deeply. 'It really is me!'

'Bertie.' Her large dark eyes are glassy with emotion. 'When that cat came to see me, I couldn't quite believe it. Then I saw you through the glass and—'

'I'm sorry I couldn't rescue you as planned.'

'It doesn't matter. Honestly. This was more important.' She rubs my nose with her own. 'Dearest Bertie, I've missed you too. More than I can say.'

'But how is this possible? Why are you here?'

'My owner said there was a lost boy, and we all had to come out to hunt for him. But I had no idea he was your human. That you would be here too.'

'Yes, he's my human, my Sam, and I found him. Me, I found him.' I bark excitedly and turn in a wild circle, then nuzzle against her body again. 'Oh, Molly, don't ever leave me again. I tried to get you away from the pinch-faced woman, but then we couldn't work out how to open that door, and last night Sam went missing. I wanted to come for you, I really did.'

I hesitate, suddenly remembering. 'Kitty . . . Wait, didn't you see her? I sent her to tell you why I couldn't be there to rescue you last night.'

Molly stares. 'So that's why she was in the house. I knew

there was a cat upstairs, I could smell her. But I didn't know who or why. When Camilla – that's my owner – got up this morning, she opened the toilet door and a cat ran past her and down the stairs. Camilla let the cat out of the front door, and she ran off at top speed.' She blinks. 'I never even had a chance to see who it was.'

I feel bad for my fellow Paw Print Club member. 'She must have jumped inside, like the night before, then found the door of the room was shut. But then couldn't get back out again. Her brother Rico was watching the house, and said the window looked like it was shut.'

'The window swung shut and trapped her,' Molly explains. 'She must have knocked it when she jumped inside. Oh dear, poor Kitty. Stuck in the toilet all night.'

'But at least we've found each other again.' I lick her face and she giggles, her tail wagging. 'Now all I need to do is persuade my owners to adopt you and —'

'Oh, Bertie, that's such a wonderful idea. But I couldn't leave Camilla.'

'But —'

'No, she's lovely. And she needs me.' She bends close, and whispers, 'She's very lonely, you see. People think she's mean. But it's not her fault. She's too shy to make friends easily. She gets tongue-tied, and never knows what to say, so everyone gets the wrong impression.'

'I see.'

'Camilla's really very nice. In fact, we're best friends.'

There's something in my sister's voice, the appealing tilt of her head, some new and unexpected emotion. Is that . . .

love? For her human? That must be how I sound when I talk about Sam, I think slowly. And Mr Green. And Granny Margaret. I'm relieved that she has made such a good friend of her owner, of course. But it makes me realise how drastically things have changed since we lived together at the Mintons', and how little I know about my sister's life now.

There's so much we need to catch up on. And so little time in which to do it.

I look at her, crestfallen and a little sad. 'So you don't want to . . . to come and live with me and Sam?'

'I love you, you know that. We're family, we always will be. And I want to see as much of you as I can now that we've found each other again. Please believe that. But Camilla is my owner. And she needs me too.' She looks up at the woman with obvious adoration. 'We need each other.'

It's hard but I try to understand. All this time I've been imagining our reunion, and how grateful my sister would be for having been rescued from the pinch-faced woman. But now it turns out that she is perfectly happy where she is, and does not need to be rescued. I am pleased for her, but it's hard to come to terms with the fact that, even though we've found each other again at last, we will not be spending the rest of our lives together as I had always dreamed.

'But Kitty and Rico – the cats who live with me and the Greens – they saw your owner going into old people's homes, and coming out with a basket. As though . . .' I hesitate, not wanting to hurt her feelings, then decide it's better for her to know the worst. 'Well, I'm sorry to say, it looked as though she was stealing from them.'

Molly does not look concerned. In fact, she laughs. 'Camilla does charity work, Bertie. Helping old people stay connected to each other, even when they can't get out much any more. She carries things like letters and cakes between elderly friends, that's all. Sometimes she's collecting, sometimes delivering. Not *stealing*.'

I say nothing. But I feel a little foolish.

'Bertie, there you are!'

Sam and Mr Green appear. His dad's arm is lying across his shoulder, and Sam is leaning into him. Both their faces are wreathed in smiles. It looks like Sam understands now that his mother's death was not his fault at all, and that his dad loves him very much.

I am so pleased for them both, all I can do is stand and wag my tail.

Which is my downfall.

Before I can escape again, my lead is grabbed up by Mr Green, and I'm being tugged away from Molly. 'Come on, Bertie,' Mr Green tells me happily, 'it's home time. The police have talked to me and Sam, and everything's been sorted out. Granny M says a trip to the butcher is in order before they close for the Christmas holiday. You deserve a bone for today's work!'

That bone is very tempting. I can't deny it.

But Molly is a thousand times more important than a juicy bone.

So I bark, and pull away from my owners, even growling a little to show how passionately I feel. I don't care if it means getting into trouble for yet more disobedience. I haven't found my sister again only to be parted from her immediately.

Sam shakes his head, looking disappointed. 'Oh, Bertie, come on. Not now! I've got tons to tell you.'

'Sam, wait. Look at that other little beagle, he's the spitting image of Bertie.' Mr Green sounds astonished. 'Only slightly smaller.'

'He's a *she* actually,' the pinch-faced woman – who I must remember is called Camilla – tells them, and then smiles shyly at him and Sam. What Molly said is true, I realise with a start. Her smile does indeed transform her face, so she suddenly looks soft and open, and very, very kind. 'Pardon me for asking, but did you get your dog from the shelter?'

'Yes,' Mr Green says, looking at her in an odd way.

'I thought as much. You see, I have a suspicion they may be brother and sister. I did want to take them both, but sadly I didn't feel confident enough to handle two dogs at once. I've never owned a dog before, you see.' Camilla looks down at Molly affectionately. 'Though Molly is a sweetie, she really is. I've never been happier in my life since bringing her home.'

'So, you mean, these two are litter mates?' Sam demands, staring from me to Molly and back again.

'I think so, yes. And they do seem to know each other.' There's a sudden sadness in Camilla's voice. 'For a few weeks after she came to live with me, Molly would howl and cry herself to sleep every night. I felt awful then. It was obvious she was missing her sibling. I even went back to the shelter to see if I could adopt her brother too. But they said he'd already gone to a family.' She flashes them a smile. 'You, as it happens.'

Mr Green raises his eyebrows. 'I had no idea he had a sister.'

She looks embarrassed, then pulls on Molly's lead a little. 'Well,' she says awkwardly, 'I suppose we'd better go home. I still have to collect my Christmas food for tomorrow's lunch. Though of course there's not much. It's only me and Molly this year.' She looks sad again, her head bowed. 'My mother used to live with me, but she . . . passed away last January.'

'I'm so sorry,' Mr Green tells her.

I bark, and wag my tail to show I'm sorry too.

Molly barks as well, straight after me.

Like an echo.

An echo I've missed so much these past few months without her.

I look down at her bad leg, suddenly aware that my sister may be in pain. 'How's your leg? You must have walked such a long way today. Do you need me to lick it better for you?'

She smiles. 'I've missed you looking after my bad leg,' she admits, but shakes her head. 'No need though. Camilla fixed it for me.'

I am perplexed. 'What? How?'

'She saw me limping, and took me to the vet. He was very good. He took X-rays, then gave her some special cream to rub into my leg, and some exercises to do with me, and after a few weeks, it was much better. It's not perfect, of course. The vet said it will never be perfect. But I hardly feel it now.'

She shrugs. 'A little twinge when it's cold and rainy, but Camilla always rubs me dry after our walks, and rubs in the cream, and then my leg doesn't hurt any more.'

I look round at her new owner, and thank her silently in my heart. 'That's marvellous, Molly.' But I feel a bit sad too, and struggle against the feeling. 'So you don't really need me any more, Little Sis.'

'Of course I do,' she exclaims, and butts my shoulder with her head. 'You great softie, Bertie. I need you to keep me company. And to make me laugh.'

'Oh that.' I chase my own tail until I get dizzy and fall over. Molly stands over me, laughing and panting, and then licks my face. 'Faugh.'

'Idiot.'

'Nag.'

She grins and sits back, clearly delighted. 'Oh, this is going to be the best Christmas ever.'

'Isn't it just?'

Sam has been looking back over his shoulder at the slowly disappearing crowd of neighbours and well-wishers. I can see his gaze fixed on young Harriet, who waves a cheery goodbye before being led away by her mum.

He waves back, a secretive smile on his face.

Sam looks round at his dad, blurting out, 'They ought to see each other again, don't you think?' He blushes, then adds, 'Molly and Bertie, I mean.'

'Well, only if Molly's owner wants that too.' His father is still looking oddly at Camilla. 'Sorry, but you're . . . Camilla, aren't you? I think we were at primary school together.'

Camilla gives a little laugh, clearly embarrassed, not looking at him directly. 'Yes, it's me. I recognised you at once, John. You haven't changed much. But I didn't like to . . .' She glances at Sam, then says more softly, 'I read about your bereavement in the local paper. I'm very sorry.'

'Thank you.'

I watch them curiously, wagging my tail. So if these two know each other, does that mean I can get to spend more time with my sister?

'And I'm very glad you found Sam in the end,' Camilla says. 'What an adventure it's been, walking out here with everyone. I've enjoyed being part of it.'

Sam stands up, nodding to me proudly. 'That was Bertie. One of my friends, a girl called Harriet, just told me how he sniffed me out, all the way here from our house in town.'

'He's a very clever dog,' she agrees kindly, then fishes in her bag and produces a small white card, handing it to Mr Green with a hesitant look. 'Look, my email address is there. Do please let me know if you'd like Molly and Bertie to go for a walk together one day. Maybe in the park or along the canal path? We go for a longer walk too on Saturday mornings, out in the country. It would be lovely if you could join us sometimes. You, and Sam, and Bertie, of course.'

'I'd love that,' Mr Green says, smiling warmly. Then corrects himself, 'I mean, I'm sure Bertie would love . . . erm, enjoy that.'

He seems to like Camilla very much, I think, and wink at Molly.

'Well, goodbye.' The woman walks away, pulling Molly after her.

I wag my tail fiercely. 'Goodbye, Molly,' I call out, and my sister looks back at me, also wagging her tail.

'Goodbye, Bertie.' Her voice breaks a little, but then she rallies. I know that look in her large, dark eyes. It's her 'chin-up' expression, the one she uses when she's being brave for my sake. 'I'm sure we'll see each other again soon.'

I gulp, and try not to whimper as my sister is led away. She's right, of course. Now that the Greens know we are from the same litter, we'll probably see each other very soon. But it doesn't make a second separation much easier to bear, not when we've only just found each other again after months of uncertainty and heartsick yearning.

Mr Green watches them for a moment too, then suddenly calls out, 'Wait.' He runs after them while I am forced to wait with Sam, who is busy talking to some of the other people who walked out with us from town. Harriet is there, with smiling eyes; she seems to have him fascinated. I wag my tail, remembering how she said she liked Sam. He likes Harriet too; he's mentioned her name several times before. Perhaps they can become proper friends after this.

It's hard not to wonder what Mr Green is saying to Camilla and my sister though.

Granny M appears, flanked by several neighbours, friends and police officers, all of them patting her on the back. She keeps saying, 'Thank you,' her eyes shining, her face bright with joy.

'It's wonderful to see you reunited with your grandson,' Mr Bradley tells her kindly, and heads off with his son in his buggy.

Granny M turns to thank Sadiq for his help.

The burly young man shakes his head. 'Happy to help anytime,' he insists, and nods a farewell to Sam. 'This year, it will be a very happy and peaceful Christmas celebration for your family, I think.' He reaches down to pat my head. 'Good job, Bertie. You look after Margaret now, you hear me? Get her home and out of this cold weather.'

Granny M is looking a little tired and chilled, I think, and wag my tail approvingly at that idea. Definitely time to take her home, where she can sit down with her feet up and a nice cup of tea in her hand.

Once we've stopped at the butcher's, of course. I haven't forgotten the offer of that juicy bone.

'Sam, we're getting a lift home with the police. You need to come along. Bertie too.' She frowns. 'Where's your father?'

At that moment, Mr Green dashes back, a little breathless, looking slightly flushed. 'Sorry, I had to speak to —'

Briefly, he explains about Camilla and Molly. Then he adds, with a slight hesitation, 'I've invited them both over for Christmas lunch tomorrow. I hope you don't mind, Margaret. But Camilla's all on her own this Christmas. Besides, I thought Bertie deserved some doggy company after his fantastic work today, tracking down Sam.'

A wise expression on her face, Granny M looks after Camilla and Molly, then turns to study his face closely. 'No,

I don't mind at all. There's plenty of food to go round. The more the merrier.' She grins at me. 'And Bertie can play outside with his sister while we're doing the washing up.'

Everything seems to have worked out perfectly, I realise, looking up at them all with satisfaction. Sam has been found safe and sound, and is reconciled with his dad; Molly and I will be seeing each other again soon; her owner is not the wicked monster I thought she was; and even Mr Green seems to be dealing better with his grief over his wife's death.

As old Mrs Minton liked to say at moments like this, 'Life is good.'

I stop wagging my tail, amid the chaos of everyone saying goodbye to each other, and suddenly remember our old friends from the Mintons': Biscuit and Jethro, and the elegant Tina. I wonder where they are now, and if they too have found happy homes. Maybe one day I'll meet them again, walking along the street, or here by the river, or in the supermarket car park in the back of a moving car . . .

Because you never know when someone special is going to come rushing back into your life, and change everything.

'Come on, Bertie,' Sam says with a huge smile, and takes my lead. 'It's Christmas Eve, I've been awake all night and I'm zonked. Time to go home.'

❀ EPILOGUE ❀

It's still dark outside when I am suddenly woken by the bedside lamp coming on. For a few minutes, I ignore the intrusive light as best I can, allowing myself to surface slowly from a very satisfying dream about bones. I am aware of the sound of rustling and excited squeals, but do not open my heavy eyelids.

Sam gets impatient.

I jump at the sound of a loud party horn being blown right by my ear, the unfurled paper bopping me on the nose.

Ouch.

'Wake up, Bertie,' he says excitedly, and prods me. 'It's Christmas morning, and Santa's been here. Look at all this!'

Santa?

I raise my head to find a large sack on the bed, toys spilling out of it, a glittering and astonishing hoard of objects. Sam had mentioned a 'Christmas stocking' last night, but I was exhausted by then and had no idea what he was talking about, so simply went to sleep next to him. But now I see the small toys and odd items and glistening bags of sweets scattered across the bed, and share his air of excitement as I sniff the tasty-smelling packets.

Good times.

He rakes some of the toys towards himself, sitting up in bed in his blue flannel pyjamas. 'Hey,' he exclaims, and shakes a small felt hat at me. It jingles irritatingly, a bell at the tip. 'This must be for you. Clever Santa.'

I have a sudden memory of old Mrs Minton pulling a cracker with old Mr Minton, then both of them wearing paper Santa hats while we dogs waited expectantly under the dining table in the hope of turkey scraps.

He leans forward with a grin. 'Come on, Bertie. Let's see what you look like in a Christmas hat.'

Oh no you don't.

I scrabble backwards but not quickly enough, and end up wearing a lopsided felt Christmas hat. It slopes over one ear, jingling madly as I reach the edge of the bed and have to stop before I fall off.

He laughs. 'Brilliant!'

I look back at the boy quizzically. Really? I save you from spending Christmas night in the dark hollow of a tree, and this is how you reward me? With the ritual humiliation of a Santa hat?

But I'm pleased that he's looking cheerful again. Appearing ridiculous is surely a small price to pay for my master's happiness.

I dip my head to one side and the bell jingles again. Sam laughs, watching with delight. I shake my head, and he laughs more. Then I back up and fall off the bed, to the accompaniment of his snorting laughter. To my relief, the Christmas hat falls off as I hit the carpet. Back on my feet in seconds, I grip the hat between my teeth, mock-growl at the silly object, and then shake it so violently that it jingles and jingles and jingles . . .

Sam rocks with laughter, holding his sides now.

I shake the hat even more hysterically, determined to kill the bell before it kills me. My growls grow louder and more menacing.

'Hush, Bertie, not so loud,' Sam somehow manages to say between his giggles and snorts. 'It's only five o'clock in the morning. Everyone's asleep.'

But it's too late.

The door opens and Mr Green is suddenly there, in his dressing gown.

I drop the Christmas hat, looking round at him in consternation. He must be here to tell Sam off for making so much noise.

But to my amazement, Mr Green is smiling. He turns on the main light and exclaims at the bed strewn with toys and sweets. 'What's all this? Has Santa been?'

'Sorry, Dad. Did we wake you?'

'Don't worry about that. Waking up while it's still dark is what Christmas morning is all about.' Mr Green sits on the edge of Sam's bed and throws his arms round his son, giving him a loving hug. 'Merry Christmas, Sam.'

As he hugs his dad back, Sam's grin couldn't get much wider. 'Merry Christmas, Dad.'

'I see Bertie doesn't like his Santa hat.'

'I think he's okay with the hat, actually. It's the bell he doesn't like.'

'You can't have Christmas without bells, Bertie.'

There's fluff in my mouth from the felt hat. I spit it out, and they both laugh. So I pick up the hat again and shake it some more, to entertain them with jingling.

'Santa Bertie,' Sam dubs me.

'I can just see him as a reindeer, pulling Santa's sled.'

'He'd drag it so hard, he'd end up pulling the sled right over and spilling all the Santa sacks in the snow. I expect Father Christmas would be *furious*.'

Mr Green smiles, looking very relaxed and mellow. 'No, he'd forgive Bertie, of course. Just like we do. Look at that little face. How can you not love him?'

Their laughter and smiling faces make me feel happy again, I realise. Happier than I can ever remember feeling before. I have found my sister, and Molly is happy too, with her new owner Camilla. I managed to find Sam too when he ran away, and everyone told me how clever I am. And I still have the Christmas turkey to come, and whatever scraps I can beg from the table.

The door creaks open, and there's Granny Margaret, in her housecoat and slippers, peeping in at us. To my surprise, she does not look annoyed either to have been woken up in the middle of the night.

'Merry Christmas, Sam,' she says cheerily. 'Merry Christmas, John.' She studies the toys on the bed. 'How marvellous. So you were a good boy this year.'

'Of course he was,' John says at once, his arm still round his son's shoulders. 'You're always good, aren't you, Sam?'

Sam manages a lopsided smile. 'Erm . . .'

They both laugh at him.

300

Granny M belts up her housecoat and continues soothingly, 'Well, since we're all getting such an early start, I thought I'd get up and fry the giblets for Bertie and the cats before I put the turkey on.'

Giblets!

I perk up, dropping the Christmas hat, and they all laugh at me again. It seems that whatever I do today is going to amuse them.

'Pot of tea, Margaret?' John asks her.

'That sounds lovely, thank you,' she agrees, and winks at me and Sam. 'Are you two staying up here with your sack of goodies, or coming down to sit by the Christmas tree?'

Sam looks ecstatic. 'I'd love to sit by the tree.'

'I'll help you carry this lot downstairs,' his dad says, and together they begin to collect up the scattered toys and sweets and pack them back into the large Santa sack. Their efforts are a little hampered by me jumping about on the bed, but neither of them seem to mind my silly antics.

Christmas is fun, I decide, scampering downstairs after them to the cheerful strain of carols from Granny Margaret's music system in the kitchen.

'Jingle Bells, Jingle Bells,' Granny M is singing to herself as she clatters about in the pan cupboard, an apron round her waist, the kettle already on.

I run to my basket near the warm range and jump in. I turn around several times as though to get comfortable, then jump out again, too excited to settle even for a minute.

Rico laughs at me, from on top of a cupboard. 'Anyone would think this was your first Christmas.'

'It's my first Christmas here,' I explain to the cat, wagging my tail. 'And I'm enjoying every minute so far. It's very different from all my other Christmases.'

'It gets even better later,' he promises me, and yawns lazily. 'When the turkey's done. Then we'll get to eat the carcass outside. Pepper might even join us.'

'Fantastic.'

Kitty is curled up on a kitchen chair, head tucked between her front paws. She opens a large eye at the sound of Granny M clattering about with pots and pans, and looks across at me balefully, as if I am somehow to blame for the noise. From the living room, I hear Sam explaining to his dad how party blowers work, before blowing the horn very loudly several times. For once, his dad does not protest at the noise.

But then, Mr Green loves his son. And he's no longer afraid to show it.

'Isn't it a bit early for all this activity?' Kitty demands, a salty edge to her voice, not moving from her curled-up position.

'It's Christmas,' I remind her indulgently. 'Everyone gets up early at Christmas.'

'Not me,' she says silkily, and closes her eye again.

I grin. 'You're just cross because you got stuck in a toilet all night.'

She does not respond.

'Thank you, by the way,' I tell her, and give a little bark of gratitude, barely audible above the carols as Granny M turns the music up.

'For what?'

'For being prepared to get stuck in that toilet on my behalf. For helping me find my sister again. For being part of the Paw Print Club.' I wag my tail. 'It was all very kind of you.'

Kitty stares at me, temporarily rendered speechless. Then she blinks. 'No problem,' she says, then pauses and adds awkwardly, 'Merry Christmas.'

I bark again and chase my tail round and round with sheer delight until I am too dizzy to stand and stagger crazily into a cupboard door.

'Merry Christmas!' I shout, not caring. 'Merry Christmas to everyone!'

When the doorbell finally rings just before lunchtime, I skid into the hall before any of the humans can get there first, slip on the well-polished wooden floor, and somehow manage to slam my head into the wall.

'Oops.'

Staggering up, my head spinning a little, I bark at the closed front door.

'WOOF! WOOF! WOOF!'

Not an emergency this time, of course. No runaway child, no house on fire, no dangerous intruders. I simply can't help myself.

Nor am I the only one.

On the other side of the door, I hear a familiar but muffled, 'WOOF! WOOF! WOOF!' in response.

I tear round in circles, rucking up the hall runner again, so excited I feel like my head is going to burst.

'Bertie, for goodness' sake, calm down,' Mr Green exclaims.

He throws open the door.

It's Molly and Camilla on the doorstep, all wrapped up against the sharp winter weather. Molly grins at me in welcome. She is wearing a tartan coat, with a shiny Christmas bow on her collar, and her owner is holding out a bottle of wine.

'Merry Christmas,' Camilla says shyly. Then she glances down at me. 'Hello again, Bertie.'

I wag my tail fervently.

I almost don't recognise Camilla when she smiles. She looks so relaxed and friendly, nothing like the pinch-faced woman that I remember from the shelter. It just goes to show that first impressions cannot always be trusted.

Mr Green takes the bottle, not even looking at it, his gaze on Camilla's face. 'Merry Christmas,' he says, then smiles down at Molly. 'Don't you look pretty? Please, both of you, come in. Make yourself at home.'

Molly runs straight in and rubs noses with me. 'Bertie.'

'Molly.'

I wag my tail, deliriously happy.

Camilla takes Molly off the lead. Then she shrugs off her coat and watches as Mr Green hangs it up. 'I do hope we're not late.'

'Not at all,' he says. 'In fact, you've come at the perfect time. I've just finished carving the turkey, and Granny M – sorry, I mean Margaret – is almost ready to serve lunch.'

'You must let me help.'

'No, sorry, Margaret wouldn't hear of it. She is fiercely in control of her domain.'

'I understand perfectly.'

Camilla walks into the living room where Sam is playing with his new present – an Xbox. Molly and I follow at a trot, and dash through the piles of Christmas wrapping paper still lying strewn across the floor, loving the rustling noise they make.

'Hello, Sam,' she says, hesitating. 'I hope I'm not intruding. How are you now? All recovered after your scary night outdoors?'

Sam pauses the game he's playing, then jumps up to play with me and Molly, fussing us both as we stand together, wagging our tails.

'It wasn't so scary,' he tells us stoutly, then grins when his dad makes a face. 'Well, maybe a bit. I won't be doing that again in a hurry, that's for certain.'

Mr Green raises his eyebrows. 'Glad to hear it.' He turns to Camilla, saying wryly, 'As you can see, Sam's favourite Christmas present is the Xbox. He's been nagging me to get him one for ages. I don't have a clue how it works, so he's on his own with it at the moment. Though apparently he's invited a friend over tomorrow who knows everything about these games, so Boxing Day should be very quiet.' He hesitates. 'We could take the dogs out for a long walk together then, if you're not busy tomorrow.'

'No, not busy at all,' Camilla stammers, her cheeks a little flushed. 'That would be lovely.'

'Can I offer you an aperitif?'

'Thank you.'

The two grown-ups wander through into the kitchen, where Granny Margaret has been banging and bashing about with steaming pans for the past few hours, all to the backdrop of loud Christmas carols on the radio. Mr Green did offer to help her earlier, but Granny M chased him out with a large frying pan, only calling him back when the delicious-smelling turkey had come out of the oven and needed carving.

She sounds cheerful enough now though, bursting into song at her favourite bits while serving up the Christmas lunch.

And the smell wafting through is mouth-watering.

I look at Sam, my head on one side, then give a short bark of enquiry.

Sam grins at me, and rubs my ears. 'Remember that girl yesterday, Bertie? Harriet. The one I told you about?'

He lowers his voice, so only me and Molly can hear. 'I meant to tell you but it slipped my mind in all the excitement of last night. When we were at the river yesterday, Harriet asked where I'd been hiding. So I took her and Dad to the old oak tree, to show them the hollow. While Dad was climbing up to look inside, I plucked up courage to tell Harriet how much . . . how much I like her. And she didn't laugh. It was amazing.'

I wag my tail approvingly.

'Plus, she has an Xbox and is pretty good at it. So as soon as I unwrapped my present this morning, I had to run and phone her, first thing. She's coming over tomorrow to play it with me. How cool is that?'

He goes back to his game console, and makes a face. 'Her dad sounded a bit grumpy though, when he answered the phone. But I suppose it was only half past seven by then.'

Molly watches him play his game for a moment, then grins, glancing round at me. 'I like your little man. He's funny.'

'I like your new owner too. Now that I've met her properly, that is. She's not at all the way I imagined her.' I listen to the voices in the kitchen, now raised in loud song. Granny M and Camilla, both joining in with the chorus to 'Good King Wenceslas'. 'And I think the Greens like her too.'

'Especially . . . Mr Green, perhaps?'

I bark, and wag my tail. 'Let's keep our paws crossed for that, shall we?'

Suddenly there's the loud sound of a dinner gong. And Mr Green appears, carrying several hot plates of food.

'Into the dining room, Sam,' he says. 'I hope you've laid the table for Granny M.'

Sam nods cheerfully as he leads the way into the dining room, with me and Molly running back and forth, and getting underfoot. 'Knives and forks, and spoons for the Christmas pudding,' he chants, ticking off the items on his fingers, 'and candles and flowers, and proper glasses for wine and water – plus pop for me – and a big Christmas cracker for every place setting. Just like Gran said.'

I jump up to look, nearly pulling off the white tablecloth. 'Bertie, get down!'

I drop down at Mr Green's admonition, and wag my tail apologetically.

Molly shakes her head at me. 'Trust you to be a nuisance,' she whispers.

I look up at the humans, worried that I may have spoilt the moment. But Mr Green is too busy studying the table to pay much attention to me. He smiles. 'This looks amazing. You've done a great job laying the table, Sam.'

To my relief, Mr Green does not sound angry. Far from it, in fact. He seems relaxed and amused by my antics. Maybe the Greens are getting more used to me. Though of course I must be careful not to be too naughty.

I won't though. Not now I have Molly to keep me in line.

'I tried to do everything the same way Mum used to,' Sam says proudly, then pauses, looking up at his dad with a suddenly apprehensive expression.

Mr Green places the hot plates on the table, then rubs his son's hair. 'That's right,' he says warmly. 'This is exactly the way Mum used to lay the table every Christmas.' He places a hand on his son's shoulder. 'It's okay to talk about her, you know.'

Sam nods, his eyes very bright. 'I know. Thanks, Dad.'

Mr Green nods, seems to swallow a lump in his throat, then leaves Sam to guard the table while he goes back for more plates.

The table does look marvellous though, shining with glassware and cutlery, the tall Christmas candles already lit, and colourful crackers with their big glossy bows beside every setting. And the whole house is deliciously fragranced with turkey.

Mr Green comes back in, then glances down at us. 'Sam,' he says with a smile, 'time for the dogs to go outside. Granny M has put down food for all the animals, out on the patio. I believe even Pepper has been invited from next door.'

He grins when I cock my head at him, surprised. 'Yes, I opened that gap again in the fence, since you were all pining for Pepper's company. Go on then, have a great time in the garden.' He bends to stroke us both. 'Merry Christmas, Bertie! Merry Christmas, Molly!' Then whispers, 'Thank you, Bertie,' as I wag my tail.

Excitedly, we run through the hot kitchen after Sam, nearly knocking over a singing Granny M, who does not swear but merely wishes us both, 'Merry Christmas!', and Camilla, juggling a gravy jug, who grins at us as we dash past.

There on the patio are five bowls, all heaped with tasty Christmas scraps, and three big juicy bones, one for each dog. Kitty and Rico are already there, with Pepper, the three of them tucking in with alacrity. They raise their heads as we arrive, interested to see Molly next to me, and Pepper barks enthusiastically.

'A new member for the Paw Print Club!'

Molly looks at him, her head on one side. 'The what?'

'I'll explain in a minute,' I tell her, and nudge my sister towards one of the bowls. 'Go, eat. Enjoy yourself.'

Sam crouches down to stroke my head. 'Thanks for everything, Bertie,' he says very quietly, for my ears only, his voice trembling. 'I'm so glad you came to live with us. I'll never forget Mum. She's in my heart for ever. But because of you, I know now it wasn't my fault that . . .' The boy suddenly hugs me tight and says, 'Merry Christmas!'

Then he runs back inside for his Christmas lunch, shouting, 'Hey, don't pull any crackers without me!'

Once the door is shut and we are alone on the patio in the cold, wintry sunshine, we crowd round each other. There are all the necessary introductions, with Pepper excited to meet Molly at last, and very eager to hear all about our adventures yesterday on the way to the river, as her owner refused to let her go. 'Fussy old fool,' Pepper moans, then grins. 'But I forgive him. It is Christmas, after all.'

Kitty looks at Molly coolly. 'Sorry about yesterday morning.' She means when she dashed past after being stuck in Camilla's toilet all night. 'I didn't intend to be rude. I just wasn't up to a conversation.'

'I'm not surprised. That awful pine smell in your nose all night.' Molly shudders. 'Bertie shut me in the loo once when we were puppies. Everyone was out, so I was trapped in there for hours. Horrid.'

'Accidentally,' I point out, in my defence.

'Oh yes, accidentally. His tail caught the door, he *claimed*.'

'Honestly, I was just wagging away, and then . . . BANG. And I tried, but couldn't get the door handle to turn. So we had to wait for someone to come home from shopping.' I shrug, looking sheepishly at my sister. 'A dog can't help the way his tail wags.'

Rico grins appreciatively. 'That sounds like Bertie all right. So he was a total pest as a puppy too?'

'Absolutely. There was this one time, when we'd just arrived at the Mintons' house, when Bertie managed to get his head stuck in a vase,' my sister begins, and I smile at her, only half listening to the old, familiar story as I gnaw on one of the juicy bones Granny M has given us.

This is how Christmas is always meant to be, I think, looking round at them all. No tasteless slop, no arguments, no sitting alone staring out at a cold world. The humans are all enjoying each other's company inside, eating Granny M's delicious Christmas lunch together, pulling crackers, exchanging jokes and smiles. Sam looked lost in a dream of happiness when he brought us outside. And me and my sister are together again. Bertie and Molly. With our friends around us. We have lost touch with the other dogs from the Mintons', which is sad. But now we have new friends, and lovely new families, and a new member for the Paw Print Club. It's Christmas Day, and we're all together, enjoying this tasty grub and each other's furry company.

We're all members of the Paw Print Club here. May we never be parted.

Happy and reunited at last.

Molly and me.

THE END